# Just Like You

# Just Like You

## NICK HORNBY

R A N D O M   H O U S E
**L A R G E P R I N T**

Copyright © 2020 by Lower East Ltd.

Published in the United States of America by Random House Large Print in association with

Riverhead Books, an imprint of Random House, a division of Penguin Random House LLC, New York.

First published in Great Britain by Viking, an imprint of Penguin Books, a division of Penguin Random House Ltd., London.

The Library of Congress has established a Cataloging-in-Publication record for this title.

ISBN: 978-0-593-29556-4

www.penguinrandomhouse.com/large-print-format-books

FIRST LARGE PRINT EDITION

Printed in the United States of America

10 9 8 7 6 5 4 3 2

This Large Print edition published in accord with the standards of the N.A.V.H.

To Mangerton, young and old

Were we to evaluate people, not only according to their intelligence and their education, their occupation and their power, but according to the kindliness and their courage, their imagination and their sensitivity, their sympathy and generosity, there could be no classes. Who would be able to say the scientist was superior to the porter with admirable qualities as a father, the civil servant with unusual skill at gaining prizes to the lorry driver with unusual skill at growing roses?

—MICHAEL YOUNG, **The Rise of the Meritocracy**

# 2016

# 1

How could one say with any certainty what one hated most in the world? It surely depended on how proximate the hated thing was at any given moment, whether you were doing it or listening to it or eating it at the time. She hated teaching Agatha Christie for A level, she hated any Conservative education secretary, she hated listening to her younger son's trumpet practice, she hated any kind of liver, the sight of blood, reality T.V. shows, grime music, and the usual abstractions—global poverty, war, pandemics, the imminent death of the planet, and so on. But they weren't happening to her, apart from the imminent death of the planet, and even that was only imminent. She could afford not to think about them quite a lot of the time. Right now, at 11:15 on a cold Saturday morning, the thing she hated most in the world was

queuing outside the butcher's while listening to
Emma Baker going on about sex.

**She had been** trying to move out of Emma's orbit
for a while, but the movement was imperceptible,
and would, she guessed gloomily, take another
four or five years yet. They had met when their
children were small and went to the same play-
group; dinners were offered and reciprocated and
offered again. The children were more or less the
same, then. They hadn't developed personalities,
really, and their parents hadn't yet decided what
kind of people they were going to be. Emma and
her husband had chosen private primary education
for theirs, and as a direct consequence, Lucy's boys
found them insufferable. Social interaction eventually stopped, but you couldn't do much about
living near someone, shopping in the same places.

**It was a particular stage** of the queuing that she
hated: the point at which one was right outside
the door, kept shut in winter, and one had to
decide whether there was room inside the shop.
Go in too early and you had to squash up against
somebody while running the risk of anxious
queue-jump faces; too late and somebody behind

would toot her, metaphorically, for her timidity. There would be a gentle suggestion, a "Do you want to..." or a "There's room in there now, I think." That was what it was like: pulling out at an intersection that required aggression. She didn't mind being tooted when she was driving, though. She was separated from other drivers by glass and metal, and they were gone in a flash, never to be seen again. These people were her neighbors. She had to live with their nudges and disapproval every Saturday. She could have gone to a supermarket, of course, but then she would be Letting Local Shops Down.

And in any case the butcher was just too good, so she was willing to spend the extra. Her sons ate neither fish nor vegetable, and she had reluctantly decided that she probably did care about them ingesting antibiotics, hormones, and other things in cheaper meat that might one day turn them into female Eastern European weightlifters. (If they chose to become female Eastern European weightlifters one day, however, she would fully endorse and embrace their decision. She just didn't want to impose that destiny upon them.) Paul helped with the boys' beef habit. He wasn't mean about money. He felt guilty about everything. He kept enough to live on, if that, but gave her the rest.

**The tricky in-or-out part** was probably another ten minutes away, though. The expense and the quality were attractive to the residents of this particular London borough, so the queues were long, and the customers took their time once they had forced their way inside. Emma Baker's obsession with sex was happening right here, right now, and it was intolerable.

"You know what? I envy you," she said.

Lucy didn't reply. Terseness was her only weapon. From the outside it probably looked useless, because the words would keep coming, but any attempt to answer the question would result in an unstoppable torrent.

"You're going to have sex with someone you've never had sex with before."

This didn't seem particularly enviable to Lucy, in the sense that if it happened, it wouldn't be much of an accomplishment. It was, after all, a future open to most able-bodied people in the world, whether they chose to exploit the opportunity or not. But Lucy's single status drew Emma back to the same subject over and over again. For Emma, married for many years to a man whose inadequacies, in the bedroom and in every other room, she made no attempts to hide or defend, divorce meant sex—paradoxically and/or idiotically, Lucy thought, seeing as her experience of it to date was that it meant no sex. In other words, Lucy's single status provided a screen on which Emma could project endless fantasies.

"What are you looking for? In a man?"

Either in real life or in Lucy's head the queue had become stiller.

"Nothing. I'm not."

"So what's the point of tonight?"

"No point."

The answers told a very small part of a very long story. Indeed, the words "nothing," "not," and "point" could even have been plucked at random from a very long story by some kind of textual artist, in order to convey a meaning ironically at odds with the storyteller's intention.

"Hygiene," said Lucy suddenly.

"What?"

"That's what I'm looking for."

"Come on, girl. You can ask for more than that."

"Hygiene is important."

"You don't want handsome? Or funny? Or rich? Or good in bed? Someone with a penis that never lets him down? Someone who loves to give oral sex?" Behind them, somebody sniggered. Since the rest of the queue was by now entirely silent, there was a very good chance that Emma had been the trigger for the sniggers.

"No."

Again, a very short answer that didn't tell the whole truth, or any part of it.

"Well, that's what I'd go for."

"I'm learning more about David than I want to know."

"He's clean, at least. He smells like James Bond most of the time."

"Well, there you go. He has none of the things you're telling me to look for, and you're still with him."

Now she came to think about it—and she hadn't really thought about it until earlier on that week—hygiene was more important than just about any other quality she could think of. Imagine that Emma were in a position to provide a potential partner who possessed every single idiosyncrasy and attribute that she wanted—or, at least, those that Lucy could think of, now, on the spot, in the queue for the butcher's, when she didn't even know what to say. Imagine that this unlikely man loved fresh flowers and the films of Asghar Farhadi, that he preferred cities to the countryside, that he read fiction—proper fiction, not novels about terrorists and submarines—that, yes, he enjoyed both giving and receiving oral sex, that he was kind to her sons, that he was tall, dark, handsome, solvent, funny, clever, liberal, stimulating.

So this guy turns up to whisk her away to dinner somewhere quiet and smart and fashionable, and she notices straight away that he smells awful. Well, that would be the end of it, wouldn't it? Nothing else would be of any use whatsoever. Bad hygiene trumped everything. So did unkindness, criminal records for—or even merely rumors of—domestic violence, and unacceptable views on race. Oh, and a dependency on drink and drugs, although that went without saying, given everything that had happened. The absence of key negatives was much more important than any positive.

Lucy noted glumly that they were approaching the crunch. It was chaos in there, she could see. There was a double queue that now stopped at the far end of the shop, so it wasn't simply a question of finding enough room just inside the door. Just inside the door was where those in the **middle** of the queue were standing, the U-bend in the snake, so in order to join the back of the queue one had to push one's way through the crowd—and it was beginning to resemble a crowd, rather than a line—thus causing even more stress to both the pusher and the pushed.

"I think we can both get in there," said Emma.

"There's hardly room for one," said Lucy.

"Come on."

"Please don't."

"I think you can probably get in there," said the woman behind them.

"I was just saying to my friend we can't," said Lucy sharply.

A couple emerged from the shop with groaning white plastic bags containing hunks of bloody meat that, if consumed over the next seven days, would make them seriously ill with heart disease and bowel cancer, and shorten the queue the following week.

Emma opened the door and went in.

"You let her in the queue," said the woman behind.

Lucy had forgotten that.

"And now she's inside and you're not."

There was a metaphor in there somewhere.

**A hundred and twelve quid** was a lot of money to spend on meat. Joseph wondered whether the couple would try and reduce the bill, get rid of the fillet steaks or the rolled loins, say, but they didn't. And there was no flicker of anything when he told them what they owed. The first time he'd asked a customer for a three-figure sum he'd made an apologetic face—more like a grimace, really, as if he were about to cause the woman actual physical pain. But there was no pain caused, as far as he could tell, and he'd ended up feeling as if he'd done something clumsy. The next time it happened, he played it cool, but the guy felt obliged to explain—relatives coming, couldn't afford to do that every week, and so on. The people who lived in the neighborhood weren't posh, in the sense that they wore jeans and didn't sound like Prince Charles, but they obviously had money, and sometimes that seemed to create some kind of embarrassment. Joseph didn't give a shit, really. He wanted what they had, and one day he would get it. Just because he earned a hundred and ten quid for a day's work in the shop didn't mean he hated people who spent a hundred and twelve on meat.

He was more worried by the loud blonde woman who'd pushed her way in when the three-figure couple left. She was trouble, of a very particular kind: every Saturday she tried to flirt with him. She made jokes about sausages and pork loins, and Joseph had no idea what he was supposed to say or do in return, so he smiled with his lips but not the rest of him. When it first started he tried to avoid serving her, but he quickly worked out that this was worse, because she'd ignore Cass or Craig or whoever it was who had to deal with her and joke with him about sausages anyway. So then the embarrassment became impossible, because it involved Joseph, his customer, the loud lady, and whoever was serving her. If he timed it right he could contain the trouble.

**He didn't have** to do anything tricky. She was his next customer.

"Good morning, Joe."

He wasn't Joe. He was Joseph. It said so on his name tag. But recently she had decided that she needed to be on friendlier terms.

"What are you after?"

"Ah. Well. There's a question."

At least she had the decency to say it quietly, so only the three or four people immediately beside and behind her heard. They looked at him, to see whether he was going to play along. He gave the loud blonde woman his no-eyes smile.

"I know, I'm wicked," she said. "Or I would be, given half a chance. Can I have half a dozen pork and leek sausages, please? Not chipolatas."

Even that was supposed to be a joke.

"Gotcha."

He got her the sausages, and then some sirloin steaks, and then four chicken breasts. She was going to say something about her breasts, or breasts in general, he could tell, so he talked over her.

"Cass, will you go out the back and tell them we need more sirloin?"

"Lucy."

The loud blonde was gesturing at her friend, trying to get her to come to the counter, and the friend, smaller, prettier, dark hair, was waving her off and making an embarrassed face. It was as if the people in the queue were extras in a film about women who are best friends despite being opposites. "I'll see you outside," said Lucy.

Loud Blonde shook her head in despair, as if her friend's refusal to push through a crowd of people so that she could be served when it wasn't her turn was precisely what was wrong with her in all areas of life.

"No helping some people," Loud Blonde said to Joseph as she was entering her pin number, and she looked at him. He tried not to shudder.

**"I could eat him up,"** said Emma when they were both back outside.

"Who?"

"Joe. The kid who served me."

"He didn't look like he was interested in being eaten up."

"He doesn't know how I'd cook him."

Lucy wasn't sure this metaphor worked. Knowing how you were going to be cooked hardly made the prospect of being devoured more enticing.

"Don't you think he looks like someone? Some sexy film star or singer?"

"Maybe."

"I know."

Lucy knew Emma's frame of reference, and it wasn't broad. She had almost certainly been reminded of a young Idris Elba, or possibly a young Will Smith.

"A young Denzel Washington," said Emma. "Don't you see it?"

"Nope," said Lucy. "But I can see that, of the three black faces available to you in your memory bank, he probably looks most like a young Denzel Washington."

"I know loads more than three. I chose the person that actually looked like him."

Emma was an occasional freelance interior designer, and Lucy would be amazed if she'd ever had a black client. All the other fields of endeavor that might have provided her with comparative options—sport, music, books, even politics—she had no interest in. Lucy had had enough conversations with kids and colleagues to understand how deep this sort of thing cut, but how did one even begin, with someone as oblivious and as unreflective as Emma? So she didn't, and she wouldn't.

They were walking home together. Emma lived two streets farther on, in one of the larger houses down the hill. They had been neighbors, once upon a time, but after the separation, that house had been sold and Lucy and the boys had moved to a smaller place.

"Are the boys with Paul this weekend?"

"Yes."

"So if it does go well tonight…"

"I'm not going to sleep with anyone tonight."

"You don't know."

"Have you ever been unfaithful to David?"

"Lucy! Really!"

"What?"

"You can't ask that!"

"Because?"

"It's private."

The information Emma did not wish to divulge was that she had been entirely faithful to her husband for the duration of her married life, Lucy knew that. It was her deep, dark secret: that despite all the talk about eating people up and pork loins, Emma had done nothing and would never do anything. Yes, it was pathetic, but the truth was she was just another depressed and lonely married woman who wouldn't give up on the idea that a young man might want to fuck her. And what was wrong with that, really? Whatever got you through.

"Why is my sex life open to discussion when yours isn't?"

"Because you're single."

"Single people are allowed a private sex life."

"But you know David."

"I wouldn't say anything."

"That's not what I mean."

"So you have been unfaithful."

"Let's change the subject."

And thus Emma's honor was spared.

**She liked the new quiet** of Saturday afternoons. In the winter, when it was too wet to play football on the playing field with their friends, one of the boys watched people watching football on the results program while listening to grime and playing a game on his phone, and the other played FIFA on the Xbox while shouting at friends through the headset. That was a lot of different noise she didn't want to hear. Now that they spent Saturdays with Paul, she could read, do the crossword, listen to music that would have made her sons snort with fury (Mozart) or amusement (Carole King). It was the early evenings she didn't like. A family house, even a family house that had shrunk due to force of circumstance, belonged to a family, and the seven o'clock silence seemed a failure of sorts. It wasn't her failure, at least in her opinion, but it didn't matter who claimed it.

**And tonight she** didn't even have to cook, an activity that was much more important than she'd realized before the lonely Saturdays. Cooking kept the evening away from the afternoon—it was a punctuation mark, stopping the long sentence of the day from tripping over itself and becoming garbled. So then what, without the cooking of pasta and the chopping of onions? She refused to be one of those women who filled in the time before a date by trying things on in the bedroom. In the movies, these sessions always came in montages, and maybe she would try on her whole wardrobe if the changes didn't involve undressing at any point, if the clothes just magically appeared on the body while there was a song about new tomorrows playing on the soundtrack.

Anyway, to actually think about her appearance would be giving the evening a gravity and investment it didn't deserve. She didn't know this man, and he didn't sound terribly exciting. His name was Ted and he worked in consumer publishing. If Ted represented a new tomorrow, she might simply stay in bed until Monday. Maybe she wouldn't even change. She looked perfectly presentable, she thought. If he didn't like women who wore jeans and a T-shirt on a date, he could fuck off. Maybe she'd put a proper top on, though. She looked at the crossword. "Across solutions all refer to a theme which is otherwise undefined." Great. You had to discover the theme before you could get the solutions, and you had to get the solutions before you discovered the theme. She seemed to spend most of her life doing that. She put the T.V. on instead.

**They smiled** at each other.

"So."

"So."

They'd done the ordering drinks bit, and they were now pretending to look at the menu. He was probably five years older than her, and he was neither unattractive nor handsome. He was balding, but he had accepted it, so the remaining hair was shaved neatly but not aggressively. The crinkles around his eyes showed that he smiled a lot, and his teeth were straight and white. Only the shirt, which was regrettably both black and floral, rang any alarm bells, but it looked like it might have been purchased specially for the occasion. If so, this was both sweet and sad. All in all, he looked exactly like the kind of man she might have expected to be meeting on a blind date set up by a mutual friend: pleasant, damaged, harmless, and with a blind faith in the power of another woman to lead him out of his loneliness. She wondered whether he was feeling some kind of version of the same thing, but she didn't think she gave off the same melancholy. Maybe she was kidding herself. She knew within seconds there would be no second date.

"Who's going to go first?"

Who's going to go first? Dear God. This was conversation as lavatory, where there was only room for one at a time. You go first, she wanted to say. There's never a queue for the gents. But then, they weren't here to have fun. They were here to find out whether they could bear to contemplate some kind of substitute sad-sack relationship, and in order to do that, stories—stories about pain, loss, mismanagement, and wrongdoing—had to be got out of the way. She could tell from his atmosphere of defeat that the wrongdoing was not his.

"You go."

"Well. I'm Ted. Which you knew. And I'm a friend of Natasha's."

He made a gesture toward her, an unfurling arm, as if he were asking her to take a bow. This was to indicate that Lucy too was one of Natasha's friends, which was why they were pretending to look at menus together in the first place.

"I have two girls, Holly and Marcie, thirteen and eleven, and I'm very involved in their lives but I'm no longer with their mum."

"I'm glad to hear it."

"Oh," said Ted. "No. I don't know what Natasha has told you, but Amy's not a bad person. I mean, she made some mistakes, but..."

"I'm sorry," said Lucy. "It was a silly joke."

"I don't get it."

"Well, if you were still with her, you shouldn't really be out on blind dates."

Ted pointed at her. She'd only met him five minutes ago and there'd already been the unfurled arm thing and a point. He'd make a good crossing guard, but that wasn't necessarily what she was looking for in a partner.

"Ah. Yes. That would be funny. Funny peculiar, I meant."

"My joke was supposed to be funny ha-ha."

"No, no. It was a good joke. But if that's what I actually was doing, it would be funny peculiar."

"Am I allowed to ask what happened?"

"With Amy?"

"Yes."

He shrugged.

"She met someone."

"Ah."

The shrug did not indicate acceptance. The shrug was a carefully casual way of disguising acute and undigested pain.

"I don't know. It takes two to tango and all that," he said.

"Well. There were two. Her and him."

"I wasn't talking about, you know. The other party."

"You were tangoing too?"

He really didn't seem the type, but what did she know?

"No! Not if tangoing means…What does it mean?"

"I suppose I was asking you whether it took four to tango?"

"Four? How did we get from two to four?"

"You and someone."

"Oh. No. God, no. No."

"So in what way were you tangoing?"

"I wish I hadn't started with the tango."

"Let's stop."

"I suppose I was trying to say that if someone is properly happy in a marriage, then there's no room for somebody else."

"Oh, you're one of those."

"Is that bad? Are we bad?"

Perhaps she had sounded too withering.

"No, no. Not bad. Just…too thoughtful."

"Really? Can you be too thoughtful?"

Of course you couldn't. It was just that some-how, Ted's over-thoughtfulness had tipped over into wetness and self-pity.

"The thing is, I don't know how unhappy your wife was."

"I didn't either."

"So she probably wasn't that unhappy."

"How do you know?"

"You seem like a reasonably sensitive guy. You'd have noticed. She was probably just medium. Neither happy nor unhappy. Like most people."

She didn't know what she was talking about, but she was beginning to see that blind dates, especially unsuccessful ones with no promise of a future relationship, could offer all sorts of riches. You could provide uninformed and unasked-for opinion, and you could be as nosy as you wanted. Lucy frequently felt the urge to go up to strangers—someone reading an unlikely book, say, or a young woman in tears on her mobile, or a white cycle courier with long dreadlocks—and ask them what the deal was. Just that. "What's the deal here?"

Well, if she wasn't worried about finding a

partner of any kind, for life, sex, or even tennis, she could sit down at a table like this one, with a man like Ted, and ask him what the deal was, and he couldn't tell her to mind her own business because they were here to cut to the chase. Until relatively recently, she had believed that the phrase had something to do with hunting, and that therefore it had been in English usage for hundreds of years. But one quiet Saturday afternoon, after a crossword answer, she had googled it, and she now knew that it came from the early days of cinema, and meant more or less exactly what it said: get to the exciting part as quickly as possible. Hal Roach, the man thought to have coined the phrase, probably never imagined it would be used to describe the moment in a meal where two divorced people talked about their disappointment and oversensitivity. But then, that was the way life went. Lucy was forty-two, and unlikely ever again to find herself strapped to a railway line while a locomotive bore down on her. She had been through that with Paul.

"That's what I thought," said Ted. "I thought she was medium."

"Well, when you're medium, there's always room for a third party."

"I hadn't thought of that. So that's what I should have been watching out for, you reckon?"

"No. You can't watch out for medium. That's the whole point. If everyone ran off with other people when they're medium, nobody would stay married for five minutes."

Lucy wondered whether they had good sex, and then remembered that she was on a first date and there wouldn't be a second. She could ask anything.

"Was the sex OK? Did it . . . was it regular?"

"Amy was very attractive. Is, I should say. More attractive than me. I probably married out of my league."

"I'm not sure I understand."

"I've probably got a picture somewhere."

He started to search his jacket for his phone.

"No, no, I understand what attractive means. I don't see how it relates to sex."

"I was always a bit intimidated."

She had no idea what that meant, or how it might be applied to the subject under discussion, but she had reached the limits of her appetite for detail.

"So you're looking for someone plain."

"I know that sounds weird, but I really am. And I should say that when I saw you walk in, I was a bit disappointed. Sorry. Once bitten twice shy and all that."

"You're quite a smooth talker, you know that?"

He laughed.

"Your turn."

"Oh, dear. Already?"

"'Fraid so."

"Lucy, friend of Natasha's, two boys, Dylan and Al, ten and eight, very, very involved in their lives, probably more than I want to be, no longer with their dad."

"And you're an English teacher."

"Yes. Head of Department at Park Road."

"We had a look at that for the girls."

"And found it wanting?"

"No. It was very impressive. But Amy wanted them to have what she'd had."

"Private."

"Well, yes. Not just that. Smaller class sizes, more people…"

"Smaller classes, more people? That's some school."

"No, no, more people that…"

Lucy knew lots of people who sent their kids to private schools, and they never failed to make a mess of explaining how they had arrived at their decision. The reasons usually involved some kind of complex, barely comprehensible sensitivity that prevented the child from attending the local comprehensive, so even though the parents would have loved to send them up the road, it just wouldn't work in this particular case, what with the shyness, or the undiagnosed dyslexia, or an extraordinary talent that needed the kind of excavation and nurture the state was in no position to provide. Lucy decided that she would have sex with the first father who said, simply, are you fucking kidding me? That school is full of psychopaths, gangsters, kids who don't speak English, teachers who don't speak English, twelve-year-olds who stink of weed, eleven-year-olds who will beat my daughter up simply because she reads Plato in her lunch break.

"More people that are…"

"Like them?"

Ted looked at her gratefully.

"I suppose that's it. There are actually lots of Asian girls at Bluebell. Chinese and Indian. So it's not…"

"I understand. It's fine."

"Where are your boys?"

"Francis Bacon."

"Oh, I've heard good things about that."

He seemed relieved, as if the boys' attendance at a half-decent school provided proof that she wasn't a complete ideological lunatic.

"And why… Well, why are you here?"

"Why am I single? Natasha didn't say anything?"

"A little bit."

"Well, the headlines tell the whole story."

"How's he doing now?"

"OK. He's clean. Rehab, counseling…He's done everything he should have done years ago."

"And he doesn't want to come back?"

"Oh, yes. He can't see what the problem is."

"And what is the problem?"

"I hate him."

"Presumably that can change."

"I don't think so."

Everyone seemed to think that forgiveness was just within reach, there, on the next table, and all she had to do was get up and turn on the tap, but perversity and bitterness were stopping her. She was angry, yes, but there was no tap. Paul had spent all their money. Paul had ruined too many birthdays. Paul had called her a bitch and a cunt too many times. Paul had hit a Deliveroo driver, and brought cocaine and dealers into the house where his children lived. She would know him for the rest of her life, and one day, if they put enough years between the past and the future, she could imagine the rage subsiding. But subsiding rage was not the same thing as love. Maybe Ted would have seemed like an attractive option to some women who had endured something similar, but she didn't need someone to be kind to her. She wanted intellectual stimulation and sexual excitement, and if she couldn't have that then she didn't need anybody.

"Natasha says you're a big reader," said Ted, who clearly didn't want to talk about hatred any more.

"Oh. Yes."

"I tried to do some swotting up, but I'd be lying if I said it was my thing."

Lucy wondered what the swotting up had entailed. Had he read the books pages of the **Sunday Times**? Had he read a book, or read every book published in the last five years?

"That's OK."

"I'm much happier with a good series on Netflix."

Lucy liked a good series on Netflix too. They got through the rest of the evening easily enough. Lucy was not young, she knew. She was roughly halfway through her life. But surely she was younger than this?

**2**

Seven minutes of the game left, nil-nil, and Lucas took a massive swipe at the ball with his wrong foot, missed it completely, and whacked the opposing winger in the stomach, right in the middle of the area, right in front of the referee. The other kid went down, not because he was looking for a penalty, but because all the air and maybe even a couple of internal organs had been thumped out of him. Joseph was fond of Lucas. He wasn't much good at football, and he wasn't very bright, but Joseph had been coaching him for three years, and he'd never once missed training or a match. He was a good kid despite his father, who was not a good or even a reasonable man, and who, like his son, turned up to every game. Parental pride often rendered him temporarily blind, and when the referee pointed to the spot, there was a volley of abuse that wasn't shocking because Joseph had heard it all before.

"Are you fucking kidding, ref?"

This was delivered at such a volume that the referee, fifty yards away, turned round and stared at him.

"Keep it down, John," said Joseph.

"Were you watching?"

"Yes. It was a nailed-on pen."

The opposing winger was still lying on the ground, being comforted by the opposition coach.

"He never touched him."

"He hasn't moved since he got kicked."

"He'll be right as rain in a moment, you watch."

"You're not even supposed to be standing here, mate."

He wasn't. He was supposed to be with the other parents behind the goal—only coaches and the substitutes were allowed on the touchline. The rules didn't apply to John, though. Lucas was the third of his sons to play for the Turnpike Lane Under-12s, which meant that he predated the rules.

"Ref. Ref. Ref. Ref. Ref. Ref."

The ref was refusing to look at him now, so he kept going.

"Ref. Ref. Ref. Ref."

Finally, some attention.

"Ref, you're a fucking cheat."

The referee crouched down to check on the injured boy, then turned and jogged toward them with a great sense of purpose.

**A couple of years ago,** Joseph had run into his old deputy head in the Wood Green shopping center, and Mr. Fielding had asked him what he was up to. "Ah," said Mr. Fielding. "A portfolio. You're portfolio working. That's the future. Except not for you. It's the present for you."

Joseph hadn't known there was a name for it, nor even that anyone else was thinking along the same lines, but Mr. Fielding's explanation made him feel better about what he was doing. Until that moment, he'd been worried that he'd just cobbled together a way of making a living, taken on part-time job after part-time job as a way of avoiding a full-time job. He worked more hours than anyone else he knew, but at least he'd never had to make a decision about his future, the kind where you went one way and not the other and that was that. He did Saturdays in the butcher's, two evenings a week coaching and one supervising the Friday-night games, three mornings at the leisure center, the after-school care for Marina's twins with the odd bit of babysitting thrown in, and the D.J.-ing. He hadn't yet earned

a penny from the D.J.-ing, the job he wanted to
do most, and in a couple of months it would actually cost him money. He was going to spend six
hundred quid on the Ableton Live 10 Suite—he'd
been using a crack for a while, but it didn't work
properly, and if he was ever going to get anywhere,
he knew he'd have to invest. That meant not
going out much, which meant not hearing what
other D.J.s were doing, which meant not knowing
whether the kind of thing he was working on
now was a waste of time, because it wasn't what
people wanted or because it was already dead.

**Joseph knew he** wouldn't regret leaving the butcher's or anyone in it if the D.J.-ing worked out, and he
wouldn't be bothered about the leisure center either.
He'd call in to see the twins, because he was very
fond of them, and their parents. He'd always
thought he'd miss the coaching the most, but it was
getting harder and harder—kids who didn't show
up even if you called them two hours before a
match, abusive parents, opposing coaches applaud-
ing their players when they stopped an attack with
a shirt-pull or a rugby tackle. And everyone—kids,
parents, uncles, and aunts—saw football as a way
out. Any middle-aged white bloke wearing a hat
was a scout from Brentford or Spurs or Barcelona,

and if there was no middle-aged white bloke in a hat, it was somehow Joseph's fault: the team wasn't good enough, Joseph didn't talk up the boys in the right places. Only one player from any of the Lane teams had ever been scouted since Joseph started coaching, and Barnet let him go when he was seventeen.

Some of the parents and grandparents who came down to watch talked about John Terry and Jermaine Defoe and Sol Campbell playing for Senrab over in Wanstead Flats, but those days were gone, Joseph thought. The Lane boys were no longer competing against kids from Wanstead or Liverpool or Dublin for places in the big teams. They were competing with kids from Senegal and Madrid, kids who didn't eat junk food and smoke weed the moment they turned thirteen. You had to play against the rest of the world now, and the rest of the world was both big and good at football.

Someone like Lucas's dad, John, would say there were too many foreigners here, and the English kids didn't stand a chance, but Joseph didn't see why football clubs should commit to picking players who would make them uncompetitive. It wasn't the same argument that his father made. According to him, all the Eastern Europeans who had put him out of a job worked for less than half his old wages, lived five to a room at the end of the Central

Line, went home when they'd saved a few quid, blah blah blah. You couldn't say Sergio Agüero and Eden Hazard and the rest were doing anything on the cheap. They were putting people out of a job because they were miles better than the locals, and Joseph didn't have a problem with that. England was the richest footballing country in the world, but it was nothing to do with the English, not English players, anyway.

"**Why don't you** take a moment, John? Go for a little walk?" said Joseph.

"I can't now, can I? He's walking over here. It'll look like I'm running away. If he wants a fight I'll fucking give him one."

"He doesn't want a fight. He wants a word."

"I want a fight."

"No, you don't."

The referee arrived, out of breath and angry.

"What did you call me?"

"A fucking cheat."

Joseph noted with interest that in these situations, repeating the accusation put the accused at something of a disadvantage. The referee's question rather presumed the answer "Nothing," or maybe an apology, or maybe a change of subject. The repetition demanded action, which placed the referee in a difficult position. He was a referee. He wasn't supposed to punch people. He settled for a push in the chest instead, a push hard enough to knock John over.

"Right," said John. "That's you reported."

"Be my guest," said the referee. And then he handed Joseph his whistle, his notepad, and his cards.

"I'm done," he said, and he walked off toward the changing rooms.

"Result," said John, still sitting on the ground. "You'll have to ref. When you get on there, you can change his mind about the penalty."

John was forty-five, the ref looked as though he were in his mid-fifties. Joseph was twenty-two. He went onto the pitch and told the kids that the game was abandoned. Sometimes he didn't want to be the only grown-up at York Road.

It poured with rain all Saturday morning, and the shop was quiet. People would come in eventually, but they were putting it off, which meant that the afternoon would be busy. Mark got them sweeping and scrubbing and sorting through the condiments, but by eleven even he couldn't pretend that there was much to do, so Joseph and Cassie left Saul on the counter and went next door for a cup of coffee. Cassie was a student at the University of North London, and her Saturday job was a torment to her, due to the exertions of the night before. Because she was more or less the same age as Joseph, she tended to presume that he was in a similar state, even though he never was. After the game he'd made himself dinner, watched a bit of T.V. with his mum, and gone to bed. He never told Cassie that they were different. It was too important to her that they were the same.

"I'm fucked," she said, when they had collected their order and sat down.

"Yeah?"

"House party."

"Ah."

"Some of them were still going when I got up for work. Anyway. Don't mess around with Ket when you're working nine o'clock the next morning."

"I'll remember that."

"I try. But then I take Ket and forget."

She didn't, really. She turned up, and she sold people meat, although he was guessing that it wasn't her in the shop, only her body. He couldn't know for certain, because he'd never seen her any other way, but he hoped there was more to her than she ever showed him on a Saturday.

"What did you get up to?"

"I had a quiet one."

"Right." She wasn't really listening. He could tell she was distracted, and not just by her pitiful condition.

"Would you mind if I asked you something?" she said eventually.

"Probably not."

"You sure?"

This was a white student version of the sentences that began, "Not being funny, but…" What followed wasn't ever funny, and was always, always about race. He preferred Cassie's approach to the same subject, but that wasn't to say it was welcome, or appropriate.

"Not a hundred percent, no. That's why I said 'probably.'"

"Shall I not ask, then?"

"I can't really tell. But if you think there's any chance of offending, maybe you shouldn't."

"I don't think there is. But just say stop and I won't go on."

Joseph said nothing, to indicate his levels of both enthusiasm and resistance.

"Is that you saying, 'Go on'?"

"It's me saying nothing."

"Right. I've sort of forgotten what you saying nothing means."

"Jesus, Cassie. Just get on with it."

"It's about dating."

"Oh, well. I know everything there is to know about dating. I can see why you've come to me."

"Well, it's not just about dating, I suppose."

"You amaze me."

"It's about dating black guys."

"It's now legal in just about every part of the world, as far as I know. But obviously in some places it will get you in more trouble than others. North London is OK."

"Oh. Yeah. No. I didn't mean..."

"I was joking."

"Right."

"So...?"

She took a deep breath.

"Is it true that black girls don't like white girls who are dating black guys?"

"Are you seeing a black guy?"

"Not seeing. I hooked up with one. I'd like to hook up again."

"I'm sure he wouldn't mind."

Cassie never looked her best on Saturdays, but Joseph could see that she wouldn't have that much trouble hooking up with anyone, if she set her mind to it.

"Yeah, but am I doing the wrong thing?"

It made him tired, this shit.

"How am I supposed to know?"

"Would you go out with a white girl?"

"Why don't you ask me whether I have gone out with a white girl?"

"Oh. Have you?"

"Of course I have."

"And did anyone, like, disapprove?"

"Yeah. Her granddad."

"Was he a racist?"

"No. He was a vegan. Didn't like me working here."

"Really?"

"No. He was a racist."

"OK. But I'm talking about, you know. People in your community."

His community. He still wanted his community to be the place where he lived, a community that contained old white women, young Muslim men, Lithuanian kids, mixed-race girls, Asian parents, Jewish taxi drivers. But it never was.

"No," he said. "The neighbors were fine about it."

"Why did you split up?"

"Because I cheated on her and she found out. You won't learn very much from that."

She looked at him disapprovingly.

"I was nineteen," he said. "It happens."

"Every relationship I've ever had ended because someone cheated on someone," said Cassie.

"I suppose that's how it goes," said Joseph. "Until you marry someone and stay married, and one of you dies."

They thought about this in silence, and did not return to the topic of relationships.

**The pretty dark-haired woman** came in when it was still raining, and there was hardly anyone in the shop. He almost pushed Cass out of the way to serve her. She'd stopped coming in with the loud blonde woman, and Joseph couldn't work out whether it was a coincidence, or whether it was something to do with him. He'd been pondering this for the last three weeks or so, he couldn't seem to stop himself. So while he was wondering whether the dark-haired woman was coming in without her friend because she was trying to flirt with him, he had also started wondering whether there was something wrong with him. Maybe he needed a girlfriend. It had been a while. Maybe a lack of sex was making him imagine that women who were asking for lamb shanks and free-range chicken breasts were actually asking for something else. Maybe when the loud blonde said something about pork loins, she was literally talking about a cut of meat. Perhaps he should find out whether Kayla was still seeing Anthony T.C.

"Hi, Joseph."

"Hi."

"So. What do I want? Oh, yes…"

"I'm sorry, I don't even know your name, so I can only say 'hi' back. Seems a bit rude."

"Oh, don't worry."

Was she saying don't worry to assure him that she wasn't offended? Or was she refusing to give him her name? If she was refusing to give him her name, he was going to train himself out of wondering anything ever again.

"So. Steak. Lots of steak. And burgers."

"Right. How much steak is lots of steak?"

"They'd eat as much as I bought, but I can't afford it and it's not good for them."

So no name. He didn't often feel stupid, especially around women, not that he knew many women of her age, and not that he knew how old she was. (Thirty-five? He hoped she wasn't any older than that. He could cope with a ten-year age gap, even though that would mean it was a thirteen-year age gap, but nothing more than that. What the fuck? Who was asking him to cope with anything? Not her, that was for sure. She wouldn't even tell him her name.

———

**How had this even started?** The first time he noticed her was when she came in with the loud blonde, so maybe back then he'd somehow ended up asking himself which one he'd choose with a gun to his head. Sometimes questions like that passed the time. And then the next time he saw her he'd realized that the gun wouldn't be necessary, and hadn't even been needed the previous week. She had beautiful eyes, a smile that warmed even a refrigerated room, and she looked like she had gone through something that had wounded her. That wasn't a good thing, of course, but so many of the people who came in here looked as though they'd never gone through anything. He hadn't been through much, not compared to other young men in his "community," but every time he got stopped by the police when he was coming home late at night and was forced to turn out his pockets, it took him further away from all the journalists and actors and politicians to whom he sold organic beef on a Saturday. He couldn't see her shape because it was February, then March, and she'd been lost inside a giant parka. And he knew shapes weren't import-ant, except they were really if you were playing games in your head, and guns were involved. And in his defense the loud blonde had the sort of body that was supposed to tip the balance, but if he tried to think about her in that way, all he could see was stupidity, and all he could hear were loud embarrassing jokes. Perhaps the best thing to do was use the lovely brunette as a model. He would remember her, her eyes, warmth, and sadness, and try to find someone of his own age who came somewhere close.

"Lucy," she said suddenly. "My name. You must have thought I was being weird."

Someone else came into the shop, a guy with a dog. The dog wasn't allowed in, but Cassie could deal with it.

"Oh. No. I just thought, you know, why should she tell me her name?"

"But now you can think, why should Lucy tell me her name?"

He laughed, to show a) that he got it, b) that he was friendly, and c) that he absolutely wouldn't need a gun to his head. She probably wouldn't get the gun part of the laugh. That was complicated.

"Do you live around here?" she asked him.

"Not far. Tottenham."

"Oh."

She seemed disappointed. If twenty minutes on the bus was too far, then she probably wasn't that bothered in the first place.

"I'm looking for a babysitter for tonight, and I

wondered if you knew any responsible young people around here."

"I do quite a lot of babysitting. You know Marina. With the twins? She comes into the shop on Saturdays?"

"Oh, yes. I know Marina."

"Except I can't really do tonight."

He couldn't really do tonight? He couldn't do tonight at all. He was sitting for the twins again, the third time in the last six weeks.

"Oh, well. I don't usually have my kids on Saturdays. Their dad has them. But this week... Well, he hasn't got them. It's OK. I'll just cancel my thing."

"No, no. Don't do that. I'll sort it out."

"Are you sure? That would be fantastic."

"No problem."

"You'd better give me your phone number and I'll text you the details."

Cassie wasn't dealing with the dog. She was just ignoring it and serving the guy his bacon. Joseph looked at her and nodded toward the dog. Cassie looked at him and shrugged.

"Sure."

He took one of the business cards from the little Perspex container on the counter and wrote his number down.

"Thank you so much," said Lucy. She tucked the card away and left.

"Would you mind taking the dog outside?" Joseph said to the customer the moment she'd gone.

"I'm nearly done," said the customer.

"Yes, but you'll get us into trouble if our boss comes in here and sees him."

"You'll get into trouble if you inconvenience customers."

"Just tie him up out there," said Joseph.

"Don't worry about it," said Cassie to Joseph. She handed the guy his bacon.

"Thank you," said the guy. "Nice to see that not everyone in here is unreasonable and aggressive."

Lucy came back into the shop.

"I didn't buy any meat," she said to nobody in particular. "Oh, hello, David. Hello, Senna."

David was the man, Senna was the dog. Joseph guessed that he'd been named after Ayrton Senna, because this guy was just the sort of arsehole who liked Formula One.

"How's Emma?"

Joseph was pretty sure that Emma was the loud blonde. If this was her husband, then it all made perfect sense: they spoke at the same volume, and were equally convinced that everyone would want to hear what they had to say.

"Fine," said David, but he wasn't very interested in the question. His head was still in the argument. "If I were you," he said, "I would make sure you're served by the girl, not the chippy kid."

"Just take the dog out," said Joseph. "Don't stop for a chat."

"I beg your pardon? I'll stop for a chat wherever I feel like it."

"Let's go outside," said Lucy.

For a moment David looked as though he were going to resist. Joseph wouldn't have been surprised if he'd started feeding the dog raw meat in the middle of the shop, just to make the visit last longer, but he sighed, shot Joseph a look, and followed Lucy into the street.

"That's nice," she said to David the moment she thought Joseph couldn't hear them.

"What?"

"Throwing your weight around in there."

"I was just about to pay for my bacon when he tried to chuck me out."

"First of all, he's not a boy."

"Oh, here we go."

"And why was he chippy? Wasn't he just trying to enforce the rules of the shop?"

Such was Lucy's indignation that she'd misquoted

him. He hadn't called Joseph a boy. He'd called him a kid. There was a difference, but she wasn't going to tamp her indignation down. He was the sort of man who might have said "boy," and the sort of man who would know nothing about the history of the word. That was enough for her.

"I didn't know there were no dogs allowed."

"I think you should go in there and apologize."

David barked an incredulous laugh.

"Yeah, that's not going to happen."

"I didn't think it would. I was just telling you what normal people would regard as the decent thing."

"Nice to see you, Lucy. I'll send your love to Emma. Come on, Senna." And then he started whistling, to show just how insouciant he was.

She didn't want to go back into the butcher's— for the third time—until she'd calmed down. She knew that her fury was out of all proportion to the event, and she had to at least try and work out what was going on before she saw Joseph again. She was worried that he wouldn't like her interference, that there was something complicated in it that wasn't good or healthy. Had she overreacted because David was white and posh? Why was it her business to intervene? Had she wanted to show Joseph something? Maybe that she was on his side, not David's? Why?

Joseph arrived on the dot of 7:30. She wasn't ready—and this time she was going to make some kind of effort—but she showed him around and introduced him to the boys, who were playing Xbox.

"This is Joseph. Joseph, this is Dylan and Al."

"Which one's which?"

They both put their hands up. Lucy rolled her eyes.

"They're clever at school. Not so smart at home."

"I'm Al."

"No, he isn't," said Lucy.

"Is that in-form Ronaldo?" said Joseph.

The boys looked at him with interest.

"You play FIFA?"

"Yeah."

"When did you start?" said Al.

"FIFA '06.'"

"'06'? Wow."

"They weren't born," said Lucy.

"I'm old," said Joseph. "Anyway, I'll beat both of you."

Dylan offered him a controller.

"Wait a minute," said Lucy. "I need to tell him some things before I lose him down a black hole."

"What time's bedtime?"

"They're staying up late to watch something or another. A sporting event."

"El Clásico?" said Joseph.

"Of course," said Dylan.

"Wow. So I play FIFA and then watch El Clásico? We don't have Sky at home. I hope I can afford all this."

"It's all free," said Dylan.

"Right, but I must have to pay your mum something?"

"She's going to pay you," said Al, in the manner of someone delivering amazing news. "You're the babysitter."

"I think he was joking," said Lucy.

"Kind of," said Joseph.

"Anyway, El Clásico. Whatever that is. And straight to bed."

"Gotcha."

"I'm not being tricked, am I? El Clásico isn't something that lasts all night?"

"It's just a football match."

"Fine. And help yourself if you want something to eat or a drink."

"I might have a beer once they've gone up."

"I'll be back no later than midnight."

"Whatever. Text me."

After she'd got ready and kissed the boys good-night, she could see that they could scarcely believe their luck.

**The boys were with her** because Paul had got drunk last night, his first lapse. He had woken this morning sick and wretched, but at least he'd had the decency to call and tell her. He didn't try to get out of his weekend obligations to his sons. On the contrary, she knew that he looked forward to them, and they made the battles he was fighting easier for a couple of days, gave shape and purpose to a time otherwise only defined by absence. She knew he was angry with himself, and she knew this weekend was going to be terribly hard, unless he spent it drinking, in which case it would be ruinously easy. If he'd gone even a couple of days without booze she would have tried to convince herself that forty-eight hours of parenthood would do him good, but the freshness of the calamity meant that the risk was too high.

She would have canceled the evening in most circumstances, but she'd been looking forward to it. Her college friend Fiona and her husband, Pete, had invited Lucy to dinner, and even though Fiona hadn't said as much, she was setting her up with a recently divorced writer, a novelist whose work she liked. He was ten years older than them, but he had kids of the same age, and Fiona had been careful to mention that his ex wasn't up to much. She'd worked at his publishers, and Fiona said it was a fling that had gone terribly wrong. Lucy just wanted to flirt with someone. It had been awhile.

**Michael Marwood's books** were sober, quiet, and short, but Michael Marwood the person did not seem to prize brevity, and he drank two glasses of wine while Lucy was watching him speak. He was in the middle of a long story about a reception at 10 Downing Street to which he had been invited, a story with lots of famous people but no narrative or subtext, as far as Lucy could tell, and he barely broke off to say hello. He had a rapt audience (there was another couple there, neighbors called Marsha and Claire) and he wasn't about to relinquish it for anyone. Even when Pete disappeared into the kitchen and came back with the food, Michael showed no inclination to let anybody actually eat it.

**It was a round** dining table, and he was sitting to her right.

"I was hoping this might happen," he said conspiratorially, but as nobody else had started talking, they all heard.

"What?"

"That we'd be sitting next to each other."

"Well," said Lucy. "Fifty-fifty chance."

"With six of us? I must be luckier than that."

"Well. I'd be two of us, because I could have sat either side. And you're one."

There was a silence for a moment, while they both tried to work out whether this was right, and then gave up on the calculation at exactly the same time. Michael shrugged and laughed, and Lucy wondered whether she might be able to forgive him for his boring story.

"Were you listening to my boring story?" he said.

She laughed.

"I caught the end of it."

"Was it terrible? I drank three glasses of wine quite quickly, and I suddenly found myself in the middle of it. I mean, those things really did happen. But so what? I'm so sorry. I've sobered up now."

She found his apology rather disarming, and now she began to notice other things about him, better things. He had a smart but age-appropriate haircut and a neat, speckled-gray beard. And he smelled good, some kind of limey old-school gentleman's cologne that was probably part of a shtick. But smelling nice was good, however one got there.

"So," he said. "How are *you*?" And yes, he placed the stress on the second word.

Lucy rolled her inner eyes, and then immediately hated herself for being so judgmental. Perhaps she would be better off on her own, with occasional sexual adventures. Who would want to live with someone who got irritated by one of the simplest and most commonplace questions in the English language? But you couldn't ask strangers how they were. You asked friends how they were. The inquiry presupposed some kind of knowledge of the past, a context in which to set the answer, and he had nothing. Only those young charity people who stopped you in the street used that particular route in, which told you something about its insincerity.

"Hello," said Lucy.

She had confused herself. She had meant to say something dry and acerbic along the lines of, "I've had a sniffle but it's cleared up now," and he might have realized that the question was synthetically intimate and unanswerable, and laughed at himself. Instead, he looked at her as if she were mad.

"Hello again," he said.

The others were all talking now, so there was a

little bubble of privacy around them. Michael wanted to make the little bubble even smaller, though. He leaned in, and started murmuring things that she couldn't really hear. She was pleased to learn that he had a volume control knob, because there had been no sign of one before dinner. However, it wasn't a dial, as such, more of a switch, with a choice of two settings.

"I'm sorry?"

"Did you know beforehand that we were being paired off?"

"I knew a single man was coming. Does that count?"

"Did you mind?"

"Did I mind that Pete and Fiona were inviting a single man for dinner?"

"You know perfectly well what I mean."

"No, I didn't mind. I was pretty sure there was no pressure on me for a long-term commitment."

"Ah. I see. You prefer shorter-term commitments. I shall bear that in mind."

"The length of a dinner party is fine."

She was quite enjoying herself now. She didn't mean to be unkind, but he kept placing her in situations where the put-down was so inviting as to be unavoidable.

"I've read your books."

She cursed herself. Now she was the gauche one.

She had never sat next to a writer at dinner before, especially one who had been brought along for the purposes of evening up the numbers.

"All of them?"

"I don't know. How many are there?"

"Seven, if you don't include the poetry collections."

"Oh, I haven't read the poetry. Should I?"

"Not if you don't want to."

"You're on the syllabus now, you know."

"So I've been told."

"What does that feel like?"

"It's very flattering."

"So it doesn't make you want to hang yourself?"

"No! Should it?"

"All those children hating you."

"I went to talk to a class and they seemed very enthusiastic."

"Where was that?"

"Highgate."

"Oh. Right." Of course he'd been to Highgate. "You don't mind going to talk to private schools?"

"I haven't been invited to a state school. I'll come to yours, if you want."

"We wouldn't know what to do with you."

The head wouldn't be pleased if he ever found out that she was gaily turning down offers from Michael Marwood, even if he was unlikely to know who Michael Marwood was. He was very interested in feathering caps, and he didn't mind which bird the feathers had fallen off.

"Well. That's telling me."

"Sorry. We're not a terribly literary school. We're happy if they read anything."

"Am I not anything?"

"What would you say to them?"

"I'd tell them how lucky they were to have you as a teacher."

"You have no idea what I'm like."

"I wasn't talking about your classroom management."

And he looked at her. Lucy was beginning to suspect that he might be what the girls at her school would refer to as a "fuckboy," a word she discouraged them from using because of its first four letters but which in all other ways seemed an entirely welcome neologism. There had always been tarts and slags and sluts, and now there were fuckboys, and the contempt with which the girls spat the word out gladdened her heart. If she had to guess, she'd say Michael Marwood's marriage had ended because he was a fuckboy, or a fuck-man, at least, and his wife's nightmarishness was neither here nor there. Marriages ended, and marriages ended because unhappy or dissatisfied people met somebody else. But when unhappy and dissatisfied people met somebody else and then somebody else and somebody else again, you could be forgiven for wondering whether the unhappiness and dissatisfaction were incurable.

There was nothing wrong with fucking a fuckman, of course, as long as one understood the terms in advance. Lucy hadn't had sex for a year, hadn't had sex with anyone other than Paul for twelve years, and even the sex a year ago was an oasis in the desert, which was almost certainly the wrong metaphor to describe a moment of weakness and unhappiness in the middle of a whole lot of confusion. Her mental energy was almost entirely spent on the boys and work, but there was a little bit left over for herself, and increasingly it went on fantasies, or speculation, at least: when, who, where. So why not Michael Marwood?

She excused herself, partly because she needed to pee, partly because she thought she should check her phone, and saw that she'd missed five messages from Joseph.

**It was as Joseph** had described. Paul was outside, sitting on the pavement with his back to the front wall. Joseph was standing guard in the doorway. As she was paying the cab driver, she couldn't help thinking about how cold the house must be.

She stood over her ex-husband.

"What are you doing?"

"That fucking kid assaulted me."

"We talked about that before it happened," said Joseph. "I told you I wasn't going to let you in, and that I'd use physical force to stop you. I didn't hit him," he said to Lucy. "I pushed him and he fell into the hedge and then he crawled out there."

"Thanks, Joseph. Close the door and sit with the boys, would you?"

"Ring me if you need any help."

"Thank you."

The light cast onto the pavement from the doorway disappeared, and Lucy stood there for a moment, not knowing what to say or do. She wanted to sit down next to Paul, to show some kind of love and solidarity, but it wasn't even ten o'clock, and she had no wish to explain to a neighbor putting out the bins or returning from the cinema that . . . Actually, there was no explanation she could come up with, other than the truth, which was that she had been summoned home from a dinner party because her ex-husband, formerly an ex-drunk, was now a drunk again, although he was not her husband again. She had wanted to stay married to him, because staying married to anyone is an accomplishment, but there were circumstances beyond one's control, and here were several of them. (Were these circumstances beyond her control? Or were they her fault? The therapist had told her off about this way of thinking, but every now and again she found herself wondering whether Paul's dependency was a product of their relationship, rather than an act of God, or genetics, if those two causes weren't the same thing. Maybe if she hadn't asked for or refused to be more this, or less that, then none of it would ever have happened. The therapist could say whatever she wanted, but who knew, really?)

"Can you stand up?"

"Why?"

"Because I don't want to have to call the police."

He looked at her, hurt.

"Why would you call the police?"

"Oh, Paul."

"It's not about 'Oh, Paul.' Don't give me any 'Oh, Paul.' There's too much 'Oh, Paul.' And not enough…"

He clearly couldn't think what there wasn't enough of, compared to the excess of "Oh, Pauls," but he pursued the thought nevertheless.

"Not enough just normal Paul."

"When I say, 'Oh, Paul,' I'm expressing sympathy and despair. I have plenty of both, and I can't do much about the latter, but I can cut out the former if it helps."

"Just stop saying stupid stuff about the police."

She had the feeling that his rage was spent, and there would be no police. But if it happened again, what was she supposed to do? She understood Paul from the inside out, two kids, nine or ten parents' evenings, eleven or twelve Christmases, eight or nine holidays in France, five seasons of **The Wire**, however many hundred fucks and takeaways. (Could it be thousands? Four figures if you added the fucks and the takeaways together, probably, although there was no earthly reason why you would.) Where did the police fit into that? But if one of her friends had told her that her husband had come round while she was out, attempted to get into the house, and grappled with a babysitter, she'd have told her to get an exclusion order.

"I'm going to call Richard."

"No. Not that cunt."

"He's your brother and he worries about you. And no more c-word, please. You can stay with him and Jude tonight."

Paul responded to this with an enormous puke on the pavement and a lot of bad language. She was relieved about the puke. He would now feel wretched but regretful.

"Can I come in? I don't want to sit out here anymore."

"I don't think that's a good idea. The boys are watching the football."

"On a Saturday night?"

"El Clásico."

"Oh, fuck." And then, at the top of his voice, "FUUUUCCCK." And he punched the wall.

The first "fuck" was simply, oh, I forgot, I'd have liked to watch that instead of sitting in the street. She presumed that the second, longer expletive came as a result of him remembering the plans that had been made last weekend. They were going to get pizzas, had already chosen the toppings, and they were going to place bets, real bets with real money, on Paul's betting app. (The bets were never more than a pound, he assured her, and the idea was to combine a whole series of improbable events so that the returns would be astronomical. It was good for their maths, he claimed, and in any case they had been uncorrupted by wealth so far.) But he'd wrecked it all, destroyed an evening all of them had been looking forward to, and the obscene howl of anguish (and the wall punch, less ambiguously) contained proper self-loathing.

"I don't think they should see you like this. When did you start drinking?"

"I was all right until five. But five is a difficult time at a weekend when you're on your own."

"I know what you mean."

"Do you?"

"Yes. It always feels weird when the boys are with you on a Saturday."

"I couldn't be with the boys today because I got drunk. So I got drunk again. Fucking hell."

"I know."

He started to weep quietly. No noise, just a few tears rolling down his cheeks. It was all agony. It was agony for him, and it was agony for her, and the two agonies combined until they were no longer distinct—simply a cloud of grief and pain that enveloped them, on a dark wet pavement smelling of vomit. She had to get out, take her own cloud away with her, somehow, otherwise they would both be incapable.

"Let's walk down to the end of the road and get you an Uber." And I'll tell Richard you're on your way."

"What's the name of the guy that assaulted me?"

"His name's Joseph. It's his first time babysitting."

It would probably be his last too, she realized.

"Will you say sorry from me?"

"Even though he assaulted you?"

"That's not the whole story. As you probably guessed."

"Yes."

"I approve, by the way. I'll bet the boys got on with him."

"You might want to use him one day."

They both knew that Joseph was very likely to be unavailable that evening, but it was an imagined future of sorts, and she could see that it had a moderately cheering effect. She called Richard, walked Paul down to the Broadway, persuaded a reluctant Uber driver to let Paul into his car, and walked home. The boys were double-screening, much to Joseph's disgust. They were watching football and YouTube and they had headphones on and they'd missed the whole thing.

**"You're early,"** said Dylan. "You said Joseph would be putting us to bed."

"Yeah, well. I'd finished my main course and I didn't like the look of the pudding so I came home."

This was the kind of logic they understood. It was hard to imagine that they would behave any other way, even when they were forty and going to their own dinner parties. They would hover by the door and say, in one unbroken word, "ThanksverymuchfordinnerI'vefinishednowand I'veputmyplateinthedishwasher."

"What?"

"Take your headphones off."

"I've only got one ear in. What did you say?"

"I said, I'd finished my main course and I didn't like the look of the pudding so I came home."

"What was the pudding?"

"Why is Mum home?" said Al.

"She didn't like the look of the pudding."

"What?"

"Take your headphones off."

"They are off."

They weren't off.

"MUM DIDN'T LIKE THE LOOK OF THE PUDDING."

"What was the pudding?"

"She won't tell me."

"Fruit, probably."

"Just fruit?"

"Probably."

"Not much of a pudding."

"Der, that's why she came home, penis-head."

"Will you please stop saying that?"

"Sorry."

"Anyway, you can stay up a bit longer. I'm having a cup of tea with Joseph."

"What?"

Lucy felt that the latest "what?" marked the end of the conversation, so she went through to the kitchen. She didn't want a cup of tea, though. She wanted a drink, but she felt awkward about it. If you needed a drink because your drunk ex had come round and got into a shoving match with a babysitter, was that post-facto enabling of some sort? Or inappropriate dependency? Alcoholism by proxy? She imagined that there might be support groups for all of these conditions, if you looked online. Islington Post-Facto Enablers probably met every Thursday in the basement of St. Luke's church.

"Would it seem really inappropriate if I had a glass of wine?"

"Well," said Joseph. "I suppose it depends whether you're an alcoholic who will want to fight me when you've knocked it back."

"No."

"Fine by me, then. People drink."

"Do you?"

"Sometimes."

"Would you like one?"

"You don't have any beer, do you?"

"I think the Indian might have given me a free one with the last takeaway."

She rummaged around at the back of the fridge

and found it, a bottle of Kingfisher. He drank it straight from the bottle, the first half very quickly.

"I'm so sorry," said Lucy when she'd poured her glass of wine.

"It's fine."

"Well. It isn't. I didn't warn you it might happen, and you weren't expecting it."

"Has it happened before? I mean, to other babysitters?"

"No. Plus, it didn't cross my mind. I suppose in my defense it would have been like warning you about a, a burglary. Or a lightning bolt."

Joseph spent longer than he should have done wondering what was wrong with this comparison. He knew about burglars and lightning bolts, and had assessed the risks accordingly. He didn't know that Lucy had an alcoholic ex-husband who might turn up at any moment. He was a bit more than a lightning bolt. He was more like a loaded gun, or a forgotten knife in a pocket.

"It's not your fault." It was a tiny bit her fault, by the loaded-gun calculation.

"I know. But I'm so embarrassed. It's like something out of . . . **EastEnders.**"

"Maybe that's why people like **EastEnders.**"

"I suppose so. But I'm the Head of English at a

secondary school. I'm supposed to have an orderly life."

"Is that what you honestly think?"

"Yes. Of course. Half the kids have got drunk fathers turning up and causing a scene. I can't be a part of all that."

Lucy would have liked to claim that she spotted the danger as soon as she'd uttered the phrase, but it wouldn't be true. Joseph was on it before she'd had a chance to reel it in.

"What's 'all that'?"

"Drunk parents turning up and causing a scene."

"Well, you already are a part of 'all that.'"

"Yes, but not..."

She stopped. She saw it now.

"Your drunk husband is different from their drunk fathers?"

"I see what you mean."

"Do you?"

"Yes. My mess is the same as anyone's mess. There's no such thing as Head of English Department mess."

"Yeah," said Joseph. "Here's the thing. The moment you're related to somebody else, you're in trouble."

"We're all related to someone else, from the moment we're born."

He nodded.

"That's what I'm saying."

He was quicker than her. Or rather, she thought she could get away with not being her quickest self, because she was older than him, but she couldn't. She could probably beat him in a quiz about Jane Austen, but that was about it.

"Is there chaos in your family?"

Joseph knew that this was probably the time to offer her something in exchange, but he didn't feel like exposing his own family, his wayward cousins and his bad-apple uncle, just to make Lucy feel better.

"There's chaos in everyone's family."

He finished his bottle of beer.

"I'm going to head off."

He felt flat. There had been a fantasy that involved him staying the night and sneaking out in the morning before the boys woke up—a quite involved fantasy that he'd been finessing while watching the football with Al and Dylan, before Paul had arrived. The fantasy hadn't survived the events of the evening, though. If he were ever going to sleep with Lucy, there would have to be some kind of serious plan in place, with every possible move and countermove thought out in advance. He wasn't very good at chess, and it wasn't a particularly sexy game anyway. All that thinking killed the vibe.

"Oh. OK."

Did she feel flat too? If she did, that was as close as he was going to get to any kind of sexual spark. And mutual flatness wasn't the same as mutual attraction.

# 3

When Joseph got to work on Saturday morning, Cassie was on the pavement, staring at the window.

"What's up?"

"What's he done that for?" she said.

"What?"

She nodded at the poster. It was the sort of thing Joseph never took any notice of. It looked boring. It just said **VOTE LEAVE ON JUNE 23rd** in black letters on a Union Jack background.

"Well," said Joseph. "He probably thinks we should vote leave on June the twenty-third."

"People won't like it."

"People won't give a shit."

"Round here? You're joking."

"Really? The bloody E.U.?"

Joseph hadn't really thought about it until that

moment. It was April, so the referendum was still weeks away. He was probably going to vote to leave, like his dad, but he couldn't see that it would make much difference to his life one way or the other. There'd still be meat, leisure centers, kids, football.

"My parents wouldn't shop here if they saw that," said Cassie. "They hate Nigel Farage and Boris Johnson."

"Your parents don't live round here, do they?"

"No. They live in Bath. But same sort of thing."

"Bath is the same as London?"

"This bit of London is the same as their bit of Bath. Dad teaches theater, Mum teaches creative writing. I mean, they wouldn't be able to afford it round here, but a lot of the people we serve remind me of them."

"And they wouldn't vote leave?"

"No. Of course not."

Joseph had no idea that there was any "of course" about it. He thought everyone was going to vote differently. Obviously there were only two choices, but he'd presumed that, say, Cassie's mother might vote differently from Cassie's father. It looked like it was going to be an us-and-them thing, except he wasn't too sure who was on either team.

"I must admit I'd forgotten about Nigel Farage," said Joseph.

"Everyone hates him," said Cassie.

"Are you two just going to look through the window all day? Because I'm not paying you for that," said Mark from the doorway.

They went into the shop.

"Are you sure you want that poster in the window?" said Cassie.

"What's wrong with it?"

"A lot of people round here won't like it," said Cassie.

"Shall I put the other one up?"

"What does the other one say?"

"'Stronger in Europe.' With the first two letters of Europe in red, so you see the E.U. bit. Quite clever."

Only Mark could come to the conclusion that this was clever, thought Joseph. You didn't have to be a genius to work out that the first two letters in the word "Europe" could be used for the E.U.

"Hold on," said Cassie. "You'd switch from one poster to the other, just like that?"

"I don't give a shit, do I?"

"Don't you know how you're going to vote?"

"I'm voting to leave. Too much red tape. Too many Albanians."

"Albania isn't in the E.U."

"Who is then?"

"Spain, France, Poland, Ireland, Germany, Italy... You want me to name them all?"

"Poles, then."

"So why put a poster saying the opposite in the window?"

"If you're telling me it's good for business, why wouldn't I?"

"Because it's not what you believe."

"Listen. I can't stand liver, but I sell it, and I want everyone to buy it. What's the difference?"

"Liver isn't a personal philosophy."

"It sort of is, to me."

"Not liking liver is a personal philosophy?"

"I'd say so. But I'm a businessman first, philosopher second."

Second? Joseph thought. That was a generous ranking system. Mark was a ballet dancer more than he was a philosopher, and he was six foot two, twenty-odd stone, and in his mid-fifties.

Cassie seemed to give up at that point, and Joseph couldn't blame her. They went into the back to put their aprons on.

**Mid-morning he got** a text from Lucy. They hadn't spoken for three weeks or so, not since the babysitting. She hadn't even been into the shop, unless she was timing it very carefully so that she

could avoid him. She'd texted him to apologize
and he sent one back telling her not to worry, but
that was it. She was embarrassed, probably. He
missed her, though. He got a boost when she came
in, a spark that gave the morning a glow. He went
to the toilet to read the text because Mark didn't
like them on their phones in the shop.

She was asking whether he had a lunch hour
and, if so, whether he'd like to drop in for
eggs and bacon. The boys would like to see him.

She lived a couple of minutes from the shop, so
it wasn't as though he'd lose any of the break
commuting.

**am I babysitting** he texted back. It was a joke.

**Oh. No. Sorry.**

That was how she texted. Capital O capital N
capital S, with all the full stops. You could tell she
was an English teacher, but it was something
Joseph liked about her, on top of all the other
things. He couldn't quite say what it was. He
didn't get any other texts as precise as that, so
partly it was a sense of being introduced to someone different. And it was sexy, kind of. Why using
punctuation in a text was sexy, he couldn't say, but
he found himself wondering what it would be like
to sleep with someone like that. He was going to

try to be as careful with his messages, at least with her. He couldn't imagine that she'd find no punctuation as attractive as he found punctuation. She had kids. He didn't want to be another one.

**I get off at 12:30.** She wouldn't be expecting "12:30 am," would she? Or was it "a.m."? Except it wasn't, was it? It was "pm" or "p.m." He decided to leave it as it was. She'd get the idea.

**Fried eggs OK?** she texted back.

**Yes.** And then he added an exclamation mark. **Yes!**

That sounded friendlier, he thought.

**See you then.**

**Al answered the door.** He was holding a tray containing a glass of orange juice, and he had a tea towel over his arm, like a waiter.

"Do come in," he said. Joseph took the glass and Al disappeared.

He'd never done anything on a Saturday lunchtime apart from buy a sandwich from next door and eat it out the back. But he walked into a room smelling of coffee and bacon. And there was sunlight, toast and marmalade on the table, jazz on the Bluetooth speaker, Lucy at the stove, her hair tied back in a scrunchie. The three-minute walk had taken him into a different universe. She turned to him and smiled.

"Hello. Did he spill the juice?"

Joseph nodded at the glass in his hand. He was trying to work out why she looked different from anyone he knew. She wasn't wearing very much makeup. And she was wearing a long gray cardigan that by rights shouldn't have done much for her. It seemed to hang nicely in some way that he couldn't have described. It wasn't tight, it wasn't baggy, and there was no brand visible anywhere. Oh, and the eyebrows: they hadn't been shaved off and painted back on to make a thick dark line. He didn't know whether he liked all this because it was different, or because it was her. He knew it was weird, zoning in on the eyebrows, but eyebrows had become a thing the last couple of years, and they freaked him out. He didn't know what function eyebrows were supposed to perform, but whatever it was, they weren't there to be looked at. So if you ended up looking, it seemed to him that something had gone wrong.

"Good," she said. "Are you hungry? I didn't ask if you were vegan, or Muslim, or anything."

"Nothing that stops me eating eggs and bacon."

"But you're something?"

"Yeah. Sort of. I suppose. Christian."

"Oh. What does that stop you from doing?"

He was sure she didn't mean it to sound flirta-tious. She didn't look away from the pan, and all he could hear in her voice was curiosity. But he could feel his voice thicken, and as a result his answer, which was supposed to be neutral and reassuring, came out like a desperate bark.

"Nothing."

She laughed.

"That's the kind of religion I like."

"I mean, it stops me from staying in bed on a Sunday morning, but..."

"You go every Sunday?"

"I try." He didn't need to get into the endless Sunday arguments with his mother.

"And you believe in God."

"The short answer is..."

He didn't know whether the short answer was yes or no. Maybe he believed that God created the universe, but he didn't know where that got him. And when he saw the old ladies on Sunday in the first couple of rows, he wondered whether God let too many people off the hook. They'd had depressing, difficult lives, the people who'd come over decades ago, and they still turned out every week to thank God. He didn't have a lot of time for the idiots who'd looted the electrical stores in Wood Green five years previously, the only night his mother had ever locked the door to keep him and his sister inside. But if he had to choose between chucking a brick through a window and sitting around waiting to die so that he could enter the Kingdom of Heaven, he wouldn't have to think for too long.

"Sorry. You only came round for eggs and bacon. Boys! It's ready!"

The boys came in, spudded Joseph, and sat down. They wanted to talk about football, in its physical and virtual incarnations, and they wanted to know when he would be babysitting again.

"I haven't been asked," he said.

"We're asking you," said Dylan.

"I need somewhere to go first," said Lucy.

"What about tonight?" said Al.

"I definitely haven't got anywhere to go tonight," said Lucy.

"Next weekend, then."

"OK, next weekend," said Lucy. "If you're not busy."

"No," said Joseph.

"Neither am I," said Lucy, and laughed.

The coffee was out of a pot, and the bacon was crispy, and the jam was homemade by a colleague at Lucy's school.

"This is to say sorry," said Lucy. "And we hope you'll give us another chance."

Joseph looked at her and widened his eyes, as in, are we allowed to talk about that?

"The boys know," said Lucy.

"Oh," said Joseph brightly.

"Dad got drunk and started a fight," said Al. "And you pushed him over."

Joseph didn't really know how to proceed.

"Yeah, well," he said. "I shouldn't have done that."

"Oh, you should," said Dylan. "When Dad's drunk, he's horrible. I'd push him over, if I was strong enough."

"You never will be," said Al, matter-of-factly. Al was the younger of the two, and much bigger than his older brother.

"Yeah, but I go to judo. So I can smash people bigger than me."

"You won't be smashing me, mate. I can just hold you off with one hand."

"We're here to say sorry and thank you to Joseph," said Lucy firmly.

"You don't have to say sorry," said Joseph. "Any of you."

"We just don't want you to think it would always be like that if you look after the boys."

The boys had already finished eating, and their desire to see Joseph had been extinguished.

"Can we get on with our games? We're both in the middle of FUT Drafts."

"Oh, well, in that case," said Lucy. "Are they being rude, Joseph?"

"It's fine by me."

He didn't want to seem too keen to get rid of them, so he tried to say it casually. They were gone almost before he'd finished the sentence. Lucy shrugged.

"More coffee before you go?"

"Thank you." He held out his mug. It was orange and white, and said GREAT EXPECTATIONS CHARLES DICKENS on the side. He wasn't going to say anything about Charles Dickens. He'd cross that bridge if the bridge ever got built. There wasn't even anything for the bridge to go over yet.

"I don't even know what you do the rest of the time."

"Oh, a bunch of stuff. Some child care, some football coaching, a couple of days in the leisure center, some D.J.-ing."

He should have left out the D.J.-ing. It was both the most interesting thing in the list, and the one that wasn't strictly true. But it was the thing that stopped him from being someone going nowhere with a string of unconnected jobs.

"Oh, you D.J.? Cool."

Shit.

"I'm more...There isn't so much D.J.-ing at clubs and parties yet." Not so much. "I spend a lot of time working on my own stuff."

That much was true. Or rather, it was closer to the truth than the stuff about D.J.-ing at clubs and parties.

"And then what do you do with it?"

"You play it for people. You develop a following. Someone hears it and you get offered a deal."

"That still happens?"

"Yeah."

"Well, good luck."

"I'll probably see you again before I make it."

He knew what she was thinking: everyone wanted to be a star. She probably had kids who wanted to be YouTubers, with followings of millions; she probably taught kids who wanted to be on **The X Factor** or **Love Island**. And here was another one. He knew he was good, and he knew he had ideas. But he wasn't daft. He also knew that he'd be managing a leisure center in fifteen years' time, if he was lucky.

"Why haven't you been in the shop recently?"

"I was embarrassed. I thought I needed to thank you properly, not by text or over the counter."

"How did the boys find out about the, the fracas?"

"Paul told them."

"Oh. Why?"

"I don't know. Well, I do know. Honesty is very important to him, when he's going through this. He's got a sponsor and all that. It's something to do with him. But it wasn't a shock. They've seen him do stupid stuff before."

"That must be hard for you."

"I think it's harder for him. He's made a mess of his marriage and his parenting."

"Is it too late?"

"Marriage, yes. Parenting, no. I hope not, anyway. Maybe when they're older they'll get properly angry. Now it comes and goes. Do you want kids one day?"

"I suppose. I don't really think about it."

It was stupid, but he didn't want to talk about what he might or might not want to do with another woman. (He was pretty sure it would have to be with another woman. They'd have to get a move on, if it was going to be Lucy.) He looked at his phone.

"I should go."

"Thank you for coming."

"Ah, no. That was so nice. The best Saturday lunch I've ever had. Hey, can I ask you something?"

"Sure."

"You know the referendum? How are you going to vote?"

"That's a very personal question, young man."

"Oh. Yeah. I'm sorry."

"I'm joking. I'm voting to stay in."

"Do you know anyone who's voting out?"

"My parents. But they read the **Daily Telegraph** and live in Kent."

"That's it?"

"I think so."

"OK. Thanks. We were talking about it at work this morning."

For a moment he wondered if he should tell her about the voting intentions of the people he knew, his father and some of the people at the gym, but she seemed to think that she'd given the right answer, an insight into the minds of everyone in the world of adults, so he let it go.

She walked him to the door, and as he was leaving she kissed him on both cheeks. She smelled of something that none of the girls he'd ever kissed would have worn. It probably wasn't even a perfume—it didn't nuke your nostrils the way a perfume did. It was a cream, or a soap, and the subtlety and lightness felt grown-up. The kisses and the scent were like the gray cardigan and the eyebrows. They took him out of himself. On the way back to the shop he felt a little bit shaky. If he didn't start seeing someone, he was going to make an idiot of himself. He'd already begun to make an idiot of himself in his head. He needed to forget about eyebrows. And he wasn't about to start reading Charles Dickens just because of a coffee mug.

**He met Jaz** because he wasn't looking for her, although there had been many times in his life when he might have been. He was in the leisure center, putting away the badminton nets and putting out the five-a-side goals, when she came up to him to ask if there was a women's five-a-side league.

"Asking for a friend," she said.

"Well, tell her there isn't at the moment, but we're trying to get one started."

"I'm the friend," she said.

"Who are you a friend of?"

"That's what people say, isn't it?" she said. "Asking for a friend. Like, 'Do you know how I can get talking to the fit guy who works in the gym and never takes any notice of me? Asking for a friend.'"

"I'm lost."

He wasn't, really.

"OK, so say there's a peng guy who works at the gym."

"Yes."

"Well, how can I get talking to him?"

"I could introduce you."

"What if it was you?"

"Me?"

"Christ. Yes."

"And do I know the friend?"

He was winding her up, and taking pleasure in both the flirtation and the irritation.

"I'm the bloody friend."

"You're the friend AND her friend?"

"There is no other person. Only me. I am the person wondering how I can get talking to the fit guy—you—at the gym."

"We've been talking for ages."

"Not about what I want to talk about."

"What do you want to talk about?"

"When we can go out."

Only now did Joseph begin to take notice of her. All things being equal, the eyes usually swung it, and not just because it was the eyes that made the face beautiful. The eyes were everything— they contained the first indication of whether someone was smart, kind, funny, hungry in all the right ways as well as some of the interesting wrong ones. Jaz had great eyes, big and brown and alive. But all things had to be equal, and, without examining Jaz too closely, he could tell that there was a great deal of equality.

"Thursday," he said.

"Is that because you've got a girlfriend and you see her at the weekends?"

"It's because I have a load of jobs and I'm working Friday night."

"Good answer."

She'd plucked her eyebrows, but it was all within the bounds of reason. He'd only just noticed, for a start, which meant that they weren't leading the attack. She seemed more concerned to accentuate the equality of all things, although that might just have been the natural properties of gym wear. She'd chosen to approach him while wearing it, though, so she certainly wasn't trying to hide anything.

"I see my girlfriend Wednesdays and Saturdays."

Jaz laughed and punched him on the arm. That seemed like a good sign.

"I'm Jaz, by the way."

"Hi. Joseph."

"Not Joe?"

"Never."

"Got it."

They put numbers into each other's phones, and Jaz went to find her spin class.

---

**Lucy wasn't expecting** to hear from Michael Marwood after her sudden disappearance from the dinner party, but he called one evening, just as she was preparing tea for the boys.

"Oh, hi."

She had the presence of mind to keep the last vowel short. Elongating it, she felt, would have suggested an enthusiasm and excitement that she'd rather not reveal. There was a great deal of excitement, she realized the moment she heard his voice—not necessarily for him, but she knew that he'd have phoned Fiona to get her mobile number, and Fiona would have teased him about it a little, and he'd plowed through the teasing anyway and here he was. There was intent. Intent was always enthralling, or it used to be, back in the days when someone might phone with it.

"What are you doing tomorrow? I wanted you to be my date for something. A film premiere. But I should warn you, I don't think the film is very good."

"Oh."

"And as a consequence, the premiere won't be very glamorous."

"Oh."

"Sold?"

She laughed.

"Sold."

"But please don't judge me on the bad films that are made from friends' books."

"Is that what we're going to? A bad film made from a friend's book?"

"I'm not going to that," said Al, who was sitting at the kitchen table doing his homework.

She shook her head at him and made a face.

"Will you meet me there?" said Michael. "It's in Belsize Park. Seated by seven p.m."

"I'll see you tomorrow."

**Joseph was in the leisure center,** sitting on the lifeguard's chair, when he got her text. He wasn't supposed to be on his phone, but there was one woman in the pool, and she was walking her lengths. A lot of the older people did that when they'd hurt themselves somehow. She wasn't about to drown any time soon.

**Are you free tomorrow night?**

And then, before he'd had a chance to respond,
**I'm going on an actual date.**

**Ha,** he said. **I've got one too.**

**Anyone nice?**

Don't know her really. And then, But she's hot.

Hot is good.

Oh, I'm free btw...by the way.

Lol, I know btw! Mine's not hot. Too old. But attractive.

So hot then.

Middle-aged hot. Warm.

How old is he?

I don't know. Fifty-something?

How old are you?

Ha. What? Well, how old are you?

Twenty-two.

Oh. I was hoping you wouldn't tell me. And then, after a short pause, I'm forty-two.
Christ. He would just ignore that.

What time?

**Early OK? 5:30/6?**

Joseph started to text a joke about middle-aged dating and then deleted it.

**Fine.**

He was just about to put the phone away when there was another ping.

**What makes her hot? Interested.**

**Ah basic stuff.** And then, **Not proud.**

**But she's nice?**

**No idea yet.**

He had to say something, now they were this close to the subject. He had to say something, while at the same time he knew already that whatever he said he would regret bitterly as soon as he sent it. The trick was to be vague.

**There are all kinds of hot.**

That wasn't so bad. He didn't want to run to wherever she was and snatch the phone out of her hand, at least.

---

**There are all kinds of hot.**

Was it pathetic to imagine that he was expanding the definition to include her? Or was he talking about Michael? But that would make no sense. They had moved away from the subject of Michael, surely? If he was talking about her, telling her that she was one kind of hot, in his opinion, and his Thursday-night date another . . . Well, it wouldn't mean anything, surely? If Joseph's mother went out on a date, and she looked at herself in the mirror, wouldn't a devoted son say something like, "There are all kinds of hot, Mum"? Almost certainly. She imagined that Joseph would be a kind, supportive son.

So that was it. She was hot like Joseph's mother was hot. The conclusion depressed her, inevitably. She didn't want to be Joseph's mother in this or in any other context. She read through the thread again, just to make sure. **Basic stuff . . . not proud . . . no idea if she's nice . . . all kinds of hot.** If she showed this exchange to a friend, she was pretty sure that the bolstering-mother theory would be demolished very quickly, partly on the admittedly solid grounds that she wasn't Joseph's mother. But then, that was the trouble with friends. It was their job to bolster too. And it was

impossible to ascertain which of the two competing bolsterings was closer to the truth. The whole
point of bolstering was that it wasn't very interested in the truth.

She was in her office, more or less on her own:
Missy, a Year Ten student who had been sent out
of a junior colleague's lesson for throwing a book
at a love rival, was sitting in the corner, apparently
revising. Missy would almost certainly be able to
interpret the troublesome text with insight and
empathy, but it would be inappropriate to ask her.

**How many kinds of hot are there?** she wrote. It
was some minutes after the original exchange, so
she felt she had to repeat some of the key words, in
order to remind him of the subject. Her neediness
was naked.

She deleted what she had just written and wrote,
**How many?** But he wouldn't understand that. **How
many different kinds of hot are there?** she wrote.
She deleted it again. **How many?** she wrote. If he
didn't understand, then she wouldn't explain—
unless he asked her to, that was. And then suddenly
she sent it, and she wanted to run to wherever he
was and snatch the phone out of his hand.

# 4

There was a little knot of people standing outside the cinema, and Michael was having his photograph taken with a man of his own age, presumably his friend, who looked uncomfortable and apologetic. The photographer was a young woman, and she was using her phone for the shot, so it was hard to imagine that it would be featured on a tabloid website, or in **Hello!** magazine. Lucy guessed she worked for the publisher of the unfortunate writer whose book had been butchered, according to Michael.

When Michael saw her, he excused himself and came over to kiss her on both cheeks. The young woman with the iPhone smiled in her direction, and took a couple of shots as Lucy and Michael embraced.

"Oh," said Michael. "No. No. You see…"

"Oh," said the young woman. "Shall I delete them? I'll delete them."

"They don't need deleting as such," said Michael.

"Right. So. Keep them?"

Michael turned to Lucy and laughed awkwardly.

"Would you forward them to me?" said Lucy.

"Sure. Give me your number before the end of the evening."

"That's very sweet of you," said Michael when the photographer had gone. "And hello, by the way."

"Hello."

"Like I said, I'm not sure it's going to be an evening you'll want to remember forever. But I'm flattered that you wanted the photos anyway."

She didn't want the photos. She'd wanted to stop the excruciating conversation about whether they should be deleted or not. And now, within seconds of her arriving, Michael Marwood had come to the conclusion that she was overexcited about both the premiere and the date.

"Will you send one on to me when you've got them?"

She could tell that he was saying this because he thought he had to, otherwise it would seem as though the evening meant nothing to him.

"I don't want them," she said.

She had now gone too far the other way.

"I only said I wanted them because the poor girl was embarrassed about having taken them in the first place."

"Oh," said Michael. "I see. Well. That's put me in my place. You're good at that."

"I mean, I'm sure I will want to keep them. Eventually. If I…If we…Actually, I'm just not going to give her my number."

Michael laughed.

"OK then."

How else was one supposed to deal with the problem of being captured for all eternity, or until the young woman ran out of storage space, in the first ten seconds of a first date?

**Heartstrings was the story** of two lonely people living solitary lives at the opposite ends of the country, who meet online through their shared love of medieval music in general and the lute in particular. If you wanted to learn about the lute, then **Heartstrings** was the film for you: who knew, for example, that the town of Haslemere in Surrey, where the instrument makers Arnold and Carl Dolmetsch lived, loomed so large in lute folklore? Or that there was a Dutch church in London, where lute recitals frequently took place, and where the couple eventually meet? Or that, if you listened to the lugubrious sound of the lute for nearly two hours, you wanted to gather up every lute in the country and burn them on a gigantic bonfire?

**Lucy could see** what the filmmakers had been pitching for. They wanted Lucy's mother, and every other middle-class retiree in the country, to flood their local cinemas on a weekday afternoon when the tickets were cheap, and then tell all their friends to go the following weekday afternoon. The trouble was that the film was too boring even for Lucy's mother, and, worse still, was psychologically opaque. Why did the lonely woman give her lute away to a dim-witted teenage girl just when she seemed to be finding happiness with a member of the lute-playing community? Why did the lonely man have a small collection of whips in his bedroom, clearly visible on the wall beside the mirror, but never explained?

"In the book, he was up to no good with the whips," said Michael afterward. They were in a French bistro not far from the cinema, but tucked away at the back in case the butchered author and his entourage should happen to choose this particular restaurant for their wake.

"Really? The whips were put to use?"

"Yes. On young men. It was quite an odd book. And I think at one point they wanted to preserve some of the darkness but then they changed their minds in the edit. Decided to go for the **Best Exotic** crowd instead. But let's not talk about them."

Michael clearly thought that the gap between the cinematic preferences of Britain's pensioners and seduction was too wide to bridge elegantly, and he was right: he had failed to pull it off. Lucy laughed at the gear change, and Michael looked puzzled.

"We can talk about them if you want," she said.

"Well, do you want?"

"I'm happy to talk about anything." And then, with a twinkle, "It won't make any difference."

Michael looked at her.

"To what?"

"To anything that might happen at another time, I suppose."

She was going to say "later" instead of "at another time," but that seemed a little too bold, even for her current mood. She could see now that she had merely been confusing.

"Which other time?"

"Well. Later." She'd said it. "Or anytime after that." She'd retracted it again.

**For two reasons,** she had decided on the way to the cinema that she would sleep with Michael. Her ridiculous text conversation with Joseph had troubled her. If she was going to make a fool of herself by mooning over a young man nearly half her age, she should at least find out whether an enforced period of sexual abstinence had anything to do with it.

And in any case, all inappropriate thoughts of Joseph aside, a single woman having sex with a reasonably attractive single man didn't and shouldn't require an enormous amount of consideration. What was the big deal? It hadn't been a big deal before she met Paul. She wasn't slutty back then, by any stretch of the imagination, but neither had she regarded each potential sexual experience as an episode of **The Moral Maze.** She wanted to take the weight off it all, or at least see if it was possible to do so. She was almost sure it was, but it had all been so much easier before.

A lot of things, she remembered, were done vertically—not sex, very often, but drinking, and talking, and dancing, and all these vertical activities seemed only inches away from a kiss, and the kiss was only a few more inches away from a bed, and horizontality. Now there were films about lutes, and menus to study, and awkward, self-aware conversations. There was psychology! What use had she had for psychology when she was drunk and twenty-five? Years and years of being a grown-up had given her entirely obstructive clues to what was going on in the minds of other people. They half revealed themselves in everything they did and said, and Lucy wished she could ignore it all.

"I'm still not sure what will make a difference to what," said Michael. "Or what might or might not happen as a result."

"I can see that," Lucy said.

"Do you know what you fancy to eat? The **steak frites** is very good here."

"'Is'? Or 'are'?"

"I see what you mean. But isn't it '**le steak frites**' in French? It's one dish. Not one steak and many **frites**."

The **steak frites** was twenty-five pounds. She was glad that Joseph wasn't here, although it was hard to imagine the circumstances in which he would be. In her guilty imagination, he already thought they were mad for occasionally spending eight quid on a piece of meat. What would he say if he knew that they would then spend another ten or fifteen paying someone to cook it for them? She was glad that Joseph had no access to her mind, because then he would know that she was almost certainly patronizing him. He had probably long got used to the prices in his shop. And he probably knew how much meals cost in nice restaurants. If he lived at home and worked several jobs, it was possible that he had as much disposable income as she did. But to be on the safe side, she decided to give meat a miss.

"The squash risotto looks nice."

"Are you a vegetarian?"

"I have two meat-obsessed sons. I eat meat every other day of the week because I'm too lazy to cook two dinners."

This was a perfectly plausible explanation, she thought. She didn't need to tell him about Joseph, and money. And then it occurred to her that if she did invite Michael back after the meal, he would meet Joseph.

"You'll meet our butcher if you come back for a drink."

There was a baffled pause, and then Lucy laughed, embarrassed. This was a more direct invitation than the reference to nothing making any difference, but she had somehow managed to make it sound like a small reception for local shopkeepers at the same time.

"Jolly good," said Michael.

"He's our babysitter."

"Ah. I see. He needs extra money despite all the meat you buy from him?"

"He works in the shop. He doesn't own it. The boys love him."

"Because of their meat obsession?"

"Because of his knowledge of football and his skills on the Xbox."

She was talking more about Joseph than she'd intended.

"Anyway. None of that is relevant. But if you'd like to come back for a drink, you'd be very welcome."

"Thank you."

He wasn't leaping up and down in gratitude and celebration, but neither was he saying too quickly that he had to be up early in the morning and therefore he would have to politely decline the offer. Maybe the jumping up and down was too much to expect at their age, especially as, from the sound of it, it wasn't the first time Michael Marwood had been invited back for a drink. Maybe the jumping up and down was too much to expect at any age, come to think of it.

"I'm spared all that."

"Sorry?"

"Xbox. Two girls."

"Oh. Yes. Lucky you. What replaces it?"

"Books, mostly."

Lucy shot herself in the head with her fingers. He laughed.

"Sorry. They're not good books, if that makes any difference. Lots of dystopian misery."

"Oh, awful. I'm glad my boys are spared all that and sit with their mouths open looking at a screen all weekend. Do the girls live with your ex?"

"Yes. They stay with me every other Saturday night. The old story."

"How do you feel about that?"

"Oh, it's painful, of course."

Lucy wondered whether she'd hear some version of this for the next ten or fifteen years, until she started dating men whose children had gone to college. She wondered too whether one of them would ever say, it's fucking great! I see them and I pay for their upkeep but the rest of the time is my own. She doubted it. For a start, it wasn't allowed. She'd have to withhold all sexual and emotional contact from a man like that, however refreshing the sentiment.

"I can imagine."

There. They had observed the traditions, and they could move on.

Their starter was a shared garlicky prawn dish, so of course she began to think about whether she had any chewing gum in her bag, and whether he'd be offended if she offered him some on the way home. And then she wondered about the message that would send, its directness and its prissiness, and then she worried that he'd notice she was thinking about everything that might or might not come afterward and not noticing the conversations they were having now. She shook herself down and banished all anxieties about chewing gum.

They talked about writing, teaching, the referendum. (Michael scoffed at the idea that a country would ever vote against its own economic interests, and Lucy was reassured by his confidence.) They talked about the failure of their respective marriages, and his explanation for the misdeeds that brought about the end of his was neither glib nor self-servingly self-loathing. She liked him. She invited him back for a drink, and he looked at her and pantomimed fear. But he was smiling too.

"Joseph, Michael. Michael, Joseph."

They shook hands.

"Like the publisher," said Michael.

Joseph looked at him blankly.

"There's a publisher called Michael Joseph," said Michael.

"Oh," said Joseph.

"Yes," said Michael. "Not the kind of books I'm interested in, particularly," and he chuckled.

"Michael is a writer," she said, in a desperate

attempt to explain why he'd mention the publisher Michael Joseph within ten seconds of meeting someone.

"Cool," said Joseph.

He wasn't going to ask Michael what he'd written, she could tell. The information would be of no interest. Lucy had invited local writers to speak to her kids, sometimes, and the visits were always met with utter indifference. It used to frustrate her—she had only ever been introduced to dead authors when she was at school—but many of her ex-students were all grown-up now, and they had become nurses, policemen, travel agents, shop assistants, London Underground workers. There were two professional footballers, one accountant, one vet, and a rapper. They were becoming valuable and valued members of society without the help of fiction.

The two men stood for a moment, staring at the floor, and Lucy tried not to think about anything when she looked at them. It was only Michael, a novelist she'd just had dinner with, and Joseph, the babysitter who worked in the butcher's. In particular she tried not to think about the physical differences between them: Joseph's unlined face, Michael's graying stubble, Joseph's height and lean body, Michael's liver-spotted hands and his little paunch. If you added the ages of the men together and divided them by two, you would arrive at a number that was more or less Lucy's own age, but the trouble with life was that you only traveled in one direction. She was rushing away from Joseph and toward Michael; she could, she felt, only look at what was in front of her, not behind her.

"Did you have a nice evening?" said Joseph.

"I'll let Lucy answer that," said Michael.

"Well. Neither of us liked the film very much, but the dinner was good."

"It's better that way round," said Joseph, and Lucy laughed, perhaps more than the witticism deserved.

"Have the boys been OK?"

"Fine. We had fun."

"Xbox?"

"They did a bit of homework too."

"They chose to do homework?"

"No. I asked them if they had any, and then they did it."

"Oh. Wow."

If anyone had ever asked Lucy to provide a list of things that she considered sexy, the word "homework" would not have been required, even if this list were hundreds of pages long. But there was a sudden, familiar but almost forgotten, pang of something. Had she got to an age where responsibility and firmness were attractive characteristics? And how did Joseph get there decades before her?

She gave Joseph forty quid, the pain of the expense slightly less sharp than when she and Paul had spent a scratchy evening in a noisy restaurant, and showed him to the door, leaving Michael alone in the kitchen.

"Thank you," she said, and she kissed him on the cheek before she had even thought about what she was doing. He grinned and walked off down the street.

She shouted after him.

"Hey, do you want an Uber?"

"No, I'm fine."

He stopped and walked back toward her.

"I take it back," he said. "There's only one kind."

"Sorry?"

"Just . . . what we were saying. Aargh. Forget it."

And this time he broke into a jog toward the end of the street.

**She opened a bottle** of wine, got a couple of glasses, ushered him through to the living room and pretended to take an age choosing a CD to play.

"What do you like?" she said.

"What have you got?"

"Oh, most things. Marvin Gaye?" Oh, God. Marvin Gaye sang songs about sex. "Joni Mitchell? Adele?"

"Is Adele any good? I'm afraid I haven't kept up much with music."

She didn't disabuse him of the idea that Adele was an indication of her coolness. She put on one of Paul's Dylan albums, to Michael's obvious relief and comfort, and sat down next to him on the sofa.

"Ah, Bob," he said.

"Yes."

Bob was as helpful a conversation starter as Michael Joseph had been.

There was a pause, and they both took glugs of wine. Michael put his hand on Lucy's knee, in a friendly rather than lecherous fashion.

"I should say that it's a bit hit-and-miss these days. Actually, let's not say 'these days.' Let's say 'at the moment.'"

Lucy didn't know what he was talking about.

"OK."

"It's just... If we're headed that way, I thought it better to explain now rather than for you to discover for yourself later."

"Thank you."

There seemed to be honesty and some kind of consideration involved, so thanks had to be appropriate.

"May I ask...Well, what's the hit? And what's the miss?"

"Ah. Yes. I was being needlessly opaque. So. The hit is everything working normally. The miss is...nothing going on at all."

The fog had cleared. She still thought he was probably a fuckman, but his eyes were bigger than his belly, as her mother used to say, and that must have been confusing for him.

"I just don't want to be one of these men who say, oh, this has never happened before. When it has."

"Right."

"So."

"Have you thought of...taking the medical route?"

"Yes. Of course. More and more frequently. But then suddenly everything comes back to life and I think, oh, I'm over it. You hear such awful stories, don't you?"

"Do you?"

"Yes. Of things...lasting too long, and discomfort, and excruciating embarrassment."

This, then, was what she was rushing toward, but surely there were some other stops along the way? She'd rather presumed that Viagra and so on would come toward the end of the journey— Plymouth, say, if you were traveling to Cornwall.

But what happened to Reading, Bath, Bristol Temple Meads? She didn't know what the sexual equivalent of Bristol Temple Meads was, but she'd somehow fallen asleep and missed the stop.

"This is all incredibly unseductive, I know. But it's so confusing, the erratic nature of it all."

"Have you detected any rhyme or reason to the hit-and-miss?"

Michael addressed his wine again.

"I have developed some theories, but...I'm not sure I want to talk about them. And it's not fair on the, the...Anyway."

"Oh. I'm sorry to..."

"No, no, it's..."

What were these theories? And why were they unfair? And how would he have finished the sentence about fairness? Lucy wasn't troubled, just extremely curious. If he were about to say that it wasn't fair on the potential sexual partner, then surely the suggestion seemed to be that the malfunctions only happened with a certain kind of woman. But what kind? What if you had to be of a certain level of intelligence? That if you weren't smart enough for the prize-winning author Michael Marwood, it just lay there, leaning back, bored and unimpressed? Or, worse, it got halfway up and then gave up the ghost? But it could be anything—breast size, arse size, weight...She would have to stop thinking about it immediately before her guesses took darker and more particular turns. Something to do with his mother? The woman who looked least like her? Most like her? Least/most like his father? Why did all mental perambulations and panics lead to the parents of potential sexual partners?

"And...Obviously I'm taking a risk in telling you anything. But I would value your discretion. I understand that one particular female novelist has been entertaining people with stories of my misfortunes."

"From experience? Or hearsay?"

"Touché."

"Touché"? She hadn't made a witty or telling point. She had merely asked a question. She could only presume that in this context, "touché" meant shut up.

She hesitated.

"Can I say one more thing about it?"

"And then we talk about something else."

"There's a lot more to sex than that."

"A lot more?"

"A lot more."

She had no idea whether this was true or not. Paul's problems frequently resulted in malfunction, but they never bothered trying to overcome them—he got angry and as a consequence she didn't want to have sex with him anyway. But she knew this was a thing people said.

"I think that's true within a relationship. I'm not sure it works when you're, well. Dating. If that's what I'm doing. And you're doing. We're doing, come to think of it."

"No?"

"The last couple of years, since the end of my marriage, I often seem to be attempting sex with women who for one reason or another have lost their confidence. A husband has left them for a younger woman, or they're not meeting any-one...I mean, there are a hundred reasons, aren't there?"

"For both genders, I'd have thought."

She was thinking of poor Ted, who was looking for someone plain.

"Yes. Yes. Of course. Both genders. But I go to bed with someone, and nothing happens...Well, you can say there's more to sex than, than that, and you're right, but you can see that..."

"Yes. Yes."

She just wanted to stop him from talking about it now. There was a part of her, inevitably, that wanted to find out whether she was a hit or a miss, but it was much, much smaller than the part that wanted the evening to end as soon as possible.

———

**Joseph called his dad Chris,** and he called his mum Mum. He didn't need a shrink to understand why that might be. Chris lived just up the road from the cinema where Joseph was meeting Jaz, so he went round there for a cup of tea first. He didn't like going to see his father. Chris brought him down. Life hadn't gone the way he'd wanted it to, and that was his main topic of conversation. A lot of his unhappiness wasn't his fault: for the last few years he had been in and out of work because of a chronic shoulder injury. The injury had resulted in a dependency on Subutex, a heavy-duty opioid that Joseph suspected he was now half addicted to, and he spent much of his life looking for new doctors who would prescribe it. It was all a mess.

Chris lived in a ground-floor apartment on the Denham estate, and he had a red poster in his window: TAKE BACK CONTROL. VOTE LEAVE ON JUNE 23RD, it said. Joseph knew the moment he saw it that he shouldn't ask about it. He'd be on the receiving end of a rant that would occupy the whole of the visit. Joseph had no idea why his father wanted to display the poster, or whether he would agree with him. Past experience had taught him that when Chris had a bee in his bonnet about something, it was best not to disturb the bee.

But it was immediately clear that something had changed. The apartment was clean, and no longer smelled of either dog or cigarettes, which it used to do long after Chris had stopped smoking and the dog had died. And Chris was smiling at him.

"How are you, son?"

"I'm good, Chris, thanks."

"Did you see my poster in the window?" said Chris.

"No."

"Vote leave."

"Yeah. You said that was the way you were going."

"How are you voting?"

"Dunno," said Joseph. "Hadn't thought about it. How've you been?"

"Yeah. Good."

"Good?" Joseph wasn't sure Chris had ever used the word before, in answer to this or any other question.

"Yeah. Optimistic."

"That's great. Why?"

"Because of all this. I've got involved. Giving out leaflets and all that."

He was pointing at the poster.

"What difference is it going to make to you?"

"You haven't thought about this at all, have you?"

"Not really. I thought everyone was voting remain."

"No, mate. Not round here. Literally nobody is voting remain. Who've you been talking to?"

Joseph decided that Chris wouldn't necessarily want to know about Lucy and the other customers at the shop.

"I don't know. I just got the impression."

"Wrong."

"Well, I will think about it properly now."

"Nothing to think about. Not if you're a working man."

"You keep telling me I'm not."

"I know you work hard, son. Just because you're not a scaffolder doesn't mean you don't put in a shift."

Joseph found it hard not to gape. This was not an opinion his father had ever previously held or expressed.

"The apartment's looking nice."

"It's all about supply and demand. If they want anything built in London, they're going to have to pay people properly."

Chris handed Joseph a mug of tea. You could just about make out the words DAD OF THE YEAR on the side of the mug, nearly worn away now. Or maybe only Joseph could have seen them. He had given Chris the mug, a long time ago. He wanted to take it back. He also wanted his father to buy some new mugs.

"The thing is, I've got no problem with immigration. Immigration is why we're here. But they haven't come here to be a part of Britain, have they? All the Eastern Europeans and all them. It's a hit-and-run. Undercut the locals, earn some money, fuck off home. Meanwhile, those of us who are stuck in one of the world's most expensive cities can't make a living."

"Right."

"You know Kelvin who I used to work with at Canary Wharf?"

"No."

"Well, I keep in touch. And he reckons they'll have to pay twenty-five quid an hour if the Eastern Europeans leave."

"Have you seen Grace recently?"

"Why aren't you interested in what I've got to say?"

"I am interested. But I'm going to the cinema in a bit and I wanted to talk about something else before I go."

"She won't come round here."

Joseph's sister was renting an apartment in South London with friends. She worked as a teaching assistant in Balham.

"Have you asked her?"

"No."

"Why don't you meet her somewhere?"

"'Meet her.' Where am I going to meet her?"

In the old days, a few weeks ago, before he'd found his purpose in life, this was Chris's favorite trick: the repetition of the suggestion, followed by a question related to it that he seemed to think was unanswerable. It was a habit born of depression, but Joseph frequently had to stifle a laugh, because most of the time he could answer the unanswerable questions with a couple of words.

"The pub? McDonald's?"

"Maybe I will."

If he did, then Joseph would know that the prospect of leaving the E.U. was more powerful than any happy pill. Vote leave to bring unhappy families together.

**Jaz had made an effort**—she looked like someone who was going out on a date. She was wearing a tight spangly shirt over leggings, and there was glitter on her face. Joseph was, he supposed, regretful about the Nike track pants and top, but not regretful enough to apologize. They decided to see a horror film called **Satan's Butcher**. The poster showed a butcher in a bloody apron holding a meat cleaver. His eyes were red.

"I hope it's about a butcher who's possessed by Satan and slices people up," said Joseph. It was supposed to be a joke. The poster didn't offer up too many other alternative interpretations.

"What else is it going to be about?" said Jaz, as if he were stupid.

Happily, it did indeed turn out to be about a butcher who was possessed by Satan, and Jaz grabbed his arm every time something awful happened, which was approximately every two minutes until the last half hour, when there was no pause between one horrific assault and the next. Joseph was frequently distracted by the incompetence of Satan's Butcher. Joseph wasn't allowed to carve up carcasses himself because he hadn't been trained, even though Mark who owned the shop wanted to train him. (He didn't want to learn because he didn't want to be sucked into working there full time.) Satan's Butcher used a cleaver instead of a knife, and he cut with the grain, which was pretty much the most stupid thing you could do. Cutting with the grain made the meat much chewier, and though Joseph had never seen Mark create steaks from a human corpse, he was pretty sure that the same rules would apply. Satan's Butcher did a slightly better job with the ribs, but that was more by accident than judgment. He was still hacking away with a cleaver, which would sort of do a job for you, although not as good a job as a saw, and he seemed to think that he could sell the end ribs, whereas in fact the end ribs are full of fat, and more or less useless. (Again, this was assuming that human ribs were roughly comparable to the ribs of a cow.)

It occurred to him that Jaz didn't know anything about his Saturday job.

"I'm a butcher," he whispered to her after the Demon Butcher had laid out his steaks for display in his shop.

"Shut up," said Jaz.

"I am," said Joseph.

"You're never a butcher."

"I work in a butcher's shop, anyway."

"No, you don't."

"Why would I lie?"

"Because we're watching a film about a satanic butcher and you want to scare me."

The man in the row behind leaned forward and tapped her on the shoulder. He was probably in his forties, cropped blond hair, with a woman. He was the kind of man that Joseph always thought of as potentially troublesome. Jaz turned around.

"What?"

"I just want to join in," said the man. "I can't hear what they're saying on the screen so I might as well talk to you. What are we talking about?"

Joseph couldn't help thinking that if you had to tell someone to shut up, this was a stylish way of doing it.

"It's not your fucking business," said Jaz.

That, on the other hand, wasn't quite as cool.

"Well, don't make it my fucking business," said the man. "Shut up."

A few people were turning round now. One person clapped.

Jaz was angry now.

"Let's just watch the film," said Joseph. Jaz was pouty, but she didn't say anything else.

"**Where shall we go?**" she said as they were walking out.

There was no evidence that the incident with the man in the row behind was still alive in her, which Joseph took to be a bad sign: the implication was that a confrontation was all part of a regular evening out. He found himself wondering whether he would ever go to the cinema with Lucy. It was completely possible, of course, in the sense that very small ambitions can be achieved quite easily, if one can be bothered. He could just ask her, maybe after a couple more babysitting sessions. He could say, "Lucy, this film looks really interesting, but I don't know anyone else who wants to see it and I don't like going on my own. Do you fancy it?" And she would almost certainly say yes, if she could find a babysitter. But of course that wasn't really what he meant, was it? Or maybe it was. Maybe he just wanted to go to the cinema with a woman who was unlikely to say, "It's not your fucking business" to the person sitting behind them. Except he never went to the cinema, really, unless it was on a date, which seemed to bring him back full circle.

"Hello?" said Jaz.

"Oh. Sorry. Do you want a drink or something?"

"I was thinking more, you know, my place or yours? Except not mine. No privacy."

This whole evening, if he were honest, had been prompted by his need for sex. But now that it was apparently on offer, the prospect seemed beside the point, unrelated to anything that had happened between them so far. Was that how it worked? They watched a film about a butcher possessed by the Devil, she told someone to fuck off, and then wanted to know where they were going to do it? That felt more like finding an empty space in a bike rack than having sex. He wasn't looking for somewhere to park it.

"No privacy at mine either."

There were only two of them at home, now that Grace was gone, and his mother didn't really mind if he disappeared upstairs with someone. She'd worried when he was fourteen or fifteen, and she was right to worry, but since he'd reached an age where he might reasonably be trusted to know what he was doing, she'd relaxed.

"So what we going to do?"

"You can come home and meet my mum, or we can go somewhere."

**There was a note** on the kitchen table reminding him that his mum had started working nights. She'd left half a chicken pie in the oven for him. She refused to believe that he never touched pie.

"So there's nobody here?"

"Nope."

"Ooooh," said Jaz, and put her arms around him from behind.

"Do you want some tea?"

She let go of him.

"Have you got any vodka?"

"Vodka?"

"Yeah. Is it bad to ask?"

"No," he said, and he shrugged, the shrug suggesting the opposite, somehow.

"I don't want to get drunk. I just want to, you know. Loosen up a bit. Will you have one?"

"No, I'm all right."

"You don't seem it."

"Meaning what?"

"I dunno. You're all tense and yes-no."

He hadn't said much on the bus, but she'd been on her phone all the time. At one point she lifted it in the air and took a photo of the two of them. She showed Joseph the picture. He thought he looked puzzled. She posted it somewhere, or sent it to someone, but Joseph didn't ask where or who, and afterward she just went back to scrolling through Instagram.

He knew there was a bottle of vodka. Neither he nor his mother drank much, and someone had brought a bottle to their Christmas party. It was in the freezer, virtually untouched.

"What have you got to go in it? Coke?"

"No. We never have Coke in the house."

"You're a lot of fun, aren't you?" said Jaz. "No vodka, no Coke…"

No chicken pie, no sex, Joseph thought. What was wrong with him?

"What about orange juice?"

"Unless you want to do shots."

He was going to have to say yes to something soon, but he had no intention of doing shots either.

"I think I'll have a vodka and orange."

He got the bottle out of the freezer, the juice out

of the fridge, and a couple of glasses. Jaz watched him pour the vodka.

"We'll need a bit more than that. Won't even know we've had a drink."

He had always had this streak of…Well, he didn't know what you'd call it. Self-denial? Obedience? Something to do with the Church? A lot of it came from wanting to stay fit for as long as he possibly could. His weight hadn't changed since he was eighteen, and the shape of his body was important to him. That explained the chicken pie and the Coke, the vodka, even. He was disappointed that he wasn't more interested in Jaz, though. That was nothing to do with fitness. It wasn't anything to do with the Church, either.

"I don't even know what you do," said Joseph.

"I'm at college."

"Yeah? What are you studying?"

"Tourism and Hospitality Management at South Bank. This is my last year."

"Then what?"

"I dunno. Hotels, probably. I'd like to go and work somewhere else. Out of England."

"You don't like it here?"

"Who likes it here? Gray, expensive, pisses with rain all the time."

"I don't mind it."

He didn't know if that was true, but he felt defensive. He didn't want to move anywhere else, so unless he stuck up for the country, he'd be admitting a lack of ambition, and yet more self-denial.

"Where do you want to go?"

"The States. California."

"Don't you need a visa?"

Visas! He was depressing himself. He hated to think what he was doing to her.

"Fucking hell," said Jaz. "I thought this was going to be the easiest whatever, hookup, in the history of the world. Good-looking boy, single, seemed interested in me. And now he wants to go all negative about my travel arrangements for something I probably won't do in ten years' time."

"I'm sorry. I didn't want you to be disappointed."

"Thank you. Are you going to kiss me or what?"

"You still want to?"

"I'm not enjoying the chat much, so ..."

Joseph laughed and kissed her. He could feel himself respond, but the response felt inappropriate, disconnected. He was going back to the idea that there was more than one kind of hot. There was the Jaz kind, with the hotness apparently independent of, and maybe even fighting with, the actual person. And then there was the Lucy kind, where the heat seemed to intensify the more you got to know her. Could that be right? If so, it seemed troublesome.

Suddenly, without any warning, Jaz began to sing—Beyoncé, "Drunk in Love." The bit about waking up in the kitchen saying how the hell did this shit happen. Jaz's voice was so unexpected, so powerful and husky and distinctive, that Joseph laughed.

"Jesus."

"Yeah," said Jaz. "I got that too."

"You're incredible."

Jaz shrugged, as if to say, I told you so.

"Where's your bedroom?" said Jaz.

"My bedroom?"

"Yeah. Your bedroom. Strike while the iron is hot."

"Who's got a hot iron?"

He honestly hadn't meant it to sound smutty, or flirty. He was just trying to work out how the metaphor worked. Had the singing made her iron hot? Or did she think the singing would have conquered any lingering resistance?

"I'm hoping you," she said. And the effect of the kiss shrank away. At that moment, he realized properly that he wanted someone else.

"Yeah, listen," said Joseph. "I think this might be going a bit quick for me."

"What?"

"Yeah. Maybe we should go out a couple more times."

"What?"

She seemed to be literally unable to understand what he was saying, and he could see why. He could hardly believe it either. Something had happened to him. A beautiful girl wanted to know where his bedroom was, and he didn't want to tell her.

"I'm not interested in marrying you," said Jaz.

Absurdly, he felt a little sting of rejection.

"How did you work that out so quickly?"

"What, you want to marry me?"

"No, see, the thing is, I am sort of with somebody."

"Ah, you fucking lying bastard."

"I'm not with them with them, but..."

"What's that supposed to mean?"

"I dunno."

"Well, think."

He could understand why she would want clarification.

"I wasn't with anyone when you asked me out."

"Who asked who out?" said Jaz, outraged. That was less reasonable.

"Well, whoever asked who out, I wasn't with anyone. But since then, things have moved on."

"You asked me out two days ago!"

"Yeah. I know. But something I thought was dead came back to life."

"When?"

Given the timescale, he didn't have too many options for this answer.

"Yesterday."

"Yesterday?"

"I know. It's weird. Affairs of the heart have their own timings."

There were many things about this conversation that would later make him shrivel up inside, but this was the line that he regretted the most. Where had it come from? An old film? A book he'd had to study? He'd been groping around for something that sounded grown-up, but he'd shot right through adulthood and out the other side.

"Is that another of your jobs? Writing shit Valentine's cards?"

Joseph laughed. It was funny. But Jaz didn't think it was a laughing matter, and went home. Her voice, the power and the shock of it, stayed in the room after she'd gone.

# 5

The church they attended didn't look like a church. A long time ago, it had been a library, but it was an old building, dating from some time in the nineteenth century, and that was enough for Joseph's mother. Its high ceilings and Victorian brick meant that she could be patronizing about the places of worship, mostly African, that had taken root in betting shops and supermarkets all over Tottenham. "Those poor people," she said as they passed them on the bus, but there was no pity in her voice, only superiority. She needed the status gap.

Joseph always regretted going to church. He didn't believe in God, but the Kingdom of Heaven Baptist Church didn't believe in letting you disbelieve quietly at the back, and neither did his mother. He had to be on his feet, praising Him at the top of his voice, otherwise he'd get a nudge. One day he would tell his mother that he wasn't devout enough for the kind of effort required.

His phone pinged during the sermon, and he apologized in a whisper to his mother straight away, but she wasn't happy, and the disrespect would not be forgotten. He took the phone out of his pocket to turn it off, but not before he'd seen that it was a text from Lucy: **Free tonight? How was date?** He replied as soon as they were outside. His mother was talking to an old lady in a wheelchair, something she always did on Sunday morning. If he wanted to be cynical, he'd allow himself to observe that she seemed to make a great big song and dance out of talking to the lady in the wheelchair, like it was an enormous gesture of Christian charity.

**Date bad. What time?**

**Do you want to eat with us? 6:30?**

**Great.**

"**Your sister's coming up** for dinner tonight," his mother said when they were waiting for the bus.

"Tell her to go round and see Chris first."

"She doesn't want to see him."

"He's all right at the moment. I went round the other day. He's full of it."

"Full of what?"

"The referendum. He thinks that if we leave the E.U. he's going to be earning a lot more."

"Lord help us."

"You don't want him earning more?"

"I'm the only British person nursing on the ward at the moment. The rest are all Polish and Hungarian and Spanish. If we send them back, then we might as well pack up and go home."

"So you're voting to stay in?"

"Yes. Of course."

"He says all the Eastern Europeans are bringing his wages down."

"People say that."

"So who's right?"

"I don't know. But there are more N.H.S. patients than there are scaffolders. Anyway. We'll be eating at half six."

"Oh," said Joseph. "I'm out tonight."

"No, you're not. You're eating dinner with your sister."

"I'm babysitting. For Lucy. I'd be letting her down. You should have told me sooner."

"I didn't know sooner."

"When did she tell you, then? Because you didn't

tell me before church, and then you turned your phone off."

"Why do you have to jump when this Lucy woman says jump?"

"She's not saying 'jump.' She's asking if I can babysit. I can always say no."

"So say no."

"I've already said yes. Plus I like earning the money."

"What time do you have to leave?"

"Six."

"Six? On a Sunday? What's she doing at six on a Sunday?"

"I didn't ask her, Mum. Would it make a difference if I found out?"

The Sunday mornings his mother had worked the night before and went straight to church were to be endured, and Joseph usually managed it. She slept in the afternoons, after lunch, but before she'd eaten and gone to bed she was tired and bad-tempered. If he ever made any money from music, he'd try to get her to stop working, but she loved being a nurse, and being a nurse meant working irregular hours.

"Yes, it would. You have a family arrangement."

"Are you being serious?"

"I don't know why she can't take her children

with her to wherever it is she's going. It's early. Or maybe she could go later. It's at least worth asking the questions."

He phoned Lucy.

"Hi," she said. "Everything all right for this evening?"

"Well. My mum wondered whether you could take the boys to wherever it is you're going, because I promised to have dinner with her."

"I wasn't taking them anywhere. You were coming here to eat, and then I was going out."

"Oh. I see."

"You knew that, right?"

"Yes."

"Is she listening to you?"

"Of course."

"You should have dinner with your mum."

"No, no. I can see that."

He wasn't sure where this was going, or how to get there, but if he ended the call, the journey would be over, and for some reason he didn't want that. There was something happening.

"I don't know what to say," said Lucy.

There was a pause.

"Right," said Joseph eventually, and he hoped thoughtfully.

"How about this?" Lucy said. "If it's not tonight

it will be another night, soon. Because we were really looking forward to seeing you. All of us. I wish I wasn't going out."

That was enough. That was more than he'd expected or needed.

"Oh, no," said Joseph. "I'm really sorry to hear that. I hope she's OK. See you later."

"Her mother," he said when he'd ended the call. "She's been taken ill."

"So you must go." He knew she'd say that.

"I know."

"And don't be late."

"I wasn't going to be."

The social occasion at which his mother might talk to Lucy and discover that her mother was as fit as a fiddle was hard for Joseph to imagine. They'd get on, though, he knew that. Teaching and nursing were both jobs where you had to get on with everybody. And suddenly Joseph realized that his mother and Lucy were about the same age, and he felt sick. They were nearly the same age! He wanted to have sex with someone the same age as his mother!

"Just going on my Xbox for a bit, Mum. Go to bed."

"I need my breakfast."

He went to his room, got out his phone, and started googling people born in 1973 and 1974, people the same age as Lucy and his mother. Victoria Beckham. Penélope Cruz. Kate Moss. Tyra Banks. A lot of porn actresses he'd never heard of but who were porn actresses, which told him all he needed to know about their general lack of motherliness. There was nothing wrong with finding a forty-two-year-old attractive, judging from these pictures. The problem wasn't Lucy but his mother. Why did she look twenty years older than anyone here? She had given up on that side of life, the world of men and sex and dating, and she didn't seem that bothered. She was large, and she had trouble with her knees and her ankles. Was it just the lack of money that made her seem so old? Or had he and Grace contributed to it in some way? They had been good kids, mostly. His dad hadn't helped. But really, it was nothing to do with the behavior of people, Joseph didn't think. Maybe if his mother had been a Spice Girl and married an England international, she'd be more like Victoria Beckham now. That was a weird idea, and Joseph didn't want to spend much time thinking about it.

**While Lucy was cooking,** and the boys were playing on the Xbox, she tried, in a desultory fashion, to find somewhere to go for the evening. She'd told Joseph she wished she didn't have to go out, so she should at least make an effort to find a commitment to someone or something. She texted a couple of friends who couldn't possibly be available at this sort of notice on a Sunday evening, friends who would be dealing with tearful or stroppy children who hadn't done their homework or who were on their way back, tired and frustrated, from a trip to see grandparents. **Are you OK? Can come out if emergency,** Chrissy texted back. **No emergency,** she said. **Just thought it would be fun to listen to music or something.** Chrissy would think that these texts alone were evidence of a breakdown. Who thought going out on a Sunday night was fun?

And even if someone had taken her up on the invitation, there was every chance Lucy would have canceled at the last minute, which would only have added to the impression of irritating eccentricity. She wanted to have some sort of conversation with Joseph, although she didn't know the shape or content. Or maybe she was merely pretending that she didn't know. She was sending these texts just because she wanted to somehow fool herself into believing that the babysitting hadn't been entirely phony.

———

**The only trouble** was, she lost her nerve. She should have told Joseph the moment he came in that her evening had been canceled, but she didn't; and then, after they'd eaten, and he'd persuaded the boys not only to put their plates in the dishwasher but also to begin on the washing-up, he asked her where she was off to, and she said she was going out with a friend to see some music.

"Great," said Joseph. "What's the music?"

She could, of course, have said that she was going out for a drink, and sat in the pub for an hour on her own if necessary. Or she could have said that she was going to see a movie, and then gone to see a movie. But her mad text to Chrissy had somehow been filed away temporarily in her mouth, for immediate retrieval.

"Just this thing in Islington."

"Right," said Joseph. He was obviously reluctant to press her further, because he could tell that she was hiding something.

"Nothing secret," she said.

"I don't mind if you go to secret music."

"No, it's not the music that's not secret. I just meant, it's not a secret assignation or anything."

"OK."

He was humoring her. She was being humored by a twenty-two-year-old.

"I'm going with my friend Chrissy. To see a jazz saxophonist friend."

"Cool."

She didn't know where these details were coming from. Every word she said seemed to make life more difficult. "Chrissy"—unavailable. "Jazz"—knew nothing about it, and certainly didn't know where people played it on a Sunday evening. "Saxophonist friend"—particularly embarrassing, the pathetic fantasy of a middle-aged woman whose friends were all teachers or lawyers or had their own interior-design companies.

"Anyway," she said. "Gosh. I'd better go. I won't be late back."

And she put on her denim jacket, picked up the car keys, and walked out the door.

**She got in the car** and drove south, and ended up following signs to Regent's Park. She was glad that the clocks had gone forward, and the evenings were now light. She parked on the Inner Circle, and then walked in through the gates. It was a relief to be alone. During the drive, she'd realized that she was clueless, without a plan—and she'd always had a plan, more or less since the last couple of years at school. She had wanted to be head girl, and then she had wanted to go to college, and on and on it went, marriage, children, promotions, hurdles jumped over with relative ease. But she'd been thrown by men, first Paul and now Joseph, and she couldn't work out how to rejoin the race, or where on earth it would finish if she did.

Paul was the more violent of the two throws, of course. Nobody could have survived that without a couple of broken bones and a nosebleed. But the response, the head-girl response, was to take some time off sick, and then plod along—another promotion, maybe a sensible divorcée partner, maybe even a second marriage. But her feelings for Joseph troubled her because they were so flaky. What was she supposed to do with a twenty-two-year-old? Where did he take her? Because of Joseph, she really didn't know what she was going to do in the next five minutes, let alone the next five years. She was making things up as she went along, and the story she had come up with was wobbly and unconvincing. Her friend the saxophonist was merely a tragicomic representation of her third-rate imagination.

She walked around the lake and then checked the time: it was only 7:15. She wanted Joseph to put the boys to bed, not only because she was paying him to do so and she'd appreciate the break, but because if she simply went home, there was no real reason for him to be there, unless she asked him to stay. She went back to the car, stopped for a newspaper, and sat reading it in a quiet pub in Primrose Hill while nursing a glass of white wine. And then she went home.

"How was the jazz?"

Joseph was watching American football on T.V. The boys were asleep, and all the washing-up had been done. She tried not to swoon. Perhaps the secret to a successful relationship was to pay someone ten pounds an hour, every hour.

"Oh," said Lucy. "Well."

She could see that it was time to stop with the jazz, although the thought of doing so made her heart thump in her chest.

"Oh, right," said Joseph, and he laughed sympathetically.

"No, there wasn't any."

"Oh, no. What happened?"

He stood up, as babysitters do when one comes back from an evening out. A couple of minutes' chat about the dinner/film/play/jazz and a quick update on the kids, two or three ten-pound notes, done.

"Please don't do the babysitter stand-up."

He looked confused, as he had every right to do.

"Do you want me to sit down? Or just . . . not do that kind of standing up again?"

She laughed.

"It must have sounded like that. But there is no wrong way of standing up."

"Phew."

"Would you mind staying and talking for a bit?"

"Oh. Sure."

He sat back down on the sofa.

She sat down alongside him, keeping some distance.

"What happened was, I wanted to see you but I didn't have anywhere to go so I asked you to babysit and told you a lot of rubbish about friends who are jazz saxophonists. I don't know anyone like that. And then I drove to Regent's Park and walked around and then I read the paper in a pub and now here I am."

"OK."

"You can cut in at any point."

"Thanks."

He didn't seem to want to cut in, however, and Lucy was reminded of his youth. How could any young person make the running in this conversation? Did that mean she shouldn't be having it at all? Because of power dynamics and so forth?

"I think there's been a weird vibe between us, and I wanted to, you know..."

He wasn't going to help her out.

"Maybe look at what's going on."

"It's my fault," said Joseph.

"Why is it your fault?"

"Oh, you know, because I said there are all kinds of hot. It was inappropriate."

"Well, that's the problem. I liked it. I think."

"But you're not sure," Joseph said ruefully.

"Only because I wasn't one hundred percent certain about what you meant."

"When I said before that there was more than one kind of hot... That was wrong. There's only hot and not hot."

"Yeah, I got that."

"Oh."

"But it wasn't so hard to get. You said there are all kinds of hot. I realize that."

"So what aren't you sure about?"

"Why it was inappropriate, I suppose."

"Because I was trying to tell you you're hot. Terrible."

He shook his head, to underline the foolishness of the decision.

They had arrived at the crossroads. There was nothing further to say, really, unless they took the conversation into uncharted territory. It was like a chess match, but only in the way she played chess: she was looking for one more move that would keep the game alive.

"You're very sweet. Thank you."

She had found something. They could limp on for another few seconds.

He stood up again.

"Maybe I should go."

"Right. Any particular reason?"

"I don't want to sit here listening to you telling me how sweet I am."

"Oh. No. I didn't mean it like that."

"Like what?"

"Did you feel patronized?"

"Yeah."

"That's what I didn't want."

"I don't know what you do want."

"Really? I don't know how I could make it any more obvious without... Well, without being extremely forward."

He sat back down and kissed her, and they took it from there.

# 6

The first time Lucy and Joseph slept together came to be known as the Night of No Jazz, although the expression quickly became modified: the Night of Too Much Jazz, for example, or (when Joseph knew that Lucy wouldn't take offense) Jazz FL, a smutty corruption of Jazz F.M. Later there was a jazz festival, one Saturday night and Sunday morning when the boys were both away on sleepovers. They weren't staying the night with Paul at the moment, so the festival was a special event, to be exploited for maximum enjoyment.

"Was that a mistake?" said Joseph afterward. She was lying in the crook of his arm, on the sofa, wearing a T-shirt and nothing else.

"Not for me," said Lucy.

"Or for me."

"I wouldn't mind making the mistake again."

And that was the extent of the introspection.

**She was anxious** and vulnerable, at first. She was in good shape for a forty-two-year-old, but she still had the body of a forty-two-year-old and the shape was the result of not much chocolate and the occasional visit to the gym, rather than an intensive regime of yoga and a personal trainer. Nothing was as taut or as smooth as it once had been. She would never have thought about any of it if he had been the same age as her, but the moment he started touching her, she couldn't help but think about what he might be used to, there, and there, and even or especially there. She kept the T-shirt on as a damage-limitation exercise, but maybe that was like closing your eyes and claiming invisibility, because there were many ways for him to uncover her secrets. What was the point of trying to keep them, anyway? If he didn't like what he saw or felt, then that would be that. He seemed ardent, though. There was no sign of anything but a gratifying arousal.

At the start the sex was happy but not good, in the old **Cosmo** sense. Joseph was too eager, and she was too reliant on previous habits and routines. She didn't pretend that something had happened when it hadn't, and eventually Joseph wanted to know if there was a way of making it happen. He learned quickly, and within a few days or nights or dates or whatever they had entered a Golden Age.

"But is it enough?" Lucy kept asking herself. "Enough for what?" she answered. The answer always came quickly too, as if she wanted to shut down all doubts. She was happy, in a bubble, and the only reason to pop it was on the grounds that bubbles were not real life. But bubbles made life tolerable, and the trick was to blow as many as possible. There were new-baby bubbles, and honeymoon bubbles, and success-at-work bubbles, and new-friends bubbles, and great-holiday bubbles, and even tiny T.V.-series bubbles, dinner bubbles, party bubbles. They all burst without intervention, and then it was a matter of getting through to the next one. Life hadn't been fizzy for a while. It had been hard.

And yes, the sex made her happy, but it wasn't a purely functional or transactional relationship. Joseph didn't put his trousers on and disappear into the night, to reappear again only when the urge came upon him. They talked about their days, their work, the boys; nothing about Joseph's youth made conversation difficult. After a couple of weeks, she realized that the opposite was true. Joseph would ask her question after question, and he listened to the answers. She asked him questions, and listened to the answers. She had very few conversations like this with people of her own age. If anybody had any interest in the problems of running an English department in a troubled inner-city school, they took great pains to hide it.

He always arrived after the children had gone to bed, an arrangement that almost immediately began to cause problems.

"When are you going out next, Mum?" said Al, a couple of weeks after the Night of No Jazz.

"No plans." She knew why he was asking.

"That's not really fair on us. Because when you don't go out, we don't get to play Xbox with Joseph."

"I'm sure he'd come round for a game."

"But you'd be here."

"What difference does that make?"

"It's funner when you're not."

"Why do you like Joseph so much?"

"He's fun."

"And I'm not?"

"Not really. I mean, sometimes."

"When?"

There was a long pause.

"Well."

Dylan came into the kitchen, looking for something to eat.

"Have some fruit."

"I don't want fruit."

"Mum's asking when she's fun."

"Why?"

"She just wants to know."

"Christmas?"

"Christmas? When is she fun at Christmas?"

"Anyway, that's not her job."

"My kids at school think I'm fun."

"Oh, you'd be a fun teacher, probably."

"What's fun about Joseph, apart from Xbox?"

"He's really good at actual football, not just FIFA."

"Rainbow flicks, Cruyff turns, everything."

"That's just being good at something, though. That's not necessarily fun."

"I disagree."

"All right. I'll go out soon."

"I thought you were looking for a boyfriend, anyway?"

"Who told you I was looking for a boyfriend?"

"Dad. When we went out for pizza."

"Why on earth did he say that?"

Paul might have heard from anyone that she'd been out on a couple of dates. She hadn't kept it a secret, and he knew everyone she knew.

"He wanted to know whether it made us sad."

"What did you say?"

"We said it didn't. Didn't we, Al?"

"And was that how you actually felt?"

"I'm not sad."

"Me neither."

"Are you sure?"

"Yeah. You should be looking."

"What if I actually find one?"

The boys looked at each other. They were clearly trying not to laugh.

"We'll cross that bridge when we come to it," said Dylan, a favorite expression of his, and rarely used with such felicity; it was often brought out to deal with room-tidying and homework.

"Yes, but it wouldn't upset you?"

"You mean because of Dad?"

"I suppose so."

"No."

"No."

"Why not?"

Never underestimate the ability of children to pull you out into deep water. The conversation had begun, really not very long ago, with a request for FIFA games with Joseph. And now here they were, talking about the nature and future of their family.

"Well. It's better now, isn't it?" said Dylan.

"Yeah," said Al. "We like Dad. But we didn't like worrying about him."

"He's doing well," said Lucy.

"Good," said Al.

"But maybe that's because he's not living here anymore."

"You mustn't think it's anything to do with you," said Lucy.

"We don't. We just mean, maybe we should leave things the way they are."

"Except with more Joseph."

"Yeah, except he isn't anything to do with you."

"Because you're out when he's here."

"So he's more our friend than yours."

"OK, OK. I'll go out more."

"Thank you."


**Emma was in the line** outside the butcher's the Saturday after her promise, and she gestured for Lucy to join her.

"I can't jump the queue," said Lucy.

"These people won't mind."

She smiled at the people behind her, two good-looking and stony-faced men.

"I'll see you later," said Lucy, and went to the back of the line.

"Oh, I'd rather chat than shop," said Emma, and walked with her.

Lucy didn't want to talk to Emma. She especially

didn't want to talk to Emma about sex while they were edging slowly toward the person Lucy was having sex with.

"How's your week been?"

"Fine. Busy."

So far, so good.

"How about you?"

"Oh, wretched."

"Sorry to hear that."

"I'm married to a pig."

"Oh, dear." Pig. Sex. Lucy's love life. Hop, skip, jump. Change the subject.

"How are you feeling about the referendum?"

"I'm quite tempted to vote out, just to annoy David. He's obsessed."

"What's going to happen to him if we leave?"

"He loses a lot of money, probably. I don't know. I haven't asked him. He's so boring. And he thinks everyone is a moron except him."

"Don't vote out."

"I don't suppose I will. But the more I read, the less I understand."

"Just look at the people who want you to vote out. Farage. Boris. Gove."

"Versus Cameron and George Osborne."

"I know. Bad, but less bad."

"I'll vote in, and I hope we never have to talk about it again."

"Is that why David is a pig? Because of the referendum?"

"No."

Lucy looked at her, but no description of porcine behavior was forthcoming.

"OK."

"Cheer me up. Have you been on any dates?"

Lucy shrugged, and nodded at the people in front of them, and grimaced, and did everything she could mutely to suggest that she was unhappy talking about this subject in public.

"A-ha. So there's something to discuss. I want to discuss it. Coffee after the butcher's? Or a drink? It's lunchtime. We're allowed."

"I have to get back to make lunch for the boys."

"So let's go out. During the week. Can you get someone to be with them for a couple of hours?"

So that was the solution to one problem, although it created another: could she bear to talk to Emma for two whole hours?

"Ooh," said Emma as they approached the door. "My friend is there."

Joseph saw Lucy, smiled, and waggled his fingers in their direction. The look, Lucy felt, was unambiguous. She smiled back with as much casual neutrality as she could manage, but it seemed to her that any eye contact between two people who

are sleeping together was doomed to reveal everything to anyone within a fifty-yard radius.

"Wow," said Emma.

"What?"

"That look Joe gave you."

"I think it was for both of us."

"I wish. You know what it is, don't you?"

"No. I really don't."

"Pheronomes. Is that what they're called? Something like that. You're having sex, and he can pick
it up. It makes you more attractive generally."

"I do shower."

"It's not like that. You're pumping these things
out all the time. And he can tell there's nothing
going on with me."

"I'd have thought the plate-glass window and all
the meat would scramble the signal a bit."

"Nope. Cuts through like a knife."

"His name's Joseph. Not Joe." Lucy couldn't let
it go.

"I call him Joe."

"That's wrong."

"Why are you so sure?"

"He's been babysitting for me."

"Ask him if he's interested in a thirty-nine-year-
old blonde who'd do anything for him."

"You ask him. And you're not thirty-nine."

"I'll tell him that when he's lying broken on top of me. He'll be amazed."

"Please don't talk about him like that."

"Why on earth not? It's just a bit of fun."

"Except you want me to ask him if he'll have sex with you."

"That would be just a bit of fun too."

As usual, everyone in the queue was enjoying the conversation, Lucy could see. Those who were queuing with partners were exchanging discreet looks, and one man, presumably after catching a fragment of something in between songs, had taken his headphones off. Who wouldn't want to listen to Emma making a twit of herself?

"Why do you feel you have to protect him?"

"I don't."

"So why aren't I allowed to talk about him?"

They had reached the front of the queue.

"You go in, Emma," Lucy said.

"Ooh," said Emma. "I will. Joe's customer is just paying up. I've got half a chance."

Lucy felt unnerved, and a little sick. Some of it was straightforward possessiveness, but there was something else too: the horrible distorted mirror image of the relationship with Joseph that Emma had been holding up. Was that what she was? A rapacious and deluded older woman who had no business messing around with someone so much younger than herself? And was there something to do with Joseph's race in there too? She couldn't put her finger on it, but it felt that way. Would Emma be licking her lips if he were a handsome young white butcher's assistant? Probably. She seemed to be so frustrated and unhappy that any young man would do. So Emma was probably not guilty of that charge, at least. Lucy wondered whether she could claim a similar innocence. Was she somehow drawn to Joseph because of his race? Oh, fuck. If nothing else, he would provide her with an opportunity to think and double-think and doubt and beat herself up every second the affair lasted.

**It was Joseph's mother** who worked out what was going on first, and she did it aloud while Grace was eating with them.

"What happened with that girl?" said Grace.

They were eating his mum's chicken stew, and Joseph wanted to concentrate on it. He loved it, and he was hungry, and for some reason it had become Grace's homecoming meal, and she didn't come home all that often.

"What girl?"

"I thought you'd met someone?"

"Why did you think that?"

"You texted me."

"Oh."

Why had he done that? What business was it of hers?

"Yeah. Well. Didn't come to anything."

"He's got other fish to fry," said his mother.

Joseph felt himself going cold.

"Oooh," said Grace. "I want the gossip."

"There isn't any gossip."

Grace had been with her boyfriend for three years. Neither of them ever looked at anyone else. They would end up married. She loved gossip.

"Oh, there's gossip," said his mother.

Grace looked at him.

"Come on, then," she said.

"What are you talking about, Mum?"

"Your friend."

"Which friend? I haven't got a friend."

He was trying to sound mystified, but it wasn't coming out right. He could hear the panic in his voice.

"Well," said his mother. "I'll be the judge of that."

"Why will you be the judge of whether I've got a friend or not?"

"Yeah, Mum," said Grace. "That makes no sense."

"All I know is, he spends an awful lot of time with one particular woman."

"Ooh," said Grace. "A woman."

"That's the thing," said his mother. "That's what she is."

"How do you know anything about what she is?" said Joseph.

"You tell us, then."

"He doesn't want to tell me, Mum," said Grace.

"Thank you," said Joseph.

"So just gimme what you got."

"So there's this woman he keeps babysitting for. And now he's spending half the night there even when he's not babysitting."

"You don't know where I am when I'm not here."

"Of course I do. That thing you made me put on my phone."

Find My Friends. Shit. He'd put it on there to stop her from worrying, and he'd been under the impression that she hadn't looked at it once.

"How do you know that's her address?"

"I don't. But one night when you were baby-sitting, I had a look to see where she lived. And that's the place you keep going back to. So it's either her, or you were lying to me about where you were in the first place."

He was like a man chased down a blind alley by the police in a film. He had to keep looking for a way out, even though there wasn't one.

"So I was lying to you. So what?"

"You made up all those names?"

"Only three. Her and the kids."

"And her job, and her mother having a stroke."

He had made up the stroke. For a moment he was tempted to tell her that Lucy's mother was the only true bit.

"So what have you been doing in that street every night?"

"You go there every night?" said Grace.

He did, now. He couldn't bear not to. He'd be there within thirty minutes of walking out the front door, if the buses were OK.

"Yes," said Joseph.

"So where is it you're going, if it's nothing to do with a woman?"

"I didn't say that."

"Do you want to start again?" said Grace.

"Yes," said Joseph.

His back was against the wall; he'd tried to shin up it, but it was too high and there was no grip.

"Go on, then."

"I'm seeing the woman I babysit for."

"And why is that so shameful?"

"It isn't."

"How old is she?" said his mother.

"I dunno."

"How old do you think she is?"

"That's a bit rude."

"Rude to guess?" said Grace "When she's not here?"

"Well. If I said sixty-two and she's thirty-nine…I'd feel, I dunno. Disloyal."

"You think you might be sleeping with a sixty-two-year-old?" said Grace.

"Oh, Joseph," said his mother, despairingly.

"I don't think he's actually sleeping with a sixty-two-year-old," said Grace. "I think he's just making up a ridiculous excuse for not telling us. How old are her kids?"

"Ten and eight."

"Well, she probably didn't have the youngest when she was fifty-four. She's probably around forty, right?"

"Maybe."

"So my age," said his mother.

Nobody said anything. Grace looked at him, and he could tell she knew that Lucy wouldn't be his mother's age, even if they'd been born at the same time on the same day in the same year. They decided, collectively and telepathically, that this was not an observation anyone wanted to articulate.

"White?" said Grace.

"Yeah. And so is Scott, so don't get on your high horse about that."

Grace held up her hands in a pacific gesture.

"I was only trying to get a picture."

"So ask for a picture."

"Have you got one?"

"No."

"Is she on Instagram?"

"No."

"You sure? What's her name?"

"Listen, you don't need a picture!" said Joseph. "She's around forty and she's attractive and she's white. What's your problem?"

"But where's it going?" said his mother.

"Where's anything going?" said Joseph.

"You're not looking for something more permanent?"

"No. I'm twenty-two. I don't want to get married, I don't want to have kids."

"You will one day."

"Maybe. In ten years."

"I'll be dead by then," said his mother.

"Why will you be dead at the age of fifty-two?"

"Too old to enjoy it, anyway."

Grace picked up her phone and spoke into it.

"People born in . . . Shit. What year were you born in if you're fifty-two?"

"Fifty-two now?" said Joseph.

"Yeah."

"1964."

"People born in 1964."

"Here is what I found about famous people born in 1964," Siri said. "Keanu Reeves. Sandra Bullock. Lenny Kravitz. Michelle Obama."

"You think Michelle Obama would be too old to enjoy grandchildren?" said Grace.

They were a long way from discussing his relationship with Lucy now. They were talking about famous people a decade older than Lucy (and his mother.)

"Well, she's got Secret Service people and everything," said his mother.

"Why would you need Secret Service people to play with your grandchildren?"

"I'm just saying. She has people doing things for her. Less stress."

"You think if you need Secret Service to protect you, you have less stress in your life? She has Secret Service because a ton of people want to shoot her."

And now they were talking about whether the Obamas had more or less stress than his mother. Sometimes, when they had real problems to discuss, his family's inability to stick to the subject at hand frustrated him. But sometimes, like now, he was grateful for it. He had survived the immediate Lucy crisis, but that didn't mean it was forgotten, or that he knew what to say about it.

———

**On the bus** down to Lucy's, he thought about what he'd said to his mother, a question he'd asked when he didn't know what else to say, but which stuck with him: **Where's** anything going? What if things had gone well with Jaz, and she'd driven Lucy out of his mind and heart and body? Would he have thought, this is going somewhere? It seemed highly unlikely to him. It would have seemed highly unlikely to his mother and Grace too, if they'd met Jaz. And yes, some day he'd probably meet somebody and he might start thinking about some kind of life with her. But the weird thing about being his age was that you spent half your time dreaming about what might happen to you, and the other half trying not to think about it, and either way you were stuck living a life that didn't seem to count for much, somewhere halfway between childhood and whatever permanent adulthood might bring.

And here was the thing about Lucy: she pulled him into now. He spent his life chasing, running from job to job to job, earning the money that would maybe one day enable him to live away from home. And if that day ever came, he'd have to add a couple of other jobs into the portfolio, and he'd never stop running. The only time he ever spent on anything resembling a dream was the time he spent trying to create a track, which would maybe one day lead to some remix work and a few paid club gigs. If you'd asked him before the Night of No Jazz what made him happy, he wouldn't really have understood the relevance of the question. Now he knew the answer: sleeping with Lucy, eating with Lucy, watching T.V. with Lucy. And maybe there was no future in it, but there was a present, and that's what life consists of.

**Lucy had hoped** that Emma might have forgotten about the drink they talked about, but she texted, and then called and left a message, and then called again. She hinted at some crisis that only Lucy would understand, although as listening wasn't Emma's strong suit, Lucy didn't really know how she'd arrived at that conclusion. They went to a local Italian restaurant with the intention of both eating pasta and drinking while Joseph fed the kids and played on the Xbox. Morale was high when she left the house, but Lucy was already worried about the argument over money that would ensue the moment she got home. She had to pay Joseph, and he would feel uncomfortable to the point of refusal, but she'd have to win. The blurred lines that would then form if she lost frightened her. Joseph couldn't be her boyfriend; Joseph couldn't be some kind of stepfather. He was a babysitter that she had sex with. She would pay for the babysitting but not the sex.

"Drink," said Emma desperately, as soon as they sat down. Lucy smiled indulgently, but the best part of a bottle of red disappeared before they'd ordered, and she was still sipping her first glass.

"Tough day?" said Lucy.

"Not particularly. No worse than any of the others. My friend Sophie is coming, by the way. You remember? She used to be a mum at Wyatt."

Lucy remembered her straight away: a lithe, tall blonde, always expensively dressed, whose face seemed to suggest that life couldn't possibly have dealt her a worse hand, but whose life seemed perfectly pleasant from the outside.

"You don't mind, do you?"

"No. Of course not."

But if you already have a friend to moan at, Lucy thought, why am I here?

"How it happened was, I told her about your recent developments, and she's divorced and not having much luck, so she wanted to hear all about it."

"Right. But I'm not sure I want to talk about my, my personal life to a stranger."

"So you don't remember her?"

"I do remember her. But even so…"

"Oh, she's very nice. Her kids go to St. Peter's with mine now."

A non sequitur, but Lucy would let it pass.

"It's not the niceness."

"We don't want details. We just want to know how you managed it."

"Why do you want to know? You're not divorced."

"I'm sure I will be soon. And even if I'm not…"

She gave Lucy a look intended to convey her readiness for extramarital action.

"Listen, my whatever it is, my relationship… There's nothing to learn from it. It just happened."

"But how? Ah, here she is."

Sophie looked different. Perhaps Lucy had been muddling her up with someone.

"She looks great, doesn't she?" said Emma.

"Really," said Lucy.

She could now see a trace of the woman she remembered. Everything on her face was glossy and stretched, and though the work looked expensive, it had also turned her into somebody else. Maybe that's what she wanted. She was also displaying a cleavage that hadn't been there before. Lucy realized that she didn't really know anybody like Sophie. Lucy belonged to a tribe where prematurely gray-haired women wouldn't even dye the gray away, and though these women made her feel both defensive and sad (she would use as much dye as it took, the moment a gray hair appeared) she felt the same way as them about most things that mattered—the importance of books and serious movies, politics, the environment, the referendum. But all sorts of tribes lived in the urban jungle, and just because Lucy never came across people like Sophie, with their four-by-fours and their private schools and their new breasts, it didn't mean that they weren't out there, living close by, in streets she never went to.

"What is wrong with people?" said Emma.

Lucy understood that people, in this context, meant the men who were not dating Sophie. Lucy shook her head in sympathetic bafflement.

"Are you still doing that marvelous job?" said Sophie.

"I don't think my students would agree," said Lucy.

"She meant that you're just marvelous for doing it," said Emma.

"And Emma tells me you've been through a fair bit of drama too."

"Have I?"

"With your husband. Paul, was it?"

"Oh. I don't know how dramatic it was."

"Listen to her," said Emma.

School had helped her to put the calamitous collapse of her marriage into some kind of perspective.

There were fifteen hundred kids on the roll, representing a thousand or more families, and she'd been at the school for over a decade. Her story was dramatic compared to the stories of university friends or the middle-class mothers at the primary-school gates, but her students told, or frequently refused to tell, tales of domestic abuse, imprisonment, deportation, poverty, and hunger. You had to do better than drug addiction and divorce to capture their attention. Two of them had been murdered, one while he was a pupil, the other soon after he'd left. Stabbed, both of them. Who knew anyone who'd been murdered? Many teachers in big inner-city schools did. How was one supposed to go home and feel as if one's world was ending if it wasn't?

"I'm sorry to hear about your divorce," said Lucy.

"Best thing that ever happened to me," said Sophie.

"Oh, good."

"Look at her," said Emma, apparently making the point that with no divorce, there'd have been no Botox or breast implants, and then where would she be?

"That was a stupid thing to say," said Sophie.

"You or me?" said Emma, a little wounded.

"What you said was a bit stupid. But I was talking about me. It was a terrible thing to happen.

And I'm more miserable now than I was before, which is saying something."

"Why were you miserable before?"

"Didn't like him. Then he met someone else, so I like him even less."

"That seems logical."

"Everyone I know is miserable," said Sophie. "Everyone."

Lucy could believe it, but the misery would have mystified anyone on the outside of it. It was spring. They were well off. In a couple of months they would be going to France or Spain, for two or three or four weeks. But they were stuck, and they were bored. Sex, and the way they were having it, and who they were having it with, offered some kind of way out, they thought. Their boredom was infuriating, and Lucy began to wonder how she could cease to know them. Surely one of the points of sending one's children to state secondary school was that you could dump the parents of the kids they used to play with when they were younger.

"Except you, apparently, Lucy," said Sophie. "That's why we're here. We want to know why you're not miserable."

"We need a master class."

"Give us hope."

"Is this all because I may or may not be having sex?"

"I thought you were," said Emma.

"And also," said Sophie, "if you don't know, who does?"

"I do know," said Lucy. "I just didn't want to talk about it in the street, with lots of people listening. And now I don't want to talk about it here."

"That's not how it works," said Emma. "You're representing."

"I just think meeting someone would help me," said Sophie. "Even if it was nothing serious. Especially if it was nothing serious."

"You just need a good seeing-to, don't you, sweetheart?"

Lucy felt sick. These people and their dismal euphemisms, from which all trace of eroticism had been surgically removed, got her down. They were surely more properly applied to another area of human activity completely, boxing, say, or horse riding.

"Have you tried online dating?" said Lucy.

"Yes," said Sophie. "Three times. With three different people. I couldn't give it away."

Lucy tried not to think about what this could possibly mean, although she was sure the new cleavage would have been wheeled into the front line early in the skirmish. It might have been too big a weapon, too soon, resulting in an unhelpful retreat.

"Is that what you did, the online thing?"

"No. There was a blind date that was no good, and then I met someone at a dinner party, but that didn't go anywhere, and then... Well, I met someone else."

"How?"

"I suppose you could call him a family friend. But really. That's all I want to say. And it's not going anywhere. We're just... keeping each other company until something else happens."

"That's what I want! Exactly that!"

It might be what you want, Lucy thought, but it isn't what you need. You need books, music, maybe God. But some guy in between wives isn't going to do much for you.

**"How was your evening?"** said Joseph.

She hadn't managed to miss bedtime, but they'd asked for Joseph to put them to bed anyway. He had developed a range of voices for a series of comic novels they were reading at bedtime, and Lucy's attempts to recreate them had been met with scorn.

"Soooo bad," said Lucy. "Emma brought a friend, and they just moaned the whole evening."

"I hate that."

"Have you got moany friends?"

"No. But my dad used to be terrible."

"And he isn't any more?"

"I don't know how long it will last. But he's got involved in the referendum campaign. He's buzzing."

"Good for him."

"Yeah, but he's voting out."

"What? Why?"

"He says his money's going to go up. Supply and demand."

"He works in the building trade, doesn't he?"

"Every now and again. Scaffolding. He wants all the Eastern Europeans to go home so they'll have to pay the British boys more."

"I don't think it works like that."

"No? How does it work, then?"

He wasn't being pugnaciously rhetorical. He was looking at her for answers. She was older than him. She was a teacher. She knew stuff.

"Well. If we leave the E.U. there will probably be a recession."

"Right. And that will be different from austerity?"

"Extra misery, I suppose."

"OK. Why will we have a recession?"

"Because... Well. We have access to five hundred

million people. That's our internal market. Foreign businesses will start to avoid the U.K. because we won't have that access any more."

"Why will that mean there's no building work?"

"There won't be no building work, obviously. There'll just be less."

You could ask her anything you wanted to know about Hardy's poems and Shakespeare's tragedies, and she'd be able to answer. Ask her two consecutive questions about the economic consequences of Brexit, however, and she could feel her face start to flush. What did she know about recessions and the building trade and scaffolding?

"So that's why you're voting to stay in?"

"I think it's safer, on the whole. And I'd like the boys to be able to work in Europe, or study at European universities, if that's what they want. Plus I feel European, you know?"

This was beginning to sound a bit feeble. Joseph's dad was unlikely to care very much about preserving her sons' foreign academic opportunities if he could earn more every week.

"Do you?"

"Yes, I do. Don't you?"

"I've never been there. Well. We went to Paris for a day on a school trip. I didn't feel any more European on the way home."

"You are European."

"Yeah, I know. But I'm not really, am I? I'm British. Why do I have to be anything else?"

"Do you like being British?"

"It's not about whether I like it or not. I just am."

Lucy knew exactly what he meant. She didn't really feel European. She read British and American newspapers and novels, listened to American and British music, watched British and American T.V. programs, and movies from all over the world. She loved Italian food, but ate Chinese and Indian too—like all British people. She liked going to Europe on holiday, but she went because the sunshine was plentiful and only a couple of hours away. If she could get to Bondi Beach in an afternoon and it cost her a hundred pounds to get there, would she tell Joseph she felt Australian?

"Well," she said. "I still think your dad's making a mistake."

"Tell him that."

"I will if you want."

She didn't mean it. She preferred knowing what she was talking about.

# 7

So Emma or maybe Sophie told someone who told someone who played five-a-side with Paul on a Thursday night, and the person who played five-a-side asked Paul whether it was weird, knowing that his ex was dating. This person wasn't being cruel. He had recently separated from his own wife, and was dreading the day that he'd knock on the door of his former home and find a strange man opening it. Paul played from seven until eight. He texted Lucy at ten past, and would have been round five minutes later if she hadn't put him off. She wanted to be on her own when he came, which meant putting the boys to bed and texting Joseph.

"Is it true?" said Paul.

He hadn't had a drink since the night of the altercation. She badly wanted a glass of wine, but she put the kettle on. Paul went to the cupboard to get a glass and then to the fridge to get some orange juice. His entitlement annoyed her.

"It depends what you've been told."

"I was just told you had a boyfriend."

"No, that's not true."

"So what is true?"

"That's a hard question to answer."

"You know what I mean."

"I'm not sure I do."

"Is there some kind of bloke in your life?"

"Some kind of bloke?"

"You know what I mean."

"There's something casual going on, yes."

"Involving sex?"

Surely that was all a casual relationship involved? It was the absence of everything else that provided the informality.

"Yes."

Paul took a deep breath. She could almost smell the need for something that would take the edge off the moment. His various addictions were sweating from the exertion of jumping up and down while trying to catch the attention of their owner.

"Fucking hell."

"It was going to happen one day."

It was like the death of a parent, Lucy thought.

It was always coming soon. She just couldn't believe that it was happening now.

"I'd hoped it wouldn't."

"I know."

"So is that it? I mean, for us?"

What was the kindest answer? No element of her relationship with Joseph was an obstruction to her reconciliation with Paul, but there would be no reconciliation with Paul.

"It's nothing to do with that."

"Is it anyone I know?"

"It's not a friend of yours, if that's what you mean."

"Do the kids know him?"

She could see how Bill Clinton had got himself into such a mess. It depends on what the meaning of the word "know" is. The kids knew him, but they didn't know him as their mother's lover. Surely that's what Paul was asking? Whether they knew their mother's lover? She could formulate an answer based on the idea of two Josephs, one of whom, Babysitter Joseph, they were close to while never having met Sexual Partner Joseph.

"Kind of."

"What does that mean?"

In order to answer that question truthfully, she'd have to introduce the notion of the two Josephs, an idea that Paul was likely to find unpersuasive.

"Yeah, they know him."

"Ah, then this concerns me. If you're playing happy families with someone I haven't approved, that's not right."

"I'm not sure that's how it works. I live with the boys, and I have an independent life. I can't be asking for your approval every time I . . ."

This was going wrong too. Her chief objection seemed to be that this would turn into an administrative nightmare, with Paul sat behind a desk with a rubber stamp while a queue of prospective partners snaked out of the door.

"You have to trust me. I'm not an idiot."

"That's what every divorced mother says. And the next thing they know, their kids are being hacked into pieces and buried under the floorboards."

"Jesus Christ, Paul. If that happens, you have my full permission to say 'I told you so.'"

"It's not fucking funny."

"Also, who was the one who turned up drunk and tried to start a fight? Not my boyfriend."

"You said you didn't have a boyfriend."

She had said that, and she'd meant it. Joseph was not her boyfriend. But Joseph had stopped him from coming into the house that night. "Not my boyfriend" meant "my ex-husband, that's who." But the person who was not her boyfriend had pushed Paul over, and now Joseph was in this conversation.

"I don't. I was comparing my calm, peaceful, and sober boyfriend of the future to the man who tried to throw his weight around."

"Is that guy still babysitting?"

"Joseph? Yes."

"So presumably he knows who you're sleeping with."

"Does that matter to you?"

"Just seems like everyone knows except me."

"Nobody knows apart from me and the person concerned."

"And Joseph."

Her heart was thumping in her chest now. If she didn't tell the truth, then more or less everything she said from this point onward would be a lie.

"It is Joseph."

"What is?"

"The person concerned."

"I don't understand what you're saying."

"You came round to ask me about who I was... seeing. I'm seeing Joseph."

"That kid?"

"He's a young man."

"What's the age gap?"

"I don't think that's anything you need to know.

Apart from that he's really brilliant with the boys, and they love him."

"Thanks."

"The more people around them they care about, the better it is for everybody."

"And all the other gaps? Friends? Culture? Education? Work?"

"We have different friends and different jobs, yes. And what do you know about his education?"

There was an awkward silence, while Paul contemplated the possibility that he'd made an unfortunate assumption, and Lucy tried to work out whether a joke about anything at this point would backfire. It was bound to. She let Paul stew instead.

"No," said Paul. "You're right, I don't. But you know what I'm talking about."

"You and I had a lot of things in common," said Lucy. "It's not necessarily the best indicator."

She remembered telling Emma that she wanted someone clean, because a lack of hygiene meant that nothing else counted. Sobriety, she realized, was just as important. She might even have been thinking about sobriety all the time. Clean was another word for sober, after all. You could have the same taste in everything, have the same number of qualifications, share the same sense of humor and the same politics, but a vicious dependency would cut through it all and you were left with a thousand pieces of thread that nobody could knit together again.

**Joseph came round** as soon as Paul had gone.

"I told him," said Lucy.

"What? Wow."

"I'm sorry. If that's exactly what you didn't want."

"You told him it was me?"

"Yes."

"What did he say?"

"He pointed out all the reasons it wouldn't work."

"Right. I don't want to know what they are."

He went to the fridge, got out the orange juice, helped himself to a glass from the cupboard.

"I wasn't going to tell you."

"We know all that anyway."

"Yeah."

She tried to mimic his matter-of-fact tone, but there was a little pang, no doubt about it. Something else like the death of a parent. She knew it was coming soon, but not today, not yet.

**Joseph had been putting aside** his babysitting money, and he'd bought himself the Ableton Live

10. He'd managed to get the track he'd already half created off the old cracked software and into the new version. It took an entire evening, because he had to bounce every single track to audio first. He'd found a good drum plug-in, a free one, and he wasn't so worried about not knowing what was out there in the clubs because he was going for something that had a more retro feel, a sort of old-school deep-house thing. He'd started off with what he'd hoped was a sort of lush Latin groove, with synth strings, but it wasn't until he double-timed the beat that he was happy with it. He had this trumpet sample that he used sparingly until the last minute or so, and then he let it rip for the climax. He'd found the trumpet on one of his mum's Earth, Wind & Fire records, although his mum didn't remember it, and she said it must have belonged to his uncle. He'd had to lift some of the music too, but he'd managed to integrate it into the song without bending it out of shape.

He took his laptop to his friend Zech's house. Zech was changing his name, slowly, to £Man. It was so slow that Joseph described it as "transitioning," which really pissed Zech/£Man off. Everyone forgot that he was changing his name, on top of which, he was still at college doing a music tech course at B.M.M., and his old name was on all the computers and registers. He refused to answer if anyone called him Zech at college, but it annoyed the other students because it slowed everything up, what with him just sitting there fuming. Joseph wondered how Earl Sweatshirt and A$AP Rocky and ?uestlove and all the others managed it. You never thought of stuff like that when you were starting out.

You were allowed to say PoundMan but you weren't allowed to write it. You had to use the symbol. Zech was very fierce about that. The truth was, nobody had any cause to write it much. He had made Joseph put £Man into his phone, which did push him up the contacts list, but Joseph had to remember to look under M. For some reason the pound sign didn't count as a letter. Joseph had to admit that it was a good name, though. Americans used the dollar sign to look flash, but PoundMan sounded cheap, like Poundland. Zech meant it to sound cheap too. It was, he said, a celebration of Haringey consumer culture.

But he was a genius, and one day everyone would know it. He was a walking encyclopedia of black music. He knew about Duke Ellington and he knew about Octavian, and the tracks he was putting together were insane. He already had a deal, but nobody at his label knew what to do with him, because he was five feet tall, more or less, wore glasses with a very thick lens, breathed through his mouth because of a sinus problem, and bought all his clothes from charity shops. There was stuff up on SoundCloud, but nothing with more than five hundred listens. He'd never had any kind of crew at school, which was where Joseph had met him. He'd kept himself to himself, managed to keep out of the way of people who wished to do him harm, gone home and listened to everything ever made.

£Man found a cable buried deep in the middle of the electronic equipment all over his bedroom floor and plugged the laptop into the studio monitors he'd put together from parts.

"OK."

"Before we start..."

"Oh, here we go," said £Man. "I don't want any excuses."

"No, no excuses. I just don't know whether it's finished."

"So don't bring it round here, then."

"What, because you're so busy in the evenings?"

"Shut up and play it."

Joseph regretted teasing him about his social life. His sharp ears would be honed to a spiky point, ready to puncture all Joseph's self-esteem.

"How've you been, anyway?"

"Oh, fuck off."

"What?"

"You take the piss, then you realize I'm about to listen to your track, then you try to make small talk. I'm not an idiot."

"OK. Sorry. But listen—you're a genius. This is something different. I'm trying to make dance music, not reinvent the wheel. I'm not in your league."

"Tell me something I don't know." And then, grudgingly, "Cheers."

Joseph felt that he'd warmed him up as much as he was ever going to, pressed play, and tried and failed not to watch £Man's face. There was nothing on it, though. He just listened, head still, eyes narrowed a little. About halfway through, he leaned over and pressed stop.

"It hasn't finished."

"I know."

"The best part is at the end."

"Don't tell me. You're going to hit us with more of the Earth, Wind & Fire trumpet solo."

Fuck. Not only did £Man know the track (of course), but he'd guessed how it was going to be used.

"Oh, come on, man. It sounds great. Really."

"I'm sure. But first of all, right? 'The best part is at the end?' That's what you're telling me?"

"Yeah."

"And that's what you're going to tell people on

the dance floor who are walking off to get a drink? Don't go! Come back! Here comes the good bit! Nobody's ever going to get to the good bit. How long does a radio D.J. give something before he bins it? How long have you got before kids skip on to something else? I know the answer to that, by the way. Thirty-five percent skip in the first thirty seconds on Spotify. There's a twenty-four percent chance of them skipping in the first five."

"Yeah, but you think they would walk off the dance floor?"

"Not if the best part is at the beginning."

"OK. So what do I put at the end?"

"That's the other thing. It's not like proper EDM. It's got a tune. Nice changes. You've written a song."

"Is that bad?"

"It is if nobody's singing it."

"I haven't got any words."

"Write some."

"I don't know any singers."

"You sound like a kid trying to get out of home-work. But I don't give a fuck if you do it or not. Don't write words. Don't find a singer. You have my full permission. OK?"

"You might not be right."

"That's true. But why did you come here? Because I'm always right."

"Thanks anyway."

He unplugged his laptop and put it back in his bag.

**"Play it to me,"** said Lucy.

"Nah, you're all right."

"What does that mean?"

"No, I suppose."

"I'm not useless. I listen to a lot of music."

"No. I know. But you don't listen to the stuff I want to make."

"Does that matter? Music is music."

"What's your favorite song?"

"I'm not answering that."

"Why not?"

"First, because I haven't got one favorite song. Nobody has. And if I tell you, you'll go off and listen to it and come back and say, mine's nothing like that."

"What's your favorite dance song?"

"Michael Jackson. 'Workin' Day and Night.' Anyone plays that at a party, I'm there."

Joseph laughed.

"Yeah. Mine's different."

"In a good or bad way?"

"Bad. I did mine on a computer, I don't have a brass section, I haven't got Quincy Jones producing me. Anyway. We watching an episode?"

Lucy had somehow missed **The Sopranos**. She remembered everyone else watching it, but when it came out she had been in her midtwenties, living with Jane in the horrible apartment in Stroud Green, both working hard, both going out a lot. She could no longer remember whether they'd even had a T.V. They certainly wouldn't have had any kind of cable. Joseph, meanwhile, had never heard of it. When they googled, they found that he was four when it was first broadcast. He thought that was funny, but Lucy's laugh was a little forced. She was sleeping with someone who had been wearing nappies in the 1990s. In the end she consoled herself with the thought that they'd both been too young, in their own different ways. But now they were both addicted, and if they were at any other stage of their relationship, they would have been binge-watching. They only ever had time for one episode, though.

They were nearly done with the first season. Episode 10 was about the music business: Chris and Adriana end up doing business with a rapper called Massive Genius, although it all goes wrong when Adriana tries to produce a track by a band whose singer she used to date. Chris eventually beats him up with his own guitar. Lucy got a bit confused by who owed who money, but as the financial stuff was about sampling, Joseph was drinking it in like a vile-tasting medicine he had to down in one. **The Sopranos** made sampling look scary and violent, and Joseph was a man who'd just lifted a chunk of an Earth, Wind & Fire record.

"Have you got a name?" said Lucy when it was over.

"How do you mean?"

"Like Massive Genius."

"Ha. No. More trouble than it's worth."

He told her about the troubles £Man was having at college, and she laughed.

"But can't you just have a music name? I call you Joseph, but the world knows you as something else."

"The world. Yeah, right."

"All right then, a tiny bit of London, misery guts."

"I suppose."

"Like Massive Genius."

"Massive Genius is a great name."

"You can have it."

Joseph thought about it.

"It would be funny. And cool."

"I think so."

"Thank you." And then, before he'd had a chance to think about it, "Do you want to hear the track?"

"If you're sure."

"I've got others. But this is the one I've worked on hardest."

Lucy didn't have a sound system like £Man's, but she had her little Bluetooth, and it was better than his laptop. He linked to it and started the song. Lucy began nodding her head vigorously to the beat, and Joseph thought he might die of an embarrassment-induced seizure. He wanted to tell her to stop, but that would mean talking over his music, which he didn't want to do. Because then she'd ask why on earth she wasn't allowed to nod her head in her own living room to dance music, and Joseph wouldn't have a good answer that didn't refer to her age and her... Well, her teacheriness, he supposed. Was that a word?

After a minute or two, she started dancing. It wasn't full on, but she was moving both her hips and her feet. And it wasn't that she had no rhythm. She was clearly a good dancer. It was just that it was the wrong kind of dancing.

"I can't be in the same room," he said. "Too nervous."

And before she could say anything, he went to the downstairs toilet and locked himself in.

It was the first time he had ever felt younger than her. Or rather, it was the first time she'd ever felt older than him. And it wasn't because of the dancing, he realized. It was her enthusiasm. Yes, he could have had a girlfriend of exactly the same age as him, who did exactly the same things. But when there was an age gap, her attempts to show that she liked it, with the hip-swaying and the head-nodding, felt like the kind of approval a mother might give. She hadn't even given it three seconds before she started trying to show him she liked it. This is going to be good, she seemed to be saying, whether it was or it wasn't.

He wanted Lucy to be on his side, of course he did, but he wanted her to show her encouragement in a different way. He didn't know what that way was, though. She talked to him about her work, and he was almost sure he listened and bolstered and did all the things a friend or a lover might do. But he hoped he didn't do it in a way that reminded her of his youth.

He could hear the trumpet solo through the toilet door. There was about a minute left. He was just a kid. He could see that now. It was because everything was new that he was embarrassed and raw. He wasn't established in any field, really. He'd be bringing her stuff, like a puppy, for a long time to come, and she could only rub his belly and call him a good boy until he was an old dog with no new tricks.

**"I LOVED it,"** said Lucy. "It sounded so . . . professional."

"Thank you."

"Better than a lot of the stuff they play in clubs."

"What clubs do you go to?"

"All right, smart-arse."

"So, nothing to say?"

She hesitated for a tiny beat.

"No. Perfect as it is."

"But there's something."

"No, nothing."

There was something.

"I mean, I wouldn't play it at home."

"Why not?"

"That's not what it's for, is it?"

"No. But . . . You play dance-y things. Like Michael Jackson."

"I suppose . . . Am I allowed to say that I prefer music with a voice and words?"

"You listen to jazz sometimes."

"But that's for mood."

"So you want a singer on it."

"Maybe." She screwed up her face, as if she were telling him she didn't want to see him any more.

"That's what PoundMan said."

"Really?"

"Yes."

"Wow."

"Wow what?"

"You took the track to PoundMan because he's a genius. And he said the same thing as me."

"I think I'm going to have to find a singer. And write some words. And a tune. I'm nowhere near finished."

"Well, you must know someone who can sing."

Later, he could see that he snapped because he was disappointed, and he went for the place where she would always be vulnerable.

"What does that mean?"

"Just...you probably have loads of friends with good voices."

"Yeah, we can all dance too."

"You must know I wasn't saying that."

"How many singers do you know, then?"

"I'm a teacher. I know tons."

"All the black girls?"

"I think I should stop talking."

"If the only things that come out of your mouth are racist stereotypes, maybe you should."

"You know that's not fair. And if you really think I'm a racist, maybe you shouldn't be here."

It was a clever challenge. He wanted to walk out, because he was pissed off with everyone and everything, but by walking out, according to Lucy, he'd be telling her she was a racist. He didn't think she was a racist, not really. The two racist things she'd said were, "You must know someone who can sing," and, "You probably have loads of friends with good voices." And maybe a third: "I know tons." He'd heard a lot worse.

"I don't think you're a racist."

"OK."

"But I want to go anyway."

"I understand."

He gave her a peck on the lips, packed away his laptop again, and went home.

He was still steaming on the bus. After a little while he let himself notice the subject his thoughts were looping around, uselessly and unhelpfully, and it wasn't anything to do with Lucy, or at least the argument he'd picked with her. He was pissed off about the track. He had wanted £Man to love it, and he had wanted Lucy to love it. And he felt embarrassed that he'd played it to them without a vocal on it, because when he shut himself in the toilet and listened through the door, it seemed blindingly obvious that it needed one. So he felt stupid, and defensive, and hurt. He wondered how he was ever going to make anything, if it meant feeling like this every time. He couldn't not make music, but he couldn't expose it to the world either.

Joseph had loads of friends with good voices. Lucy had turned out to be right in her assumption, even though she might or might not have been wrong to make it. He knew people in the church choir, for a start. The church choir might have been one of the sources Lucy was referring to. Nobody in the choir was white. But he knew the person he should get to sing on the track, and she wasn't in the choir. He'd never forgotten Jaz singing the Beyoncé song in his kitchen. Now he came to think of it, he'd remembered it while he was putting the finishing touches to the track, and when he played it to £Man, and when Lucy said it needed vocals. She'd been in his head the whole time, but tucked away in a corner, behind all the other crap that was in there, Lucy and money and work. Her voice was so good that he was even prepared to text her and ask her to sing, even though she would be angry, and he was afraid of her. Nobody could say he wasn't committed to his craft.

———

"**Oh,**" said his mother the following evening. "To what do we owe this pleasure?"

"I live here."

"Not often you don't."

"I sleep here every night. That's the definition of living here."

It was true. He had only stayed the whole night at Lucy's house the once, when the boys were with friends. He would like to wake up with her in the morning, but that would mean coming out, as it were, and neither of them wanted to do that.

"Well, you're never here at this time."

She was watching T.V., a documentary about Alzheimer's that was the most depressing thing Joseph had ever seen. He was on his phone most of the time, but his mother kept telling him he'd learn something if he paid attention.

"I don't want to learn about this."

"It'll be me, one day."

"I won't let it get to that. I'll bump you off."

"Lovely. The last thing I ever see, my own son strangling me."

"I'd use a pillow. You wouldn't see anything."

"Did I tell you I've changed my mind about the referendum? I'm voting to leave."

"Why?"

"Because of the money the N.H.S. is going to get."

"That stupid bus? Three hundred and fifty million a week? They're lying. Even I know that."

"Yes. They're lying. We were arguing about it on the ward, and we checked it on the BBC's fact-checker. But..."

"You know they're lying and you're going to vote for them anyway?"

"The BBC says it's a hundred and sixty-one million."

"Oh, so they're only lying about two hundred million a week, then. That's fine."

"A hundred and sixty-one million a week, Joseph! Think what we could do with that!"

"You're not going to get it all."

"You're not taking it seriously."

"And what happened to all the European staff you're worried about?"

"There'll still be immigration. But it'll be like in Australia. Points-based. The more skills you have, and the better your English and so on, the better your chances."

"Who's telling you all this stuff?"

"Janine. She's voting out. Half the nurses are."

"So why aren't the other half?"

"Ask them. Or ask your fancy lady. She's in, isn't she?"

"She's not my fancy lady."

"I don't know what she is, then."

"Isn't a fancy lady like a mistress?"

"Yes, and she's married."

"Separated. Anyway, I'm not, am I?"

"You might as well be, all the time you spend round there."

His mother could sustain an argument forever, simply by switching sides right in the middle of it.

"When am I going to meet her, anyway?"

"It's not like that," he said. It was an ill-considered answer, unlikely to prevent any follow-up questions.

"What is it like, then?"

"It's not, you know, oh, I'd like to introduce you to my mum."

"Why not?"

"It wouldn't be appropriate."

"She must have clothes on some of the time."

"Oh, Mum. Jesus."

"I won't have Him brought into your seedy arrangements."

She'd done it again. She was the one who had introduced the off-key note, he was the one in trouble.

"I don't see what the big deal is. I'd like to meet these boys. They sound lovely. And I'd like to meet her, if she's worth all this time."

"It's not a serious thing."

"So she means nothing to you. Just sex."

"Yes, she means something. But it'll all fizzle out in a minute."

Every time he thought or said something like that, he felt his stomach drop, as if he were in a lift. But it was true: it would all fizzle out in a minute.

"Well, how long is a minute?"

"I don't know."

"Tomorrow?"

"No."

He felt that in his guts too. And if he didn't want it to fizzle out tomorrow, then he needed to see Lucy and apologize for calling her a racist. She might be thinking that they'd fizzled out already.

"One month? Six months?"

"I don't know. Maybe."

"So what you're saying is you'll only let me meet people you're sure you're going to marry."

"You've met my girlfriends before."

"Only because you had nowhere else to take them. This woman has her own house. Say it goes on for two more years. You're just going to disappear every evening and I never clap eyes on her?"

"I'll introduce you in two years' time. I promise. What's the date?"

"May the twelfth."

"So on May the twelfth 2018 we'll all go out to dinner. I'll pay."

"So you'll be breaking up with her on May the eleventh, I would imagine."

"Can we put something else on?"

"No. This is doing you good."

While the old man with Alzheimer's was dying, with his family round his bedside, Joseph texted Lucy and asked whether he could come over.

**I thought you'd never ask**, she said, with the apostrophe in the right place.

**He rang,** and then he knocked, but he didn't want to knock loudly. He could see the bathroom light upstairs, and guessed that she was taking a shower, maybe especially for him. He texted her, and leaned against the door, waiting, but nothing happened, and a next-door neighbor, nobody Joseph had ever come across before, walked past and then put his keys in the lock. But he could see Joseph over the little hedge that separated the two properties.

"Can I help you?" the man said.

He was in his late thirties, probably, shirtsleeves and tie, jacket slung over his arm. A City boy, or a lawyer, back late after a drink.

"I'm fine," said Joseph.

"Can I ask what you're doing there?"

"She can't hear me knocking. She's in the shower."

"Is she expecting you?"

"Yeah."

"Quite a late visit."

"I wouldn't have thought that's much of your business."

"I wouldn't get lippy, mate."

"I'm not being lippy. I'm just pointing out that it's a weird question."

"It was an observation, more than a question."

Joseph's heart was thumping in his chest. He wanted to knock the guy out, but it was an old feeling, and he knew he had to swallow it. Nothing had ever gone wrong in this street, or in this house, and now the world had caught him up.

"I think I'd feel a bit more comfortable if you came out of there."

"Where do I go?"

"Just go for a walk until she's downstairs again. If she's coming downstairs. You've presumably got her phone number?"

"Fucking hell."

Joseph walked down the little path and out into the street.

"That's better."

Joseph shook his head in disbelief and the guy let himself in. Joseph walked back to the door and rang the bell again. Five minutes later, a police car turned up. Joseph had the presence of mind to send another text to Lucy saying, **outside please come**, no punctuation or capital letters.

Two policemen got out, both white. One was very small, with red hair, and Joseph was momentarily distracted by his height. Wasn't there a minimum? If there was, he had to be under it.

"Hello, sir," said the taller one.

"Sir." That was their race-awareness training, or whatever they called it.

"Good evening," said Joseph cheerfully.

"Would you mind telling me what you're doing?"

"I will tell you exactly what I'm doing. My friend is in the shower, her kids are asleep, and I don't want to knock too loud in case I wake them up."

"I see. You often visit her this late?"

"It's ten o'clock."

"Quite late for a visit, though," said the short guy.

If Joseph had to guess, he'd say he was five feet four or five. He looked like this was the defining battle of his life, and he was seeking any opportunity to prove that being small was no disadvantage at all, when it came to arresting violent offenders. He was straining on an invisible leash.

"What is it you think I'm doing wrong?"

"I think the gentleman next door was more worried about what you might do wrong in the future."

"You wouldn't mind if we just had a quick search?"

He'd been searched before, four or five times, when he was a teenager. Nobody ever found anything. He'd never carried a knife, and he never walked around with any weed on him. But the first time, he'd gone on about his rights, like kids do, and it turned out he didn't have any.

The search wasn't voluntary. He was wearing his favorite item of clothing, a green Baracuta jacket, and he took it off and handed it to the taller guy.

"Nice jacket, that," said the short one. "I had a look at one of those, but it was out of my price range."

This was the real stuff, now. This wasn't about whether Lucy was or wasn't saying that black people made good singers. He suddenly felt the need to apologize to her. Perhaps he needed reminding that policemen quite often made pleasant-seeming conversation that was actually suggesting criminal activity.

The short guy stepped forward and patted his trouser pockets. It didn't take long. Joseph was wearing Nike track pants, and he never kept anything in them because it all fell out. Meanwhile, the tall one examined the contents of his jacket—phone, keys, wallet. The phone started to buzz in his hand. It was Lucy, Joseph could see.

"Can I take that?" said Joseph. "Because that's my friend who lives in there."

"When we're done, you can call her back," said the short one.

Joseph looked up at the sky. He didn't swear under his breath, he didn't roll his eyes.

"Is that a problem, sir?" said the little red-haired bull.

"Not a problem. Just that she could have backed up my story, and that would be the end of it. But for some reason you want to keep it going."

"We just want to make sure you're not about to get yourself in any trouble."

Lucy's front door opened, and she marched down the path.

"What's going on?"

"This young man says he's a friend of yours," said the taller one.

"He is."

"And your friends often come round to visit you at this time of night? Or just this one?"

"What business is it of yours?"

"Unfortunately, other people's private arrangements quite often become our business."

"What are you insinuating?"

The little one made a big-word face, which involved a widening of the eyes and a purse of the lips.

"I'm not sure we're insinuating anything."

"Are you searching him?"

"One of your neighbors was worried about his behavior."

"What was he doing?"

"We're trying to find out."

"But it can't be what he said he was doing?"

Lucy thought she could make this go away with a bit of moral outrage, Joseph could tell. She was a teacher, a head of department, and if these bobbies weren't careful, she would give them a piece of her mind. It didn't work like that, though. It was like multiplying a positive number by a minus number: the answer was always minus. Multiply a young black man by a white woman and the answer was a young black man, as far as the police were concerned. It would go away, but only because they'd get bored.

"We find in our line of work it quite often isn't. You didn't answer the question about whether he often comes round at this time of night."

"Why is it you're so interested?"

"It's happened before, madam. A well-meaning person such as yourself thinking they're doing the best thing by providing a helpful story."

The little redhead had taken over now. He had worked out how to push Lucy's buttons, and he was enjoying it.

"So you thought . . . what? That Joseph was going to break into my house, and I'd help him out by saying he was coming round for a cup of tea? In what world does that make any sense?"

"How do you two know each other, then?"

"I really think I should report this."

"You're welcome to."

"Come in, Joseph."

Joseph walked back down the path with her. Just before they reached the house, they heard the little one say something, and the other one laugh. It could have been about anything, but it probably wasn't. Lucy turned around to go back to them, but Joseph pushed her gently toward the door.

**"Do you want** a whisky or a brandy or something?" she said. She was pouring herself a glass of white wine from the bottle that seemed to be permanently open in the fridge.

"It's May," said Joseph. "And I wasn't out there that long."

"It was for the trauma, not the cold."

Joseph laughed, and then realized she wasn't joking.

"Fucking bastards."

"Yeah."

"You're not angry?"

"About that? Not especially."

"Well, I am. I'm furious."

He wanted to say sorry to her for suggesting that she was a racist, but if she got whipped up into a frenzy over something like that, she'd make it harder. And he didn't want her telling him how he should feel.

"I know you mean well," he said. "But forget it."

"Why?"

"Honestly? That wasn't such a big deal."

"That's terrible, then. Because it should be."

"You don't want the police turning up when there's a guy skulking around outside your window at night? I would."

"You're being flippant."

"Don't tell me what to feel."

"I'm telling you not to write it off as nothing."

"Fucking hell, Lucy. If I don't write things like that off as nothing, I'd drive myself mad."

He suddenly felt exhausted by the complication of it all.

"I'm so sorry I made that comment about the singing," she said. "It was thoughtless."

"I wanted to apologize to you about that. My reaction."

"You shouldn't. I wasn't thinking about how it must have sounded to you."

"It didn't sound like anything. I was pissed off

about the track not being right, and I hit out with the first thing I could grab."

"Are you OK? About this evening, I mean . . ."

"The police? It pisses me off but then I think of what it's like in America. Most of the time, the feds here are just arseholes who get bored and wander off. Over there, they kill you. Well. Not you."

Lucy went quiet, but you could always see everything on her face.

"Do you ever . . ."

He spoke over her straight away.

"Listen, I can only say what I feel. I can't talk about anyone else."

"It was just horrible, seeing them on the door-step."

"Try to forget it. They aren't worth bothering with. Especially the little ginger fucker."

She smiled and kissed him, a quick, sweet peck on the cheek.

Joseph looked at her and kissed her back properly then.

"See?" he said when they stopped. "We've got them to thank for this."

"Who?"

"The fucking police. It would have taken us a lot longer to get here without them."

She laughed, and took his hand, and led him upstairs.

# 8

But upstairs—and the boys, and **The Sopranos**—was their answer to everything, and Lucy was beginning to wonder what would happen when the questions got more complicated. She still loved their bubble, but there wasn't an awful lot of room in there, nor a lot of air to breathe, and they were both behaving in ways that their friends found odd or frustrating: they never wanted to see them, do anything, accept invitations out. They watched an episode and made love, watched an episode and made love, watched two episodes and didn't make love. They always watched an episode, and they nearly always made love.

"Do you play chess?" said Joseph one night. It was a Paul night, and they had made love and then watched an episode, in that order. They came to the end of Season 2, but decided not to start Season 3 immediately.

"No. I mean, I know the rules. And we've got a set. Do you want to play?"

"Ah, not if…"

"Not if I'm no good?"

Joseph laughed. "That would be the rude way of putting it."

"What about backgammon?"

"My dad taught me once, but I haven't played for years."

She went over to the cupboard where they kept the games.

"I'm sure we've got it."

She started to pull things out.

"Oh. Yes. Here we are."

She handed it to Joseph and he started to set it up.

"No dice."

"Oh, I'm sure we've got dice. There's a Monopoly here. And a Snakes and Ladders."

"Not enough pieces, either."

"Oh. Well, we could use counters or something."

"Seriously?" said Joseph.

Lucy laughed.

"We could go out one evening."

"Like the movies or something?"

"Or to eat."

"I'll bet we couldn't decide on a movie. What do you want to see at the moment?"

"There's that one with Meryl Streep about the woman who couldn't sing. I quite fancy that."

"Mmmm," said Joseph.

They didn't see it. And they never got around to going out.

**Lucy still looked back** with embarrassment on her conversation with Joseph about the recession and its effects on the building trade, but it turned out that everyone was talking about things that she was pretty sure they couldn't possibly understand, and that made her feel better. A few days before the referendum, there was a ferocious argument in the staffroom between an art teacher (remain) and a geography teacher (leave) about future trading arrangements with the E.U., an argument that Lucy suspected was built on very marshy ground indeed. Eventually, even they could see that they'd passed the limits of their understanding, but they didn't stop.

"So when you listen to all these clever economists telling you it will be a disaster, what do you think?" said Polly, the art teacher. "Do you think, oh, they don't know what they're talking about?"

"No," said Sam, the geography teacher. "I think, well, they would say that, wouldn't they?"

"Why would they?"

"Because it's all going very nicely for them, isn't it?"

"I don't know how it's going for economists," said Polly. "But they're probably worried about their house prices, like everyone else."

"House prices," said Sam. "Jesus. It's only you lot who give a shit."

"What's my lot?" said Polly. "Art teachers? We don't own many houses."

"I come from Stoke, right?" said Sam. "And you can buy a house there for a pound."

"A pound!" But Polly was scoffing, not expressing disbelief.

"Yes. A pound. Ex-council."

"So it's a scheme."

"Yes. It's a scheme. But they don't have many schemes in London, do they? They don't need to sell houses for a quid."

"I'd need to know more about the scheme."

"You know where else they had a scheme like this? Detroit. Fucking Detroit. Which is like a war zone. Stoke is less than two hours from here!"

"But what's it got to do with Brexit?"

"For a start, everyone I know at home is voting for it. And just think what's going through their minds when David Cameron says it will take thirty grand off the price of their house. I'll tell you: 'Not mine, pal. Mine's only worth a quid to begin with.'"

"Well, they'll be even worse off than they were before."

"What, their houses will be worth seventy-five p? Or fifty p? And how do you know about what will happen to house prices? You're an art teacher. You know about how to draw a nose."

"Don't be patronizing."

"You think you haven't been patronizing all the way through this conversation? Patronizing is all I ever get from southerners."

Lucy understood it now. The referendum was giving groups of people who didn't like each other, or at least failed to comprehend each other, an opportunity to fight. The government might just as well be asking a yes/no question about public nudity, or vegetarianism, or religion, or modern art, some other question that divided people into two groups, each suspicious of the other. There had to be something riding on it, otherwise people wouldn't get so upset. But if the government promised to flog every piece of art the country owned that was created after 1970 and give the money to schools... Well, there would be fist-fights. Lucy didn't know many people she wanted to fight with, and she suspected Polly, with her Doc Martens and her large earrings, was the same, and now she was discovering that she could fight with the person sitting right next to her at work. (Although why did she think that the boots and the flamboyant jewelry were an indication that Polly kept to her own kind? Why didn't Sam's Nike bottoms and blue hoodie convey the same message? Perhaps they did, but Lucy couldn't read the signs in the same way.) What would happen after the vote? Polly and Sam had just called each other names, or adjectives, anyway. Would they be able to forget it and find something else to talk about? From the looks on their faces when the bell went for the end of break, it didn't seem likely. They probably hadn't talked before, and they certainly wouldn't talk again.

Lucy liked Sam. At the school fair the previous year, he'd worn a red-and-white-striped football shirt (Stoke?) with the name of a player on the back. Lucy couldn't remember the player, but there was a q in it, and her boys had gone up to him to talk about both the shirt and the q, and Sam had asked the boys, to their enormous delight, to name five other players with a q in their names. They answered the question, Sam told them they were a credit to their mother, and they immediately started pestering her about attending Park

Road when they were old enough, as if the whole of secondary education was going to consist of naming footballers with a q in their names, or a z when they got to the sixth form. But she still wasn't on Sam's side. She was on Polly's side. She'd hardly exchanged a single word with Polly since she'd arrived a year ago, and whenever Lucy thought about her, which wasn't often, it was with a little irritation. Polly seemed affected, and managed to wordlessly convey that teaching was beneath her.

In the few days leading up to the vote, Lucy tried to make sure once and for all that she was on Polly's side, and not Sam's. She watched **Question Time**, and read the papers, and listened to the **Today Programme** in the morning, but there was no doubt about it: the people she loathed were all on the other team. Sam wasn't a bad guy, and nor, she guessed, was Joseph's dad, or Joseph's mum. But all the people telling them to vote leave were hypocrites, bullies, and racists. Then Nigel Farage unveiled his poster, the one that showed a lot of desperate brown people queuing up to get into a country that wasn't Britain but might be one day, according to him, and Jo Cox was murdered, and any remaining doubts vanished.

She showed the poster to Joseph.

"He's a twat," said Joseph.

"So why are you thinking of doing what he says?"

"Because it's nothing to do with him."

"How can you say that?"

"The money for the N.H.S. and my dad's salary, that's not him. He's just a racist tosser, stirring the shit."

"And he's on your team."

"I haven't got a team."

"We're all in teams this week. One team or the other."

"I might not vote," said Joseph.

Lucy was outraged, but she would give him a chance to reply before launching a scathing attack on his sloth and his irresponsibility.

"Why wouldn't you vote?"

"Because I haven't got a bloody clue what I think."

And Lucy laughed, despite herself.

"What's funny?"

"That's the sanest and most obvious opinion I've heard for months. But, still, you don't want to stop the racists?"

"Of course I do. But they'll still be there after all this. This is about sending people back to Poland."

"I'd have thought..." And she stopped herself. Whatever she would have thought (and what a strange tense that was), she either hadn't finished or hadn't even started thinking it. Remember the singing, Lucy. She might have that put on a T-shirt.

"I know what you were going to say. What are my family doing, voting the same way as a bunch of racists? But they're British. I thought you all wanted us to be British. Just because we're black doesn't mean we want to stay part of Europe. Half those countries are more racist than anyone here. The Italians. The Poles. The Russians. Just about every country in Eastern Europe. You ever heard the abuse our black players get when they play in those places? They fucking hate us."

She hadn't. She was beginning to feel that she didn't know very much about anything.

"When I was a kid," said Joseph, "I loved Thierry Henry."

"Everyone did."

"Anyway, France were going to play Spain, and the Spain coach was recorded telling one of his players that Henry was a black shit. And there was a fuss, and the coach got fined. But he went to court and had it overturned. Took him, like, three years, but he did it. They still make monkey noises at black players in Spain. It used to happen here, my dad says, but it stopped years ago. That's why I don't feel very European. Fuck Europe, man."

"Now I feel bad that I'm going to vote to stay in."

"Well, you shouldn't."

———

**She went to vote** after work, in a dusty little hall that only ever seemed to be used for elections. She wanted to feel a somber sense of duty, but it was hard, when it was just a piece of paper and a stubby little pencil. And usually, when you looked at the piece of paper, you would find names like Lord Cashew Nut, or political movements like the Keep Dogs Out of Lordship Park Party. America, with its machines and its hanging chads, at least tried to make things appear complicated and serious. Today, of course, there was just a question: Should the United Kingdom remain a member of the European Union or leave the European Union? For a moment she wondered whether the boxes underneath would simply say "Yes" or "No," and the whole thing would have to be scrapped, but the wording was clear. She put a cross in the first box, "Remain a member of the European Union," folded her piece of paper even though she'd been told there was no need to, and walked out into the early summer evening. On the way home she met a few people she knew, neighbors, parents of the boys' friends, members of the book group she used to go to before she wanted to kill them. They were all on their way to the polling station. One made a nervous face, another crossed his fingers and held them up, another asked whether she thought it would be all right. It didn't occur to any of them that she might have voted to leave. And of course she hadn't, so the presumption was correct. She wanted to stop them all and ask what it was they had invested in the European Union, but she didn't. She didn't want them to think she didn't belong.

**On the bus** home from the leisure center, Joseph met John, the parent who'd been pushed over by the referee at one of the kids' matches a while back. When John saw Joseph, he switched seats and sat alongside him.

"You voting?" said John. "I'm stopping off on the way home."

"Dunno. Haven't made my mind up."

"Haven't you?" said John. "I'm surprised."

"It's a complicated question," said Joseph.

"Not to me," said John.

"No? So why are you voting, then?" For some reason, Joseph thought "why" was a better question than "how." He was wrong.

"I'm sick of it."

"What are you sick of?"

"No offense, but you can't say anything these days, can you?"

"Can't you?"

"No."

"I'm not offended, by the way."

"How d'you mean?"

"You said, 'No offense.'"

"Oh. Yeah. But you're all right."

"Thanks. And voting to leave is going to help sort that out?"

"I think so, yes," said John. "But that's just my opinion."

"What do you want to say that you can't?"

"Well, you know how it is. I'm not going to spell it out. I have too much respect for you. But it's all Afro-Caribbean this, and gay that, and lesbian the other."

"But how will leaving Europe help?"

"It can't make it any worse, can it? And as I understand it, it's a lot of their laws. Brussels."

"I didn't know that."

"Apparently. Anyway. This is me."

He stood up.

"Think about it."

"I will," said Joseph.

"See you next season."

And he was gone.

**When he got home,** his mother thrust his polling card at him.

"You'll need this."

"I don't know if I'm going down there."

"Yes, you are. People died so you could have a vote."

"Who?"

"Well, you don't know them. They died a long time ago."

"All right, but what kind of people?"

"Soldiers. In the war."

"The Second World War?"

"If you like."

Joseph laughed at her vagueness.

"It's not funny."

"I was laughing at you, not people dying in the war."

"Oh, let's all laugh at me again."

"The Second World War was Winston Churchill, right?"

"Oh, Joseph."

"I'm not checking my facts. I know about World War Two. I'm trying to construct an argument. Hear me out. So that was Churchill. And you're voting to leave, yes?"

"Yes."

"Well, you know what Churchill wanted, don't you?"

"I know some of the things. Which one are you talking about?"

"He wanted a united Europe."

"Who told you that? Your fancy woman?"

"Look it up. He defeated Hitler. And then he said, enough war in Europe. Let's have a European union."

"Why are you telling me this now?"

"Would it have changed your mind?"

"Yes. Of course. He was a great man. Your grandparents loved him."

"Well, it doesn't matter. You won't win."

"Why do you say that? Everyone I've talked to in this street is voting out. But it doesn't matter. Vote. Take your card and go down to the school and be a responsible person. Like I said, people died for this."

Joseph wasn't sure that she'd proved that to his satisfaction, but he took the card and left the house. Lucy didn't know anyone who was voting out. None of his neighbors were voting in. Joseph was somewhere halfway between. Before all this business, he'd have guessed that everyone was in the middle, really, not that bothered about anything, but he seemed to be all on his own. When he got to the school hall and looked at the ballot paper, he put a cross in both boxes, because he thought both things. He wouldn't have to lie to anybody.

**He was starving,** so he went to McDonald's for something to eat. He didn't do it very often. He spent part of his week encouraging kids to get fit, and he didn't want to be caught with his nose in a heap of Chicken Selects smothered in barbecue sauce. But every now and again, the need became too great, and he hadn't asked Lucy to save him anything, and he didn't want her to cook for him when he arrived at hers. And he wasn't even sure he was going to go round and see her. She would be glued to the news, and he'd get bored, and he'd go on his phone, and though she wouldn't say anything, he'd feel judged. She would think he was stupid, or young, or something. Or maybe it would be him thinking these things about himself. Either way, maybe it was best to give it a rest for an evening.

**He took his tray** over to a corner of the restaurant in the hope of keeping his junk-food shame secret, and found himself heading straight for Jaz and one of her friends. He smiled and said hello, and hovered for a moment, in case she invited him to sit with her, but she looked at him as if he'd ordered a large dead cat stewed in its own vomit, and turned away. He sat where he was going to sit anyway, and started scrolling through Instagram.

"Is that it, then?" she said. "You're just going to sit there?"

"I said hello, and you looked away."

"I'd need much more than a hello."

"I'm not sure what I've got that's more than a hello."

"That's what I told everyone."

Joseph rolled his eyes.

"I'm only messing around. I never mentioned you to anyone. Darcy, this is Joseph. The guy I was telling you about. I'm only messing around again."

"Hi, Darcy."

"Hel-lo," said Darcy. "Have you finished with him?"

"He finished with me," said Jaz. "But I might not let that happen."

"Well," said Darcy. "If you do, let me know."

Joseph wondered whether he would be allowed any choice in the matter. He knew, because his sister had lectured him on the subject many times, that young women grew up with all sorts of body issues because of men like him. But in an extremely private conversation with himself, one that didn't even involve him moving his lips, he would admit that maybe Darcy was too large, by several stones, to be his absolutely ideal woman.

"You're too big for him," said Jaz. "I know his type."

"Is that true?" said Darcy.

"No," said Joseph. "Of course not. She doesn't know my type, and you're not too big for me."

He was trying to make amends for Jaz's rudeness, but he felt that he was overcompensating, and now in danger of committing himself long-term to Darcy.

"See?" said Darcy.

"He's lying," said Jaz to Darcy. "She has loads of men after her, so it doesn't matter," she said to Joseph.

Joseph wanted to move the subject away from Darcy's love life, and the only way he could do it effectively was to offer Jaz a chance at stardom via his track. He had intended to approach her with more subtlety, without third parties present, and perhaps not halfway through a meal in McDonald's, but those luxuries were unaffordable now.

"I've been meaning to call you," he said. He needed an introductory sentence of some kind before telling her that he wanted to record her, but that was the wrong one, inviting only scorn and bitterness.

"Oh, I'll bet."

"I was."

"What was stopping you, then?"

"I was looking for the right moment. Plus, I wanted to give it a bit more time. After the, the night we went to the cinema."

"I went back to his place afterward," Jaz explained to Darcy. "But he wasn't interested."

"Yeah, I know," said Darcy.

Of course she knew. Everybody knew, probably.

"Are you still with your girlfriend?"

"Yes."

"So why did you mean to call me, if you're not single?"

Somehow he had ended up exactly where he wanted to be.

"I was going to ask you to sing on a track."

He tried to anticipate the wounding answer, but none was forthcoming. She gaped at him.

"Really?"

"Yes. I think you're an amazing singer."

"How much?"

"Nothing."

"Oh."

"That can't be right," said Darcy.

"I'm not earning anything from it," said Joseph.

"That's not her problem, though, is it?"

"No. But if she won't sing for free, I'd respect her decision and look elsewhere."

"You can't cut her out just like that."

"Nobody's cut her in yet."

"You just asked me to sing on your track!" said Jaz, apparently genuinely outraged. "And now you're going back on it!"

The conversation about the singing didn't seem to be going any better than the conversation about Darcy's size, although that particular minefield at least offered an escape route: he could have tiptoed through it and out of McDonald's with Darcy to the nearest registry office. The way out of this one was not immediately obvious.

"Listen," said Joseph. "If I make a million quid from it, she can have half a million."

"Don't fall for that," said Darcy.

"Fall for what?"

"What he's saying is, if he makes half a million quid, he won't give you a penny. Because that wasn't the deal."

"I'm saying that if I make half a million, she gets a quarter."

"A quarter of a million, or a quarter of what you make?"

Jesus Christ.

"A quarter of a million. Half. If I make ten quid, she gets a fiver. Five hundred, she gets two hundred and fifty. I'm not going to go through every single possible amount and then halve it."

"But half of nothing is still nothing."

"Yes. Agreed. Up to you."

He hadn't eaten many of his Chicken Selects. He picked one up, dunked it in the sauce and began to chew ostentatiously, to indicate that the negotiation was over for now. The girls stood up to leave.

"I might be interested," said Jaz. "Have you ever been in that studio in Turnpike Lane?"

"No. Have you?"

"Yeah. Boy I was seeing worked there for a bit. It's for disadvantaged young people in Haringey."

"What does that mean?"

"Which word don't you understand?"

"I understand it all. I'm just wondering whether it applies to us."

"It applies to me."

"Good. I mean, not good, but…"

"And you have to take us to dinner."

"Both of you?"

"Unless it's a date."

Joseph picked up a Select and shoved it into his mouth quick, even though he hadn't finished the first one. Jaz laughed.

"I'll call you," she said, and he nodded vigorously.

**Lucy went to bed** before the result came in, and only had a vague sense of unease when she turned the light off. She was uneasy about the future direction of the country, and she was also uneasy about the future of her relationship with Joseph. She didn't expect explanations, or long devotional epistles in text form, but she was surprised and a little stung by the brevity: **Not coming tonight. Xx.** He came every night, and they hadn't talked about him not coming, and she suddenly realized that if and when it ended, it would probably be as sudden as that, and there'd be no need for long anguished conversations, or counseling. There would be no tears or accusation or self-flagellation, either, which was of course a good thing, but also implied a kind of insecurity, like a zero-hours contract. The end of a marriage was miserable and difficult, but that was because it was a living, breathing thing, and when it died, grief was inevitable. Her thing with Joseph existed only when they were together, in the same room, it seemed to her now. And if they weren't in the same room, then it wasn't anything at all. As she lay sleepless in the dark, she had to admit that she was more worried about Joseph than she was about Brexit, seeing as she wasn't thinking about Brexit.

———

**And then she turned** on the radio the next morning, and the unease solidified into fear, and Joseph wasn't anything to do with it. When there were still two possibilities, in and out, she had, she felt, made her peace with the other side, with Sam, and Joseph's dad, and all the other people who wanted something, anything, to change. Now that her desired outcome had been removed, and she found herself living in a country where the BBC were sticking microphones up to the mouths of jubilant racists, opportunists, liars, and cynics, people whose unpleasantness had made them famous over these last few months, all the ambiguity had gone.

Even the boys seemed to be listening while they ate their cereal.

"So out won?" said Dylan.

"Yep."

"Are you angry?"

"I'm a bit sad."

"I can't remember whether I was in or out," said Al.

"You were out," said Dylan. "I was in."

"Ha. Loser."

"I didn't know you were out," said Lucy. "Why?"

"Because he was in," said Al.

"That's a stupid way to make a political decision," said Lucy, before remembering that she had voted in exactly the same way. Perhaps that's how everyone had done it, in the end.

**Very few of the P.E.** teachers turned up in the staffroom before the first lesson. They were usually in the gym, or on the all-weather pitch, putting out equipment and messing around with a ball. But as Lucy was making a coffee, the door burst open, and Sam came in singing "**Championes, championes, olé olé olé.**"

One or two people smiled at his ebullience; most glowered at him. He made his way over to Polly, who was scrolling through her phone, and sat down next to her.

"Unlucky," he said.

"Fuck off."

"I knew you'd be a sore loser."

"It's not a game."

"I never said it was. But your side lost."

"Yes, and I'm sad, so why rub my nose in it? You can do that after a football match, but not when you've fucked the country up."

"But we don't think we have."

"What do you think you've done then?"

"We've told the E.U. where to stick their laws."

"You mean, 'Now we can kick immigrants out'?"

"Oh, here we go. Everyone's a racist except you."

Ben Davies, the deputy head, walked over to Sam, bent over, and said something quietly into his ear.

"Me?" said Sam, at an entirely different volume. "Why not her? She's told me to fuck off, and she's told me I've fucked the country up. Why can't she go somewhere else?"

Ben continued to say things that nobody else could hear, and eventually Sam stood up and walked out.

Lucy had been a teacher for a long time, and she had seen arguments between members of staff before, but they were about cover periods and difficult pupils—about work, in other words. These rows blew over. Understandings were reached. Jokes were made. But this was about whether Polly or Sam was a bad person. Neither of them was, of course, but it would be a while before they would be able to see it like that. How long? Who knew? And knowledge seemed beside the point anyway.

**After school she got** a text from Fiona, the college friend who had introduced her to Michael, on the night that Joseph had pushed Paul into the hedge. We're trying to cheer ourselves up with drinks and nibbles tomorrow night. A chance for a moan and a

**catch-up. Please come.** That was exactly what Lucy wanted: a moan. She wanted to listen to people like her say things that she hadn't thought about, and she wanted to let off steam. She had presumed that Saturday night was going to be a takeaway, two episodes of **The Sopranos**, and some escapist sex. But she needed to talk, and she could see that Joseph might not be the right person to talk to.

**Do you still do babysitting?** she texted.

**For the right person.**

**Proper. Payment etc.**

**OK. What time?**

She had hoped for a joke about payment in kind, but then, she hadn't made one either.

**Eight?**

**Maybe I'll come straight after work and play with boys.**

**Sure.**

**You don't have to pay for that part.**

**Worth any money. See you later?**

**Going to a party.**

**Oh. OK,** she typed, and then deleted the **oh**, which sounded wounded to her, and, now she came to think about it, was meant to sound that way to him.

**OK.**

**xx**

She doubted that they'd ever go below two kisses, as long as communication continued. Could a bubble be in the process of popping? It couldn't, really. It just popped.

**Joseph was babysitting** the twins the following Tuesday, five days after the referendum, and as he was leaving, Marina asked for a quick word.

"Listen," she said. "I know you do lots of other jobs, and you've got lots of other sources of income…"

"Yeah," said Joseph. "The money's pouring in."

"Oh, please don't say that," Marina said.

She was a nice woman. He had absolutely nothing to say to her that wasn't about her children, but she trusted him, and treated him like a grown-up. He'd never met Oliver, her husband. He was never home by six, when Joseph knocked off.

"I was kidding."

"I know, but… We're almost certainly going to have to move."

"Oh. Right. Where? Because maybe…"

"Abroad. Oliver works for a Japanese company, and if we're not in Europe, London isn't going to be any use to them. They're thinking of getting out quick and going to Paris or Brussels. They want him to open the office there."

"Oh."

"This whole thing is a walking fucking nightmare."

Joseph had no plans to go and live in Brussels or Paris, but neither option sounded like a walking fucking nightmare to him.

"Yeah," he said.

"Your generation must feel so betrayed. All these old farts gambling your future away."

"Yeah," he said. He was glad he'd voted for both sides. It made these conversations easier. But maybe when he'd shrugged it all off, on the grounds that there would always be meat, and football, and kids, he'd been too optimistic: there wouldn't always be kids. Not these kids, anyway. There would always be meat, though, and football, and leisure centers. Maybe there would be more leisure than anyone knew what to do with.

## 9

The Friday-night party was in a place called God's Village, owned by some church in Tottenham. It was a maze of halls, chapels, conference rooms, and corridors, all of them devoted to Our Lord on every day of the week apart from this one, when it was devoted to loud music, Yeezys, and discarded cans of NOS. It took Joseph a while to find Jaz and Darcy. They were in the corner of the main room, away from the speakers, in the center of a little knot of people, mostly guys. As Joseph approached, he realized he knew most of them from school, or from football, or from being in the same place at the same time. He hadn't seen them for years. Who had moved on? It didn't feel like he had.

"Nobody dancing?" he said, as a way of stopping

the girls from saying something mean, or aggressive, or flirtatious, or sexually explicit.

The boys, Cody, Josh L., Xavier, a couple of others he only halfrecognized, offered fists and leaned in for a quick hug. It felt good to be exchanging greetings with people he knew and understood. It felt good to understand the greetings, even.

"We're waiting," said Jaz. "This guy called PoundMan is D.J.-ing."

"I know PoundMan."

"Someone said he was American."

Joseph didn't ask her why an American would fly over the Atlantic and make his way to Tottenham to play at Alexa Williams's twenty-first birthday party and be called £Man.

"Nope. North London."

He wouldn't tell anyone that £Man was Zech. Some of them might remember him, especially if Joseph were unkind enough to describe his physical peculiarities and inadequacies. If Jaz thought £Man was American, then maybe the transitioning was working, even though Zech still had to get behind the decks and reveal himself at some point in the evening.

"How you been, anyway?" he said to Josh.

"Yeah, OK."

"You working?"

"Last year of college."

"Where?"

"South Bank. Game Design and Development."

"Seriously?"

"Yeah."

"Is it as good as it sounds?"

"It's sick. And I've been offered a job when I leave."

For some reason, Joseph had got it into his head that he'd be listening to stories about unemployment and supermarket jobs, and he'd feel good about himself. Now he remembered that he wasn't actually doing that well, and that a lot of his self-esteem came from the sense of direction Lucy seemed to give him. Talking to Josh made him realize that Lucy wasn't a job, as such. She seemed to offer him a way out of something. It just wasn't a way out of any of the jobs he was doing.

"How about you, man?" said Josh.

"Yeah. Busy."

"Good."

"Yeah." He felt he should give a fuller picture of his activities, without going into any specifics. "I just wanted to get on with it, you know?"

"Yeah."

"Make myself a few quid."

"I don't blame you. I'm paying off student debt for years to come."

"That's it, you see? I don't have to worry about any of that."

He hadn't thought of it like that. He was actually rich, compared to some of them, simply because there wasn't a minus number in his bank account. He had plus five hundred or so, whereas Josh had minus forty or fifty thousand.

"And are you living at home?" Josh asked.

"For now, yeah. Looking around at the moment."

As he said the words, something compelled him to scan the room, presumably so that he could not be found guilty of lying in a court of law. He was literally looking around at that precise moment. There was unlikely to be any kind of legal situation, true, but the conversation was pulling him into uncomfortable areas. If there was an opportunity for the truth, he wanted to take it.

"Seen anyone you like?" said Josh.

Joseph had been looking around the party, not for girls, but to illustrate the hunt for new accommodation. That explanation was complicated, however, maybe even insane.

"There are some very, very pretty women here," said Joseph. Now he needed to find some examples urgently, just in case Josh asked for some.

"If you had to go home with one, who would it be?"

"That one over there," said Joseph. He hadn't

spotted anyone. He would point in the general direction, and hope that someone over there vaguely corresponded to somebody's idea of a one-night stand or a potential wife, depending on which sort of going home Josh meant. Were mothers and cakes involved? Or just beds and condoms?

"Hanna Johnson?"

Probably, Joseph thought. She'd do as well as anyone.

"Yeah."

"Do you know her?"

"Don't think so."

"Come on. Let's go and talk to her."

Oh, hell. Why had he said he was looking around for somewhere to live? It was a pathetic lie, and as a consequence he was going to end up having sex or a relationship or an entire life with someone he didn't know and who wasn't his type anyway.

**Anyway, it turned out** that Hanna was exactly his type, a type he didn't even know he was interested in. She was pretty, quiet, smart, and the smartness didn't just come from the glasses she wore. Or rather, he didn't come to the conclusion that she was smart just because she wore glasses. (The glasses might well have been because of the smartness. Maybe she read so much that her eyes became strained.) She was at the university too, studying English at U.C.L. He'd never met anyone who had studied there. Later, he wondered whether Lucy had created the interest—whether he was suddenly interested in people who knew about books because of her. He asked questions, listened, didn't mention the butcher's or the leisure center (or Lucy) and to his surprise asked her out for a drink. The immediate trouble this caused came from Jaz, who seemed to know about it even before it had been planned, and who said unkind things about Hanna and about him to his face, and who before the evening was over said unkind things about him to Hanna's face.

Oh, and £Man blew the roof off.

**The queue at the shop** on Saturday morning was different—louder, more animated. People were speaking to those behind them and in front of them, and the conversations continued into the shop. It slowed everything down: sentences had to be finished and points made before orders were given. If Joseph had never worked in the shop before, he'd have presumed that some kind of coach party had just arrived, people who for reasons best known to themselves had come from a small village out of town to buy meat. Since the previous Saturday, the country had voted out and the Prime Minister had gone, and that was enough to turn the Saturday-morning volume button up. Lucy was in the coach party. He saw her through the window, talking over her shoulder to the man behind her, and when she got into the shop, Joseph tried to focus on what she was saying, as opposed to what everyone else was saying.

"I don't get it. How will a petition help, when we've just had a vote?"

She smiled at Joseph, and he smiled back.

"Eight hundred thousand signatures this morning."

"But how many people voted out? Seventeen million?"

"Something like that."

"So I'll put my name to it when it gets to seventeen million."

"If everyone thought like you, we wouldn't get anywhere."

"Most people do think like me. That's why you've only got eight hundred thousand signatures."

"In twenty-four hours."

"Hi. Could I have four rump steaks, please?"

Lucy was being served, by Cass. Joseph wondered whether he was getting the fourth steak.

"So you're just going to do nothing?"

"Oh, I'll probably moan a lot."

"Good morning."

Joseph was looking after the guy, which nowadays he preferred. He'd only served Lucy once since they'd started sleeping together, and it felt weird, both of them on the verge of laughing all the time. It felt like he was wearing an "I Fucked Lucy" hat.

"What would you like?"

"Can I have twelve of the gluten-free sausages?"

"That's twenty pounds forty," said Cass.

"I want some cubed lamb as well, please. People voted a different way from me. What else is there to say? Apart from I wish they hadn't?"

"It'll be a bloody disaster, though. It's insane."

"Anything else?"

"I'd like some of those marinated chicken skewers. Six? Yes. Six."

"Barbecue this evening?"

"Tomorrow afternoon, I think. If the weather holds."

Joseph wondered whether the man would ask him to sign this petition. He thought not. The queue was made up of one type of person. The people behind the counter, apart from Cass the university student, were another.

"Have you signed it?" the man said to Cass. Wow, thought Joseph. Wow.

Actually, Joseph was glad he hadn't been asked. What would the man who voted both ways say? Yes and no, probably.

"Yeah," said Cass. "Of course. But I don't know why I bothered."

What was it? Her accent? Her eyebrows? The little tattoo on her hand? In lots of ways, Joseph thought, he had just as much in common with the petition guy as the petition guy had with Cass. He'd talked about football with him before, during the last World Cup, and he had a kid who played in the league where Joseph coached. But something in Cass had encouraged Petition Guy to believe that in this matter at least, he thought like her. And he was right. Did Joseph mind? He did, he thought. He hadn't been invited by people he didn't like much to a party he didn't want to go to. The lack of invitation still stung.

**In the Uber** on the way to the party at Fiona's, Lucy felt a pang she didn't know what to do with. It was like flicking through a photograph album, or the last day of a wonderful holiday, or the occasional moment of motherhood when a child does something that you know won't happen again, not like that, and you want to stop time. Or this: it was like moving, leaving a house where you'd been happy. Yes, it was her house, and yes, she'd be back in a couple of hours, but the Uber that took her home would be delivering her to a new place. Her house had been happy, and then really fucking miserable, and then, just recently, with Joseph, happy again. But she could tell that the Joseph days were coming to an end. He'd be there when she got back, because he was babysitting. There was even a possibility that they would have sex. But it was all ebbing away, sweetly, sadly, and the sadness was appropriate and inevitable, the end of a movie.

**They hadn't even** said anything. Joseph had come round after work, and she'd grilled steaks on the barbecue, lit an hour before he finished work so that she could eat with them before the party, and she'd left him playing FIFA with the boys. So it wasn't conversation, or a decision. It was all body language, and missed cues, and a slightly stiff politeness that had never been there before. Where had it come from? It was something to do with the events of the week, she knew that much. Last night he had wanted to be with people who wouldn't talk about them. Tonight she wanted to be with people who would. They weren't divided in the same way as the rest of the country, she didn't think. But they were divided nevertheless.

**And when she got** to the party, she realized that she'd simply missed going out; there had been an awful lot of staying in. It had felt as though home and kids and Joseph had been providing all the necessary nutrients, but of course that wasn't true. It hadn't been a healthy diet. Even if she went to the cinema on her own, which she did occasionally, she was sitting with people who liked the films she liked. Sometimes you needed that.

The first person she saw was Michael Marwood.

"Hello," he said, kissed her on both cheeks, hugged her briefly. He was pleased to see her, she could see that, but he was still a little embarrassed. She wondered whether he recalled all the details of the evening they spent together, or whether some of them were lost in the haze of temporary mental incapacity.

"You told me that nobody ever voted against their own financial self-interest," she said.

"You know, that's the first thing I thought of when the result came in. My confidence when we had dinner."

"So, any explanations?"

"No. You?"

"Yes."

She told him about scaffolding, and Sam's one-pound houses in Stoke, and he listened, and was interested. Another couple, people who worked in publishing, came over to say hello to Michael and he told them about scaffolding and one-pound houses, and they listened too. The publishing couple were dragged away to meet someone else, but more friends, of hers and his, came over, and everyone talked about the referendum, and how depressed they were, and it was easy for Lucy to imagine that she and Michael were a couple, and to understand why she and Joseph weren't. She couldn't have gone to the birthday party the night before and listened to £Man's D.J. set with a lot of people in their twenties. She'd have looked absurd. And Joseph couldn't have come tonight. He'd have been bored and uncomfortable.

And then Paul walked in with a woman. Lucy gaped for a moment, and felt sick and panicky, and then recovered herself.

"Hey."

"Oh," said Paul. "Hi. Wow."

Wow? Why was there any wow? There was no room for any wow whatsoever. Friends of hers were throwing the party. He had previously only been to this house with her. He must have suspected that she'd be here, even if this suspicion didn't creep up on him until he was at the front door.

Lucy smiled politely at Paul's companion. She was a few years younger than him (and therefore Lucy) but nothing outrageous. Paul didn't take the hint.

"I'm Lucy," said Lucy, and they shook hands. Lucy didn't think she'd announced herself with too much emphasis, although she was immediately aware of the weight of her name, and the eyes of the young or younger woman widened before she composed herself.

"Daisy."

"Hi, Daisy."

"So."

"So."

"How come you're here?"

"Me?" said Daisy.

"I'm presuming Paul didn't bring you. He wouldn't have been invited."

"We're...we came together."

"No, I understand. I was trying in my cack-handed way to ask who invited you?" Too aggressive. "Who do you know?"

"I'm sorry," said Daisy. "I shouldn't have come."

"No, no...Honestly, I don't mind. Are you a friend of Pete's? Or Fiona's?"

"Oh," said Daisy. "I see what you mean."

She smiled blankly, as if she either didn't want to answer the question, or it was simply too hard for her.

"Daisy is a freelance researcher," said Paul. "Documentaries, mostly."

Paul was attempting to demonstrate that Daisy was neither dim nor mad, despite all appearances to the contrary.

"Good for you," said Lucy. "Are you working on one at the moment?"

"I sometimes work with Pete," said Daisy suddenly. "Fiona's husband."

"That's who she knows," said Paul. "Pete."

"Yes," said Daisy.

They were both drinking water, Lucy noticed. She wondered whether they were both alcoholics, and that was how they'd found each other. Or whether Daisy was showing solidarity, or whether she just didn't drink, or wasn't drinking tonight. Lucy was wondering too much, clearly. But how could one not be interested in one's estranged husband's girlfriend? (And she was his girlfriend, for sure. There was too much panic and embarrassment for her to be anything else.)

"No Joseph?" said Paul.

"No," said Lucy, and nothing more.

"Who's Joseph?" said Daisy.

"I told you about Joseph," said Paul. Lucy bristled.

"Is this the Joseph I met?" said Michael, who was still standing there, unintroduced to anybody.

"I'm sorry," said Lucy. "This is Michael. Michael, this is Paul, my ex. And Daisy."

"I'm not technically her ex," said Paul.

Daisy and Lucy both looked at him.

"You're not technically my ex-husband," said Lucy. "But you are my ex. Technically and in every other way."

"That lets Daisy and me off the hook," said Michael. And he smiled at Lucy fondly. He had just equated himself with Daisy, who was clearly having sex with Paul. There was no comparison, but Michael wanted to make one, for reasons unknown. Dear God, thought Lucy. What was wrong with everybody?

"Why are you off the hook?" said Daisy.

"And why were you on it in the first place?" said Paul.

"I suppose that's right," said Michael.

"What is?" said Paul.

"The expression 'off the hook' does imply that one was on it. Otherwise everybody would be off the hook all the time."

"I'm still trying to work out why hooks came up in the first place, though," said Paul.

"Oh, never mind," said Lucy.

"Anyway," said Michael. "That all makes sense.

The ex- thing. There seemed to be a lot of subtext."

"When did you meet Joseph?" said Paul.

"He was babysitting one night when Lucy and I
went out for dinner."

"Oh," said Paul. "So Joseph has returned to his
former role?"

"Ah," said Daisy. "That Joseph." And then, "I
do know about Joseph. But not a lot. Just the basic
facts."

Lucy looked at Paul and raised an eyebrow in
an attempt to suggest mild disapproval of his gos-
siping.

"No, no," said Daisy quickly. "I just meant...I
don't think I know anything, you know. Inappropriate. Paul just mentioned him in passing, really.
And yes. Alec Guinness and David Lean. Sorry. I
seem to be answering every question late."

"What was that the answer to?"

"Whether I'm working on a documentary."

"I met him once," said Michael.

"Yes," said Paul. "You said."

Paul now seemed to be working on the assumption that Lucy and Michael were together, and
that Michael was senile. This made him mani-
festly happy.

"Did I?" said Michael.

"Yes," said Paul. "You told us you met him when you and Lucy went out for dinner."

"Oh," said Michael. "Not Joseph. Alec Guinness."

There would almost certainly be no other time in Joseph's life that this clarification would be required.

"You met Alec Guinness?" said Daisy.

"Yes. In the early nineties. Some film company was interested in adapting one of my novels, and they'd sent it to him, and there was a meeting or two."

"You write? Would I know your books?" said Daisy.

"I don't know much about you," said Michael pleasantly. "It really depends on how much you read."

"You're not Michael Marwood, are you?" said Daisy. She was already thrilled.

"I'm going to find a loo," said Lucy, and once she'd found it, she went to talk to other people in another room.

**Were these her people?** Apart from the writers, the documentary researchers, the graphic designers and friends of Alec Guinness, there were the publishers and the independent film producers, the college lecturers and the tank-thinkers, the theater critics and the radio presenters. A couple who had opened a cheese shop, a wine importer, a head teacher. She knew some of them, and she talked to all of them about the referendum, the conversation that couldn't be avoided. She told them all about Sam's one-pound houses and Joseph's dad, and her knowledge of elsewhere gave her temporary authority as an expert in how the other fifty-two percent thought. On the whole, though, the guests at the party preferred the narrative about lies, fear, stupidity, and racism. They had lost an argument, and they never lost arguments. They were confused and angry.

On the way home, Lucy got a text from Michael:

**Sorry not to have said good-bye. Would you give me another go?**

"How was everything?"

"Yeah, fine," said Joseph. He was watching T.V. Lucy would have sat down and kissed him on the cheek at this point, maybe leaned into him, but Joseph seemed a little distracted.

"Do you want a cup of tea?"

"I think I'm going to head home. It's been a busy week."

"Are you still recovering from your party?"

"I don't often go out on a Friday night."

"You haven't been going out many nights."

"No."

Lucy sat on the armchair, at right angles to him. They were both watching the T.V. now.

"Do you miss it? Your mandem?"

He laughed. "How do you know about mandems?"

"Oh, I hear about mandems all day every day. It's not like singing, is it?"

"Like singing?"

"You know, when I said you must know people who could sing."

"Oh. No. Everyone has a mandem. But not everyone calls it that. And I haven't got one. Not really. You?"

"I was sort of with my mandem tonight, but they're making me feel weird. So now I'm not sure."

"I met someone last night."

"Oh."

"I mean, no big deal or anything. But we're going to go out."

"Thank you for telling me."

He looked at her.

"What?" she said.

"I dunno."

"You thought I'd have more to say?"

"I suppose. I didn't know if you'd be angry."

"Oh, how can I be angry? It's been wonderful, and I knew this conversation was coming."

She was tempted to turn off the T.V. and play some music, something quiet, beautiful, regretful, thoughtful. What did young people listen to, if they wanted all that? They didn't have k.d. lang or Nina Simone or Leonard Cohen. They had chill-out music. They chilled out. Maybe quiet thoughtful regret wasn't a thing any more. And maybe they were all better off without it. She left the boxing on.

"How did you know it was coming?" he asked.

"I don't mean I suspected anything. I just meant, this was a parenthesis for both of us."

"A parenthesis."

"Sorry. Stupid English teacher way of talking."

"That's the problem right there."

"No," said Lucy. "Don't think that. It was never a problem. Still isn't."

To her ears, that sounded like something she should have said on the first night, not the last. Well, maybe not the very first night, because she certainly hadn't talked like an English teacher then. But it hadn't occurred to her that there was this, Joseph's insecurity, on top of everything else that made their relationship so delicate, like a houseplant, with no ability to survive out in the world. And now, when it was too late, she was saying too much, as if she wanted to demolish his doubts and objections one by one. She really didn't. The time had come.

"I just meant, you and me are like something between brackets."

"Yeah. I suppose that's right. For both of us."

"Of course for both of us. I was including myself in the relationship," Lucy said.

"I mean—you'll meet someone too."

"Yes."

She knew she would, eventually. There would be someone, a cheese-shop owner or a human-rights lawyer, for her somewhere. Joseph had helped her to think that she wouldn't be alone forever.

"I have two questions," said Lucy.

"OK."

"Do you ever think about the night we were going to play backgammon?"

Joseph looked at her, confused.

"No. Why? Do you?"

"I have done once or twice, yeah. I wondered if it had anything to do with anything."

"Not as far as I know. You think I got annoyed because you didn't have the right pieces?"

She laughed. "No. It doesn't matter."

"OK."

"And will you still babysit? The boys would hate it if you stopped."

"I really love those boys," said Joseph. "And their mum."

"I'm glad. We love you too. Now I just have to find somewhere to go."

Nobody had said the words "I love you," Lucy noticed, and yet each had found a way of telling the other that they were loved. That seemed like a good place to end.

# 10

In August, Hanna suggested that they went away somewhere, just for a couple of days, to make them feel as though the summer had happened to them. They were both working hard. Joseph was doing what he always did, and Hanna was waitressing at a steak restaurant in the City. It was a hot week, and they were lying naked on top of Joseph's bed, listening to other people's music with the window open.

"Where do you want to go?" Joseph asked.

"I'd like to swim in the sea somewhere."

"In Britain?"

"England, probably. Like Brighton or wherever. Sussex. Dorset."

"Dorset. Huh."

"What's wrong with Dorset?"

"Nothing's wrong with Dorset. In fact, someone just invited me to go there."

"Seriously? I really want to go. Hardy country."

"I don't know what that means."

"Thomas Hardy? The writer?"

"I don't know who that is."

"Jesus Christ."

She was laughing, but he knew he was damaging himself. What was he supposed to do about it, though?

"He wrote **Jude the Obscure** and **Tess of the d'Urbervilles**. He wrote about Dorset. Anyway. I'd love to spend a couple of days there. I've never been."

"Yeah, but…"

"But I'm not invited?"

"You were specifically invited. By name."

"Who by?"

"You know Lucy and the boys? Who I babysit for sometimes? They've borrowed a house down there."

Hanna knew about his relationship with Lucy and the boys, but she didn't know about his relationship with Lucy, and he wasn't tempted to illuminate her.

"And she asked if I wanted to come too?"

"Yeah."

"So what's the problem?"

"You want to spend a few days with a couple of kids?"

"I like kids."

"And I don't know if you'd get on with her."

"What's wrong with her?"

"Nothing. She's nice."

Hanna made a noise, a mock-outraged laugh.

"Oh. So what's wrong with me?"

"Just because I don't think you'd get on doesn't mean there's anything wrong with either of you."

"What does it mean, then?"

"You're just different people. Chalk and cheese. Oil and water."

"Why do you get on with both of us?"

"I'm in the middle."

This was all utter rubbish. And now if Hanna ever met Lucy, she'd think he was mad. Hanna was young and Lucy was older. Lucy had kids and Hanna didn't. And apart from that, they were more or less exactly the same. They were both calm and funny; they both loved books, and had probably read more of them in the last two weeks than Joseph had since he left school. They were both attractive; they were both sociable, but seemed to be right on the edge of their social circles, as far as Joseph could tell, looking in and out. If Joseph took Hanna to Dorset, she and Lucy would probably be friends for life.

"Is it a nice place?"

"She's borrowed it off a friend. It's near the sea, and it's got a pool. And there's a little converted barn we can have."

"She's got nice friends."

"It's this guy she, you know, hangs out with a bit. A writer. He's got a few quid."

"What's his name?"

"Michael."

"Oh, that helps."

"I don't know the names of any writers, do I?"

"So will he be there?"

"I don't think so. He's in France with his kids. Anyway, she's worried that her kids are going to get bored there, and she wanted me to come and kick a football or whatever."

"And I read by the pool. Honestly? If this woman is worse than Hitler, worse than Boris Johnson even, I still want to go. What's she going to do? Throw my book in the water? I've never been to a house with a pool. Have you?"

"No, but…"

He was hoping that the "but" spoke volumes, without actually knowing what those volumes might contain. He'd never been to a house with a pool but… There must be a but, surely? No. Nothing was coming. Joseph was beginning to realize that whatever he ended up doing with his life couldn't involve strategy. He was a terrible strategist. Everything seemed like a good idea until the next idea, the opposite of the previous one, came along. He had told her why it wouldn't be a good idea to go to this place in Dorset (which he believed), and then told her how great it would be (which he also believed). They were going to Dorset, he could tell.

**His next strategic** decision was, he knew, sensible, fair, and appropriate. He would tell Hanna about Lucy before they left. And, when that didn't happen for various reasons, all of them involving his discomfort, he saw that he had no choice but to tell her on the train down. And on the train down, he saw that easily the best thing would have been to tell her before they got on the train, because the train was packed. Many people, it would appear, had hit upon the idea of escaping London for the seaside during a hot August. They found two empty seats opposite each other, but they were both sitting next to people, a mother and her teenage daughter. The girl was wearing headphones, but the mother was doing a word search in a magazine, and could hear them if they chose to talk, which they didn't. Joseph got out his phone and started scrolling. Hanna was reading one of

Michael Marwood's books. (She had made him text Lucy to ask for Michael's surname. Hanna claimed to have heard of him, but Joseph was doubtful. How could you have heard of someone who turns up in the kitchens of houses belonging to normal people?)

"Didn't you bring anything to read?" said Hanna after a few minutes.

The mother looked at him.

"My phone."

"You're not going to read when we're there?"

"I dunno."

He wanted to close the conversation down. Neither of their traveling companions was reading. Joseph didn't want Hanna to embarrass them. He played Candy Crush for a while, had a look at Instagram, then read a couple of the stories on the BBC Football website. He was finding it hard to concentrate. Would Lucy say anything? She wasn't that sort, although he'd never seen her drunk. Would Hanna guess? That seemed more likely. There was probably body language and all sorts that he wouldn't necessarily be aware of. He went through his texts, deleting the boring ones from his mother about dinner, replying to a couple of coaching-related messages he'd forgotten about. The most recent text was from Hanna, this morning, asking where to meet at Waterloo. He replied to it, and then, before he could think again about the non-Waterloo-related information the new text contained, he sent it.

She ignored the ping for a while. She was good like that. Once Joseph had received a text, he had to look at it straight away. He tried not to watch her closely, and went back to Instagram. He became deeply absorbed in photographs of Iceland posted by an Icelandic Premiership footballer who had liked a picture of another Premiership player he followed, and he forgot to feel nervous about what he'd sent. Then he received a sharp kick on the shin. The mother looked up when he reacted, so he went back to the texting.

**That actually hurt.**

**YOU HAD A THING WITH LUCY?**

**Yes.**

**AND YOU'RE TELLING ME NOW?**

**Sorry.**

Hanna didn't make eye contact. She just bashed away with her thumbs, staring down into her lap.

**When was this thing?**

**Before.**

They were both typing so urgently that it must have seemed perfectly obvious they were arguing with each other. He turned his pinger off.

**Before what?**

**You.** And then, **Maybe turn your pinger off?**
She ignored him, but at least he'd halved the number of pings.

**I'm now, as far as I know. So couldn't have been after.**

**No.** And then, **Hide your phone. She's trying to see.**

**Like I give 1 fuck.**

**It's over.**

**YES I SHOULD HOPE SO**

**Emotionally as well. Friends.**

This seemed to be true. He had never managed

it before, but Lucy made things easy. They had left it for a couple of weeks, and then she'd invited him round for Sunday dinner with the boys, and he'd played Xbox, and gone home. And the week after that he'd babysat for her while she went out for dinner with Michael Marwood. She had come back alone, made Joseph a cup of tea, and they'd talked about how things were going for them. He'd touched very briefly on the subject of Hanna, and she didn't start wrecking her own living room. She just nodded encouragingly. And now here he was, on a train to visit her with his new girlfriend, unless his new girlfriend got off at the next stop.

**You're reading her new boyfriend's book, if that helps.**

He didn't know whether this was a strictly accurate description of Michael's status, but there was a chance that it was, and it was helpful to him to share the possibly accurate information at that moment.

**I hope he's more fun than his book.**

Joseph replied with tears of laughter, although she was sitting opposite him and could see that there were no such tears, or even much amusement. He realized that when he got the LOL emoji, he frequently imagined that the other party was quite literally weeping helplessly, but this conversation had taught him that it was just a thing you did, stony-faced, to acknowledge someone's weak attempt at humor. There was no reply, and he hoped that might have been the end of the matter. He went back to Iceland, to an amazing waterfall called Gulfoss. He put in a search for Iceland and started following Iceland photography. It was incredible. He wanted to go there. His phone pinged.

**Who is better in bed?**

He sent her the rolling-eyes emoji.

**What is that?**

**Rolling eyes.**

**Not an answer.**

**Out of you and me? Me.**

**Ha ha. ??**

**You of course.**

**Why of course?**

The honest answer would have been, **Because I'd be off my fucking head to say anything different**, but it wouldn't have ended the conversation.

**Because…you know.**

**What do I know?**

He typed the word **embarrassed** in the hope that there would be a red-faced emoji. It offered him some peculiar-looking faces, and he chose one at random.

**What is that?**

**Embarrassment.**

**Looks like a sex face.** And then, **What's the point of emojis if you have to explain them all?** And then, **Why embarrassment?**

**Because I'd prefer to talk about it face to face. In our barn.**

She did smile then, with her actual face. She sent back an **OK** and some hearts. The train nearly emptied at Bournemouth, and the mother and daughter got off. He went to sit next to her.

"I am sorry," he said. "For not saying anything before."

"Is that why you said I wouldn't get on with her?"

"Yeah. That was all rubbish."

"Well, that's a relief. How did it happen?"

"It just happened. I dunno."

"Was it weird?"

"Which part?"

"I don't know. The age gap."

"Not really. But it felt like . . . something between things. A parenthesis."

"Oooh. Parenthesis. Calm down, mate."

"Can you understand that?"

"Yeah. Of course. We've all had things between things."

The trouble was that Hanna felt like a parenthesis too. Their entire relationship had taken place during the summer, while she was on holiday from college; she was waitressing in a steak house, which wasn't her real life. She hadn't told him anything about exes, but he got the feeling that she'd split up with someone toward the end of the college year, and he had no doubt that there'd be someone else when she started back again. He was part of her temporary North London life, when she'd been reunited with old friends that she'd lose touch with eventually. Hanna wouldn't be spending her life in Tottenham. Joseph was new, but he was a throwback too. They wouldn't last. He wouldn't last.

And as for the question that he would never answer: the sex was different. A couple of times he had noticed his own theories about why trying to be heard, but he didn't want to listen to them. There wasn't any point.

**Lucy and the boys** met them at Crewkerne station. Michael Marwood kept an old 2CV at the house and the top was down, and it was warm. Hanna put out her hand to say hello, and Lucy leaned in to kiss her. It was sort of like emotional porn, if there was such a thing: two hot women that he liked very much being nice to each other.

They put their bags in the boot and then looked at the car awkwardly.

"You go in the front," said Joseph.

"You've got longer legs," said Hanna.

"Yes, but I know these two scoundrels, and you don't. I don't mind squashing them."

The boys laughed, and Joseph sat between them.

"Be warned," said Lucy. "I'm quite a nervous driver round here. The roads are too narrow, and there are animals, and I keep having to reverse into hedges."

"Can you drive?" said Joseph to Hanna. "I don't know."

"No. You?"

"No. Don't see the point in London."

"Wait until you have to start picking up kids from far-flung football pitches," said Lucy.

"You can do that bit," said Hanna to Joseph.

Lucy laughed. Joseph sort of barked. It was such a weird thing to say. Hanna had never given any indication of wanting to see him the following week, and now she was suggesting that they had a family together. After that, Lucy and Hanna started chatting, and Joseph couldn't really hear them, and anyway the boys wanted to play a game they'd invented that was a mixture of Twenty Questions and Hangman, with the answer always being the most obscure footballer in the most obscure European league. Nobody ever got it.

They drove for thirty minutes, and as promised the roads became twisty and narrow, and then Lucy turned down a drive and they were outside a joke country cottage, with ivy growing up the walls and cows on the hill behind, and Joseph was embarrassed that he'd ever thought about not coming. He had been out of London, but not very often, and nowhere like this. And he didn't think he'd been to a house that was so far away from another house. There were, as far as he could tell, no neighbors. This probably wasn't what you were supposed to think—you were probably supposed to think about poetry, or God—but Joseph wished he had an amp, a deck, and a 2,000-watt QSC K12.2. That was what the freedom of the countryside meant: the ability to turn the fucker up as loud as it would go.

"I'll show you where you're sleeping," said Lucy.

The barn was part office, part spare bedroom. The double bed was on a raised platform under the roof, and you had to climb a ladder to get to it. On the floor there was a desk, a small kitchen, a couple of armchairs, and a large Bang & Olufsen Bluetooth speaker. Joseph didn't notice things like rugs, as a rule, but this one was beautiful, bright, in blocky primary colors. Joseph immediately began calculating what work he could move, what lies he could tell, to extend the stay for another couple of nights.

"Is the house as nice as this?" said Hanna.

"It's nice," said Lucy. "But I love it in here. The kids won't let me, though. And there isn't room for the three of us."

"We can swap if you want," said Hanna.

"Oh, that's kind of you," said Lucy, and then didn't say anything. Joseph was sure there'd be a "but." Where was the "but"? Come on. "BUT." He looked at her, and she laughed.

"But look at Joseph's face."

"Phew," said Joseph. "I thought you were actually going to take this away from us."

Hanna punched him on the arm. "You selfish bastard."

He shrugged.

**Lucy and the boys** went off in the car to get fish and chips for dinner while Hanna and Joseph swam in the pool at the back of the cottage. Hanna swam steady lengths, and to begin with Joseph copied her, when what he really wanted to do was see how many lengths he could manage underwater, and how long he could stand on his hands for. He thought Hanna would think he was immature, so he didn't, and then he remembered that she wasn't going to be around for the long term, so he did. When was the next time he'd get a swimming pool nearly to himself? Maybe it would never happen again. That wasn't the right way to think about the future, though. He tried to focus on a house in Ibiza, with a pool bigger than this one, bought from the proceeds of a career as a producer and D.J., or an inventor of something he hadn't thought of yet, or a tech entrepreneur.

And not a whole career, either, just the early first flush.

"You're like a kid," said Hanna predictably, when she stopped for a breather.

"You're like one of the old ladies who comes in the leisure center," said Joseph. "Although they don't usually wear bikinis like that."

"Is that a compliment?"

It was. She looked great in a bikini.

"No. Just a statement of fact. They wear swimming costumes."

"Listen. What I said in the car," said Hanna. "About you picking up kids from football."

"Oh. Yeah. You think we should take turns?"

He delivered it straight, to make her think that she'd encouraged him to think about their future together, right down to the last micro-detail.

"I don't want..."

"Lots of mums pick up the boys from matches. But they're quite often the mums who've been dumped."

"I'm not thinking about kids for years."

"Understood. That's fine. I'm in no hurry either."

"You know what I'm saying."

"Yeah. I'm only messing you around."

"I want to try and do a doctorate, maybe abroad."

"Listen, you don't need to spell it out. Neither do I."

She looked momentarily affronted, as if it were OK for her not to want kids with him, but not the other way around.

"But I can tell you where it came from."

"Go on."

"Well, she's quite intimidating, isn't she?"

"Lucy? Is she?"

"Just—I can see why you went for her."

"So you thought you'd better warn her off quick?"

"It was weird, I admit it. I suddenly went into marking-out-territory mode. Pissing on my boyfriend. I felt insecure."

"No need."

"No, I know. But there would be, if this was, you know."

"It went as far as it could. No going back."

"Why not? That's what most things do, when they've gone as far as they can. Cars. Trains. People. They go back."

"Oh, fucking hell. What do you want me to say?"

He did another handstand, demonstrating both that the conversation was over, and that he was an unsuitable partner for grown-up women of any age.

———

**There was no sex** in the barn. Joseph was expecting it, and when Hanna got into bed he kissed her in a way that had always previously led to other things. But Hanna stiffened, and Joseph stopped, and there was a sense of relief that took him by surprise.

"It feels weird."

"Why?"

He was glad she'd said it, not him. It felt weird for him, for obvious reasons. He was staying with Lucy. He used to have sex with Lucy. He was about to have sex with somebody else. But it would have been bad for him to freeze up. He couldn't have said, "It feels weird," because Hanna would have said, "I knew it!" and so on. In one way, he wished his body were more responsive to complicated situations. His obvious keenness was sort of embarrassing, oblivious. In another way, he was glad it was business as usual, because he could therefore prove that Hanna was feeling the weirdness, not him, even though above the waist he was feeling it too. Maybe when you got older, your body started listening to the rest of you. Like, no, this is weird. I'm just going to lie here until you sort it out.

"I don't know. Disrespectful or something."

"I'm sure she thought it would happen."

"Yeah, but that doesn't mean we have to. It wasn't part of the deal. At least, I hope it wasn't."

"You know what I mean. She's a grown-up."

"And I'm not?"

"When did I say that?"

"She's cool with us making love and I'm not."

"Oh, come on, Han! I'm cool with anyone making love. Consenting adults and that. But some of them might not want to do it. It's your body. Jesus. Let's forget it and have a cuddle."

"Not with that thing sticking in my leg. That's not cuddly."

"Give me a minute."

She nestled into his chest, and fell asleep. Joseph was awake for a while.

**During the fish-and-chip supper,** Lucy had discovered that Hanna loved Hardy, and there was an immediate determination to visit Max Gate, the house Hardy built, the very next day.

"And I'm not taking the boys," said Lucy.

"Why not?" said Al.

"Because you'll ruin it."

"No, we won't."

"I'm coming," said Dylan.

"So am I," said Al. "What is it?"

"You weren't listening just now?"

"You were talking about some writer's house."

"That's where we're going."

"I'm not," said Dylan. "No way."

"Neither am I," said Al.

Joseph took a similar view, so the boys stayed back at the cottage and the book lovers got in the car. In Lucy's experience, these were the two genders, boys and readers. She wished there was as much gender fluidity as people seemed to think.

Neither of them said anything for a while. Hanna was looking out of the window at the fields and the occasional front gate; Lucy was looking very carefully ahead of her. And then they both spoke at exactly the same time.

"So. Who got you interested in Hardy?" said Lucy.

"Joseph told me about your thing," said Hanna.

They both laughed.

"Different subjects," said Lucy.

"Very," said Hanna.

"My feeling is that yours wins. I don't think Thomas Hardy can ever be an elephant in the room."

"That would be like a good writing exercise," said Hanna. "Write a story in which one character has to say, at some point, 'The elephant in the room here is Thomas Hardy.'"

"I'll try it at school. I'd have to explain the expression, then who Thomas Hardy was. And then I'd get a ton of stories about either gang fights or terrible revenge wreaked on faithless boyfriends, and at some point in the middle someone would say, for no apparent reason, 'The elephant in the room here is Thomas Hardy.'"

They went back to silence.

"OK then," said Hanna. "I had an amazing English teacher."

"Hooray."

"And she used to take me to one side after class and give me books. She gave me **Black Boy** by Richard Wright. And she gave me **The Color Purple**. I was like, fourteen. She gave me **Things Fall Apart** and **Go Tell It on the Mountain** and **Their Eyes Were Watching God**. And then she gave me **Jude the Obscure** and told me it was her favorite novel."

"Wow."

"And the weird thing was, it made sense to me. In the context of the others. Because it was about outsiders and poverty and class and all that."

"This teacher sounds like a star. Where did you go to school?"

"Edmonton. St. Thomas à Becket."

"Anyone getting kids to read Hardy in Edmonton should be made Minister for Education."

"Yeah. I'm not sure it was kids plural. I was a weirdo."

She went back to looking out of the window.

"The problem was, I didn't actually ask you a

question. About Joseph. You asked me a question about Hardy and I answered it."

"Good point. So is there anything you want to know?"

"I dunno. No. Tell me something."

"Ummm. It was nice, and it came to a natural end, for all the obvious reasons. And I'm very glad he has a girlfriend who is more appropriate for him."

"The trouble is, I'm not appropriate for him either. Or he's not appropriate for me."

"Yeah. I can see that."

"Poor Joseph. Not appropriate for either of us."

Lucy laughed. She wanted to tell Hanna that it wasn't true.

"Joseph and I . . . We haven't quite got enough," said Hanna. "It's been a nice summer, though."

She didn't seem to want to say any more, so Lucy changed the subject.

"Do you like any other Victorians? Apart from Hardy? Oh, you want to know my favorite Hardy fact? Well, there are two. One—he's buried in two places. They cut his heart out and it's down here somewhere. The rest of him is in Westminster Abbey."

"Wow."

"Can you believe it? That happened in the twentieth century. And the other—he drove himself, in a car, to see a movie adaptation of one of his novels."

"No way."

"True."

And the rest of the drive passed in a blur of plots, characters, scenes.

**They poked around** the house, although neither of them felt any magic emanating from the brown furniture; they bought postcards in the gift shop, went to visit the grave of Wessex the dog. As they were leaving, an elderly lady in an anorak, wearing a badge with the E.U. logo, peered dimly at Hanna and stopped.

"Excuse me."

"Hello," said Hanna. "I like your badge."

"Oh. Thank you. What a bunch of bloody idiots. Anyway. Can I just say that it's marvelous you're here."

"Sorry?"

"I just think it's wonderful."

"Oh. Thank you."

The lady turned her attention to Lucy.

"Well done."

She nodded and walked on. Lucy stared after her.

"Fucking hell," said Lucy.

Hanna shrugged.

"I suppose there was a time when she might have stopped me to say she didn't want my type here," she said. "So, you know."

**On the way back,** Hanna asked Lucy about her marriage, and heard the sad story of Paul.

"But if he stays sober...?"

"Maybe in twenty years or something."

"You'd get back together in twenty years?"

"That's about how long I'd need to trust it. And anyway, there's nothing there. He killed it."

"He wasn't himself, though."

"I know that. But there's only one of him. So it doesn't help. The man I married was also the man who became an alcoholic and a coke addict. Now I just feel nothing when I see him, and he's lucky it's only nothing."

"And what about Michael?"

"Oh. It's..."

It was a friendship, was what it was, but Michael didn't seem to see it. Maybe that was unfair; maybe that simply wasn't what it looked like from where he was standing, but that made the friendship difficult. She had no other friends who were expecting their relationship to turn some kind of corner and end up in a bed somewhere. She did have them, once upon a time, but everything settled down in the end. Her relationship with Michael was so polite and gentle that it was impossible for her to imagine the kind of eruption, or disruption, anyway, that sex required.

"Complicated?" said Hanna.

"No. Not really. He's nice, and I like him."

"Won't that do?"

"Yes. Of course."

"So..."

"There's no 'so.' That's it. Where are you getting a 'so' from?"

"Sounds like you could do a lot worse."

"Oh, I could. And I have done. But you'll be forty soon enough, young lady. And you won't feel ready to settle for the least bad option either."

They turned down the drive and walked around the back of the cottage to find Joseph and the kids playing a violent and apparently hilarious version of water polo with a football, and Lucy wondered how many versions of a nice life she had a right to expect.

Joseph got out of the pool and sat with Hanna and Lucy, and they watched the boys play their game.

"I can't believe how nice it is here," said Hanna.

"I can't believe this house came out of a guy's head," said Joseph.

"What do you mean?" said Lucy.

"I mean, this guy just thinks stuff up, and then he buys a house with a pool."

"As well as his house in London," said Hanna.

"Does it piss you off?" said Lucy.

"No," said Hanna.

"Me neither," said Joseph. "Why should it? Does it piss you off?"

"No. It's not like he's done anything bad to get it. But."

She was getting into deep water again.

"You piss me off more than him," said Hanna. She was laughing as she said it.

"Me?" said Lucy.

"Yeah. How come you know people like this?"

"It's true," said Joseph. "We don't have any friends who invite us to their second home."

"With a pool," said Hanna.

"Neither did I, when I was your age," said Lucy, but even as she said it, she realized it wasn't true. Her friend Joanna at college went to France every summer, to the house in Nice her parents rented. Lucy had gone one year.

"You're right," said Joseph. "It's an age thing. My mum and dad go to places like this all the time."

Hanna laughed.

"Mine too," she said. "They're sick of it."

Lucy hadn't thought of that. She was a teacher—
a head of department, yes, but she still earned less
than a lot of people she knew. And yet this wasn't
the first time she'd been given access to a private
pool. She, Paul, and the boys had received invitations to villas abroad a couple of times, to Italy and
France and Spain. She was lucky to know Michael,
of course, but it wasn't a miracle. She knew other
people like him, people with the same kind of
income, and the same kind of life. Having friends
with money, she realized, didn't make her resent-
ful; rather, they provided an occasional escape
route, an extra room in one's mind, one that
stopped her from feeling shut in, and she had never
noticed that until just now.

"Sorry," said Lucy. "It was a stupid thing to say."

**They went to** the seaside on Sunday. They swam
in the astonishingly cold sea, looked for fossils, ate
lunch in a café on the beach—more fish and chips
for the boys, crab for Hanna and Lucy.

"So are you Joseph's girlfriend or what?" said Al
to Hanna.

"What," said Hanna.

"What does that mean?"

"You gave me two choices."

"No, I didn't."

"She did," said Dylan. "Girlfriend or what? First choice, girlfriend. Second choice, what."

"Oh, I get it," said Al mirthlessly.

"It wasn't great," said Dylan.

"Anyway, why is it what?"

"Why is what what?" said Dylan.

"I'm talking to Hanna. I don't understand why she's only what, not girlfriend."

"Perhaps Hanna doesn't want to talk about it," said Lucy.

The café was packed. People were ambling around with trays full of drinks that were constantly on the verge of sliding off, looking for tables, and as a consequence there was always somebody at their elbow. The hot, harassed waitresses were walking around with plates of food, shouting out numbers to customers who were too deep in conversation to hear, or who had mislaid their tickets, or who had wandered off to look at the sea. It wasn't the best environment to discuss affairs of the heart.

"Well," said Hanna. "Boyfriend and girlfriend… That's sort of permanent, isn't it?"

"Is it?" said Dylan. "I had no idea."

"Well, you know. Not permanent. That's the wrong word. Official."

"Official?" said Al. "How?"

"Well, not official like a marriage."

"Which, by the way, is not permanent," said Dylan. "As we know."

"So not permanent and not official," said Al.

Joseph started laughing.

"What's funny?" said Hanna.

"You shouldn't have started this."

"If it's not permanent and not official, why isn't he your boyfriend?" said Al.

"You sleep together," said Dylan.

"Seventy-TWO," shouted a young woman with a lobster on a plate standing right next to them and looking as though she might cry.

"Maybe I'll explain later," said Hanna.

"Would you say she's your girlfriend?" Dylan said to Joseph.

"Well, I wouldn't now," said Joseph. "Not if it's not mutual."

"What does that mean?" said Dylan.

"Well, if she's not my girlfriend, I'm not her boyfriend."

"Why did you and Mum split up?" said Al.

Both boys started giggling uncontrollably then.

"Oh, you're such an idiot, Al," said Dylan.

"You wanted to know too," said Al.

"For God's sakes," said Lucy. "What are you talking about?"

"We're not stupid," said Dylan.

"Why on earth do you think we split up?"

"Because you were together, and now you're not."

Joseph was watching her carefully, looking for some kind of guidance. Hanna was watching her too, but Lucy imagined that was simply curiosity. She'd be curious too, in Hanna's position.

"We weren't together. We were just keeping each other company."

"So why did you stop keeping each other company?"

"Because Joseph got a girlfriend."

"She's not his girlfriend," said Dylan triumphantly.

Lucy felt cold, and a little sick. Of course they'd have noticed things. As Dylan had pointed out, they weren't stupid. She could only hope that the things they'd noticed were little clues, rather than something more explicit. They'd had sex on the sofa that first time. What if one of the boys had wandered down the stairs and then fled in terror?

"Sixty-EIGHT!"

"I'd be annoyed if I was sixty-eight," said Joseph.

"Because they just called seventy-two, you mean?" said Lucy.

"We're not going to change the subject and talk about numbers," said Al. "Nice try, though."

"We do like you, by the way," said Dylan to

Hanna. "We're not protesting or anything. And anyway, Mum can't date Joseph."

"Why not?" said Hanna.

"They have a lot of issues."

Lucy was almost lured into an argument with them, but managed to resist. If they thought there were a lot of issues, then that was all for the best. And anyway, there were a lot of issues.

"What time's the train?" said Hanna.

"There's one at ten past five. Plenty of time. We'll take you to the station."

"We're going to play that game in the pool again," said Dylan. "So we won't be coming."

"I can't leave you on your own in a swimming pool," said Lucy.

"Joseph's staying," said Dylan.

"Is he?"

"Oh," said Joseph. "Yeah. If that's OK."

"It's fine with me."

Lucy looked at Hanna.

"I told him to stay," said Hanna. "He loves it here."

Hanna got a taxi in the end. Neither of the women wanted another conversation in the car, although of course they were both prepared to spend the journey to Crewkerne chatting amicably and avoiding subjects if they had to. Hanna pointed out that Lucy would be sitting in the car for the nicest part of the afternoon, and Lucy asked whether she'd mind terribly, and Hanna said of course not, and Lucy said she had the app for a local firm on her phone and they were cheap and she wouldn't dream of taking any money off her. When the cab arrived at the house, Hanna and Lucy hugged, and then Lucy ushered the boys into the house to get changed for their swim.

# 11

S he's lovely," said Lucy when the boys had gone to bed.

"Yeah," said Joseph.

They were drinking outside, by the pool, side by side. It seemed easier for Joseph to look at the water or the night sky than at Lucy.

"You should try and keep hold of that one."

"She's just gone."

"Only until Tuesday."

"Not sure."

"Not sure what?"

"Whether she's only gone until Tuesday, or whether that was it."

"You might have split up while she was getting into the taxi? Bloody hell."

"No, no."

"So what happened? I had such a nice time with you both."

"It was just all a bit weirder than I'd imagined."

"What sort of weird?"

"I dunno. Well, I do."

"Weird because of me?"

"Yeah, sort of. She loved meeting you, but she was weird about you. Behind closed doors, sort of thing. She didn't feel comfortable…Anyway."

"Oh, I'm sorry."

"I wasn't, really. I was probably a bit weird about you too. Like, a bit, you know. Squirmy."

"Perhaps it was all a bit ambitious," said Lucy.

"Did you feel weird?"

"No."

"Oh."

"Is that too blunt?"

"No. I mean, it was blunt, but not too blunt."

"It seemed right," she said.

"What?"

"You and her. A very handsome and charming young couple."

"Can we talk about something else?"

"Sure. Do you have a subject in mind?"

"No. I just don't want you banging on for the rest of the evening about why I should be with Hanna. Because I won't be for much longer, so you're wasting your breath."

"It felt really weird," said Lucy.

"What did?"

"You being here with her."

"That is exactly the question I asked you! And you said no!"

"I know. I thought it was easier not to tell the truth."

"Well. I've had a nice time," said Joseph ruefully.

"Do you think we shouldn't be seeing each other at all?" said Lucy.

"No. I just think maybe we shouldn't be double-dating just yet."

Lucy laughed.

"I can't imagine you and Michael chatting away at dinner."

"No, me neither," said Joseph.

"Are you being mean?"

"Are you? Also, are you officially seeing Michael?"

"Not officially until Wednesday. There'll be an announcement in the **Telegraph**."

"I wondered how you people did these things."

"'You people'? Since when did I become 'you people'? Why aren't you 'you people'?"

"Because I can't be, can I?"

"Why not?"

"Because if I say 'you people,' then I'm not including myself. 'Me people.' That's not a thing."

"What about 'us people'? 'Us lot'?"

"You think me and you are 'us lot'? There isn't a single way in which we're 'us.' That was the whole problem. We were only together in bed or in front of the telly."

He didn't know why he was getting so agitated about it, but he had turned up the volume, and he could feel his cheeks flushing.

"Did you want more than that?"

"Did you?"

"I asked you first," said Lucy.

"I didn't even think about it. I knew it couldn't be done. I've thought about it more since than I did at the time."

"Why is that, do you think?"

Why? Because he'd just spent the last few months drifting backward in his mind, unable to love the one he was with, and maybe not even the one before her, although they were two different kinds of disability. Lucy was older and had two kids, so there was all that; Hanna was at college, pushing forward into someplace he guessed he wouldn't be able to get to, so that was something else. Was it just that he hadn't been to uni? That wasn't quite true, because he had, but only for a few weeks. He was supposed to be studying Sports Science, but the size of the loan he was going to need for a three-year course seemed ludicrous when he didn't even know what he was going to do with the qualification. And even though his mum had encouraged him, she'd been relieved when he quit. Anyway, now he was worried that he'd only ever be attracted to women who were being, or had already been, educated out of his league.

There was something else, though, and it was serious, in all senses. He had never told any woman he was seeing that he loved her. It just wasn't done. If you told someone you loved her, she might get the wrong idea, whatever that might be—even if it was clear that there was love going on, in some form or another. They had no legal force, these words, as far as he knew, but there still seemed to be some kind of commitment that hung off them, weighing them down to the point where they seemed unusable. He knew now that he loved Lucy, and could see that he'd loved her even when he'd started seeing Hanna; he'd just presumed that he'd have to love her in a way that didn't involve monogamy, or sex, or anything very much. Anyway. That was the real answer to Lucy's question.

"Dunno, really."

That was the best answer, however.

"Oh," said Lucy. "That doesn't really encourage me to talk about why I've been thinking about it."

"You don't have to."

"I know."

"Have you ever been skinny-dipping here?" said Joseph.

"I'm not sure that's the complete change of subject you think it is."

"Ah. I see what you mean. All right. Is there a backgammon set here?"

She laughed.

"I'm not playing backgammon. I'm either talking to you or going to bed. We don't need to fill time."

"Right."

There was a long silence. Joseph stood up and hooked the football that was stuck in the corner of the pool out with his foot. He juggled it a couple of times and then side-footed it gently onto the grass.

"I'm going to tell you what I've been thinking about," said Lucy. "And if you want to get the first train back tomorrow, you can."

"Yeah, I'm not gonna do that," said Joseph.

"Thank you."

"I just meant, there's nothing you can say that will make me leave here early. If I don't like it, I'll just move my chair up the other end of the pool and sit there tomorrow. It's too nice here."

"OK. Well, that's still reassuring, in a strange way."

He was nervous. He had the feeling that whatever she was about to say couldn't be unsaid, like most of the crap that passed for the conversations he got into.

"I can't imagine myself with Michael."

"Oh."

"All the surface things are good. Nice. I can happily go out in the world with him. Nice restaurants. Cinema. All that."

"Conversations about books."

"I suppose. He tells me about novels in translation that he thinks I'd enjoy. I'm sure he's right. But I can't see myself reading them. One of them is French and doesn't contain the letter 'e.'"

"Really?"

"Apparently."

"Like, deliberately?"

"I don't think it was an accident. He didn't forget to use the words 'he' and 'she' for a few hundred pages."

"French, though. 'He' is 'il,' isn't it?"

"Yeah, but 'elle.'"

"Oh, yeah."

"And 'the' is 'le.' Anyway, I'd be reading it in English."

"Does the English one leave 'e' out as well?"

"I think so."

Joseph got his phone out of his pocket.

"What's the name of this fool? I want to look him up."

"Can we, you know, put a pin in that?"

"Oh. Yeah. Sorry."

He knew that the conversation they were about to have would be difficult, or dangerous, or something. But he didn't often talk to Lucy about books, especially French books. He was thinking maybe he could show her he was capable of a conversation, at least, even if he had no intention of reading the bastard book.

"You can't imagine yourself with Michael."

Lucy looked at him, surprised.

"Exactly," she said.

"I'm not saying that," said Joseph.

"What are you saying, then?"

"No... You said it. Before we started talking about the French book."

"Oh. Right. Yes."

She seemed disappointed. Maybe she'd thought he was about to seize the moment, tell her that Michael was all wrong for her.

"So there's this, I don't know what you'd call it," she said. "This vibe. I feel I'd be on my best behavior all the time. It's all too grown-up for me."

"You're a grown-up."

"I'm not that sort of grown-up, am I? I don't see

how you can be when you've got kids. They drag you down into the world of stupid jokes and farts and fights. Life is hard enough without reading books with no 'e's in them."

Now he didn't know whether to go back to the French writer or not. He decided not.

"Anyway, there's not much you can do about the inside world, I don't think. That's the important part too," she said.

"It's very small, though. There's a lot of outside world."

"I think maybe I'm not expressing myself very well."

"No, no, I get what you're saying."

"Right. Do you really?"

"Yeah. You need someone a bit more fun than Michael."

"Yes." And then, "It's you."

"Me?"

"I thought you got what I was saying."

"I got the Michael part. I didn't get the me part. Or maybe I did, but then I thought, she can't mean that."

"Well. There you are. I did."

"It's not a choice between me and him. It's a choice between me, him, and every other single man in Britain. Or Europe, really. If you factor in like Skype and cheap flights."

"I don't like any other single man in Europe."

"How can you say that? You haven't met..."

"Oh, don't even go there. That's the whole basis of everything."

"What?"

"You meet someone, you fall in love, you don't even want to know anyone else. You don't need to meet every single man in Europe to compare. Nobody would ever have sex again."

Joseph got the impression that the love part had just slipped out at the wrong point in the conversation, and that, he felt, put him in an awkward position. He decided to ignore it for the time being. There was still a possibility they were talking theoretically.

"Unless you have sex with every man in Europe just to help clear your head."

"Bloody hell, Joseph."

He was probably wrong to ignore it. She was frustrated and a bit annoyed with him.

"Why do you keep telling me to be with everyone else except you?"

"I keep not being sure of what you're saying."

"I want to be with you. Inside and outside."

"Oh."

She gave him a few seconds, and then she stood up.

"Right. I've said it. I'm going to bed."

"Hold on, hold on."

She sat back down again.

"Have you thought this through?"

"Can we first establish whether this is something you're remotely interested in?"

He couldn't just say yes, he was guessing. The situation required some kind of speech, or at least a sincere expression of feeling. The inside/outside relationship felt much more achievable than the words he needed to find, but his failure to find them was causing her alarm and embarrassment.

"First of all and very quickly—yes."

"OK. Really? OK."

"And… Well, there are other things about it, apart from yes. Things that don't stop the answer from being yes. They sort of add to it. But it's, you know. Not easy. Unless we're somewhere else. Will you stand up and say what you said before?"

She looked blank for a moment.

"Oh."

She stood up. "I'm going to bed."

"Will you come to bed in the barn for a bit?"

"No!"

"What?"

"You were sleeping in there with your girlfriend until this morning."

"Great."

"Isn't that true?"

"Yes. But she didn't want to have sex with me because of you. And you don't want to have sex with me because of her."

"You didn't have sex?"

"No. I told you."

"You said she didn't feel comfortable. I didn't know whether that was before, during, or after."

"Before."

"Right. But you'd have been fine."

"Men are built all wrong."

"I'm going to bed."

"Goodnight."

She didn't say "goodnight" back. She just went. After a little while, he followed her into the cottage, just in case that was what she was expecting. It was. And afterward he found it was easy to talk.

# Autumn 2016

# 12

There was more inside than outside, for the first couple of weeks. They didn't make any kind of announcement to the boys, although Joseph started staying the night and eating breakfast the next morning, and they didn't seem to require any clarification or explanation. He was a part of the family—why wouldn't he eat breakfast with them? Lucy and Joseph watched a lot of episodes of **The Sopranos** (neither of them had had the heart to continue with the series during the hiatus), and had a lot of sex. They would have gone out for a meal, but Lucy was still looking for a reliable babysitter.

When a neighbor volunteered her daughter, a seventeen-year-old who the boys knew and liked, she took Joseph to the fund-raising quiz at the boys' school. They didn't arrive hand in hand, nor did they touch during the evening; in other words, they did nothing to differentiate themselves from any of the other couples there. And many of the parents knew Joseph from the butcher's shop anyway, so they presumed that Lucy had asked him to come along because he was good at quizzes.

There were ten tables, with eight people on each. There was an Indian couple on the other side of the room, and a Korean woman on the next table, but otherwise all the contestants were white.

"Do you have a specialist subject?" said the woman who was sitting to his right. She seemed nice. Blonde, smiley, very podgy. "I'm Ellen, by the way."

"Joseph. Sport, I suppose."

"Ah," said Ellen. "Sport. Of course. So there's method in Lucy's madness."

The woman seemed to watch the words as they came out of her mouth, and they alarmed her.

"There's no madness, by the way," she said. "I don't know why I put it that way. Why would it be mad?"

Joseph smiled.

"But usually when someone brings someone along, it's because they have a specialist subject."

"Well. Let's say it's sport."

"OK. We will listen to you on all sports-related

questions. Everyone, Joseph knows all the sports answers."

"There's a whole sports round," said Ellen's husband, who was also large. "Round five."

Joseph winced. There would be less pressure on him during round five if he simply announced at the end of round four that he and Lucy were having sex.

They elected a team captain (Lucy), and drank wine out of paper cups, and pored over the picture round. By the time the sheet made its way to Joseph, eight of the ten pictures of famous people had names beside them.

"We're just missing two," said Karen, the woman sitting on the other side of Lucy.

"We think the one with the hair might be Beyoncé's sister, but we can't remember her name."

Joseph looked at the pictures and recognized both of them.

"That's Solange Knowles."

"Solange! Yes!"

"And the other one is Alex Iwobi of Arsenal."

There was a momentary silence. Everyone around the table, it seemed to Joseph, was trying to find an explanation for why the only black person in the team had recognized the only black people in the picture round.

"Two things I know nothing about," said Karen. "Football and modern pop music. Is she pop? I don't even know that."

These twin admissions of ignorance were seized upon gratefully.

"Me neither."

"I know David Beckham and that's about it."

"And Adele."

"Is Dido still going?"

"Dido! That's going back a bit."

"And Drake," said Karen's husband, Nick, quickly, conscious that they were digging them-selves into yet another hole.

"I wouldn't know what Drake looked like," said Ellen, who, it seemed, loved digging, would dig to Australia if she weren't stopped.

As Joseph was handing the paper on to Lucy, he noticed that someone had written **?? Ryan Gosling** alongside a picture of the YouTuber Roman Atwood.

"That one's Roman Atwood," he said.

"Who's Roman Atwood?"

"He's a YouTuber. He does pranks."

"Oh, well," said Nick. "That's another thing. YouTubers."

"Exactly," said Ellen. Everyone laughed, a laugh crackled through with relief. Roman Atwood was white! Hurrah! They were equal-opportunities dunces!

"These aren't my friends," said Lucy quietly while they were queuing for the Mexican buffet.

"I know."

"So you mustn't think this is what every evening would be like."

"I don't."

"What do you think every evening would be like?"

He laughed.

"I'm serious."

"How many of these evenings are there? I'll tell you one thing—I haven't got rich off babysitting for you."

"I stopped going out when we started whatever you'd call it."

"Staying in."

"Maybe we shouldn't have come here."

"Why not?"

"They're so nervous. It's like you're an un-exploded bomb. Guacamole, no salsa, please."

"White people are weird. It's like it's all they ever think about."

"That's because they never think about it."

"Everything for me, please," said Joseph.

He got nine out of ten on the sports round, and

anyway, horse-racing wasn't a sport. They were all pleased with him. But at the end of the evening, he lost his nerve: he said good-bye to them all, thanked them for the evening, and left without Lucy. He sat in McDonald's with a vanilla milkshake until she texted him to ask where he was.

**They had conversations** in bed that rarely went anywhere. The circularity and pointlessness made Joseph laugh, at first, but Lucy was serious about them: she wanted him to admit that everything was pointless and doomed.

"You'll want kids."

"Maybe."

"You can't have them with me."

"Why not? How old are you really?"

"Shut up. You know what I mean. You won't want kids for five or ten years."

"No."

"So that won't be me."

"No."

"So..."

"You're right. We should pack this in."

"That's what I think, though," she said.

"Yes. I know. That's why we should pack this in."

"I'm being serious."

"So am I."

"Will you stop this and talk properly?"

"You think we should pack this in."

"Yes."

"I'm agreeing with you," he said.

"No, you're not. Not really."

"So what do you want?"

"I want you to disagree."

"Why?"

"Because I want to know I'm not ruining your life."

"Do I look like someone whose life is being ruined?"

She looked up at him. Her head was on his chest, and he was peering down at her, pleased with himself and pleased with the world.

"Not yet. But you wait."

"You said the same thing about Brexit and nothing's happened."

"Brexit hasn't happened, that's why. It won't happen for a couple of years."

"Exactly."

"What?"

"Same thing. I'm not going to stop doing anything because of the terrible future. When we're all unemployed and I'm itching to have children with a younger woman. What am I supposed to do between now and then?"

"Look for a younger woman."

"I'm twenty-two. Any younger woman I find now isn't going to be the younger woman I have kids with."

"So I'm a placeholder."

"Fucking hell, Lucy."

It had to be something to do with being older, he thought, this obsession with spooling forward. He couldn't do it, anyway, and he didn't think he knew anyone of his age who could, or did, or wanted to.

"Say I met someone tomorrow," he said.

"Where are you going tomorrow?"

"Nowhere. This is for example."

"OK, although I don't know why it has to be tomorrow."

"Next week. Next month. Next year."

"Next year."

"Say I met someone next year. Do you think I should ask them to take a, like a test? A fertility test? Straight away?"

"What are you talking about?"

"That's how you're asking me to think. 'Oh, I might have kids with her. If she can't get pregnant, I'd better find out now.'"

"You don't need to do that. You've got time."

"Time for what? To meet someone else? I like this one. I want to be with her."

"For example?"

"For example, yes."

"You can make decisions together."

"Listen, I don't know much about much. But young people—we're shit at thinking about tomorrow. Smoking. Pensions. Junk food. All of it. You want to be with someone younger than you? You have to live with it."

It seemed like appropriate advice for the times. Lucy would try to remember it.

**Another one,** right in the middle of something:

"Hold on, hold on."

He thought it was an instruction, and he tightened his grip.

"No. No. Stop."

He stopped.

"You'll tell me when you're too disgusted to go on, won't you?"

"What?"

"When everything's drooping and it's all too much. Like, where your hands were. I can't see it. I have no idea what my arse looks like."

"I can't see either in this position."

She had thought about some of this when they were having an affair. She'd been embarrassed to take her clothes off, but when he didn't seem to mind what he saw, she forgot about it. But this was different: she was no longer worried about what he might think this minute, but what he might think at some unspecified date in the future. Now there was no expiry date, it was on her mind. It was, she supposed, another version of the baby conversation. One minute would leak into the next, one year would follow another, each of them adding wrinkle to sag and sag to wrinkle, invisible to an everyday observer until the horror was such that he could no longer ignore them.

She lay down on the bed beside him.

"I won't have to tell you, will I?" he said.

"I'm asking you to tell me."

"I'll be too disgusted to go on. And you'll know."

"I'm not going to go to Pilates seven days a week, just to keep you happy." She was surprised to hear the anger in her voice. There was a note of "**fucking men**" in there, as if Joseph had just insisted she went to Pilates seven days a week.

"OK," he said.

"I mean, I'll go for my sake. Not yours."

"OK."

"But not every day."

"Fine."

"Is that all you're going to say?"

"Well. Have we actually stopped? Because if we have, I'll try and think of something else. But if we haven't..."

"I don't know if we've stopped or not."

"When will you know?"

"When you stop saying OK."

"You mean, if I come up with a good answer to this question, we carry on? 'Cause I don't think I'm going to come up with anything that makes you happy. Let's just stop."

He got out of bed and put his trunks and T-shirt back on.

"Well, you couldn't have wanted it that much. If you can stop just like that," she said.

"You're the one who stopped, not me. You can't be that into it, if you're busy worrying about what your arse will look like in ten years' time. Do you want some tea?"

They sat at the kitchen table, Lucy in a dressing gown, Joseph in his T-shirt and pants. Lucy hated the dressing gown, suddenly. It felt frumpy. She wanted to ask Joseph what he thought of it, but if she were him, she would point out that she seemed just as unhappy and vulnerable covering her body up as she did exposing it.

"How do you manage with people your own age?"

"There haven't been any people of my own age. Only Paul. And before he came along I was in my twenties. Like you. Didn't cross my mind for a second."

"Like me. And what about with Paul?"

"We were growing old at the same time. Still are, I suppose."

"Yeah. But just because he's growing old doesn't mean he'll be into all the stuff you're threatening. The wrinkled old bum and the droopy tits."

"He'd have to put up with it."

"Why him more than me?"

"Because... That's how it works. That's the deal. You'd have to put up with it in thirty years, if you were with someone your age. But you might not want to put up with it before you have to."

"Just do Pilates seven days a week."

"When you're fifty, I'll be seventy."

"Yep. Whether we're together or not."

"If we were together, you'd have to have someone else."

"Deal. But just to get this straight—you don't want sex with me now because I might not want sex with you in whatever. 2044."

"Do you feel like sex now?"

"Not really," Joseph said. "It's after midnight, and I've got to be up early."

Even then, Lucy wondered about the dressing gown, and vowed to look for something less functional at the weekend. And then she got angry with him again, just as she had done about the Pilates. If he didn't like it, he could lump it, or find someone who didn't have anything else to think about but lingerie. And then she began to wonder whether it was possible to be driven mad by sleeping with a younger man.

**It didn't help** that two weeks later, she was another year older. Joseph didn't know until the day before. He was playing FIFA with Al, with Dylan watching on. Lucy was out.

"By the way," said Dylan. "Dad usually takes us out shopping. But he's forgotten this year."

"He might have stopped," said Al. "Because it's not his business."

"It is his business," said Dylan. "She's still our mum. And he's still our dad."

"It probably should be our business," said Al.

"We're just kids, though," said Dylan.

"What are you talking about?" said Joseph.

"Mum's birthday," said Al.

"When is it?"

"Tomorrow."

"Tomorrow? Shit. And you've got nothing?"

"Nothing."

"Dad's fault."

"Cards?"

"Nope."

"Right."

Joseph stopped the game.

"Bedrooms. Paper. Pens. Now."

"We can get cards from the corner shop."

"You don't want a card saying 'Happy Birthday You Old Fart.' Or one with a bunch of old-lady roses on it."

"I'd get the old fart one," said Al.

"Go and make your own. And what am I supposed to do? I'm working all day tomorrow."

Why didn't he know? They'd never talked about it. He had always known the birthdays of his girlfriends. The first time he'd ever talked properly to any of them, they had wanted to know when his was, and he'd told them, and they said, oh, Libra, my sister's a Libra, or something like that. And this was his prompt to ask them what star sign they were, even though he didn't give a shit, and then they'd say, Gemini, May the twenty-fifth. And once or twice, no more than that, he was still involved with the girl in question as May the twenty-fifth approached, and she'd provided a countdown, and he'd been expected to mark the occasion with a card, or a card and a gift, or, most recently, with a card and a gift and a meal. Lucy had never asked him his star sign, and he'd never asked her, and now he had nothing, even though Lucy was a bigger deal than any of the others.

He confessed his failure after **The Sopranos**.

"You didn't know because I've never told you."

"I know, but..."

"We can do something. With the boys."

"You don't want to see your friends?"

"That isn't how it works at our age."

"Why not?"

"Friends need notice. And I know the boys will be expecting to go out."

"Where do they like to go?"

"There are only two restaurants in the whole of North London—the Chinese on Kentish Town Road or the upmarket hamburger place in Chalk Farm."

"So it's on me."

"Really?"

"Of course."

He wanted to ask how upmarket the burger place was, but he suppressed the question.

"What did you do last year?"

"Oh, last year was a mess. Paul wanted a family meal, but...Well, it didn't happen. Takeaway."

"But they remembered cards and presents."

"They were reminded by their father, yes."

"I'm sorry."

"You're not their father."

"I know. But."

"You're not. No buts."

"So what am I?"

"You're not their stepfather, either. You're somewhere between a stepbrother and a step-uncle. Either way you're not related."

Maybe not, but he was growing more related every day.

**At the beginning** of his lunch hour, he asked Cassie what she'd like for her birthday, if she could have anything on sale within five minutes' walk of the shop. She was taking a smoke break; she didn't get lunch until two. She was leaning against the wall of the little community hall a couple of doors down.

"This isn't for me, right?"

"Unless it's your birthday today. And you're expecting something from me."

"But there's no price limit?"

"No. Not around here."

"I don't get this. I'm presuming this person is someone special."

"Yes."

"But you have to buy her a present this lunchtime."

"It's her birthday today."

"Oh, Joseph. That's so crap."

"There are whatsit circumstances."

"Mitigating."

"Exactly."

"Like what?"

Joseph huffed.

"You're not helping me. You're just saying you wouldn't start from here."

"When are you seeing her?"

"Straight after work."

"Where?"

"Hers. And there's nowhere between here and there. Apart from these shops."

"Are you sure?"

"Yes, I'm sure."

"Tell me where she lives and I'll tell you where to go."

"It doesn't matter where she lives."

He wished he hadn't started this. He should simply have asked for an idea, and not got into all the geographical restrictions. He felt he was being drawn further out than he was comfortable to venture.

"How can it not matter? And what are the mitigating circumstances?"

"I didn't know it was her birthday."

"Ooh. So this must be quite recent. And I'm guessing she must live near here. Which is why these are the only shops. Where did you meet her?"

"Anyway. Thanks. I'll have a little poke around."

"Unless you're going to buy her a cheap kettle or

a bet on the three-thirty at Cheltenham, I don't know what you'll find."

The area around the butcher's was coming up in the world. There were cafés in which men with beards drank flat whites, and a bar that specialized in craft beers from microbreweries. These cafés, however, had replaced kebab houses and grotty pubs. The old shops—the pound stores, the book-ies, the newsagents, the off-licenses, the funeral parlor, and the little supermarkets—had stayed stolidly in place, apparently unperturbed and certainly unthreatened by the arrival of the craft coffee.

"Perfume? From the chemist?"

"Yes. Yes. Great idea. What should I get? What perfume would you get from the chemist's?"

"Is she like me, this woman?"

She wasn't, of course, but Joseph was perma-nently uncertain about white university-educated women. Who knew what they liked? And now he came to think of it, he wasn't sure Lucy had ever worn perfume, not around him, anyway. She smelled nice, but it was all body lotions and face creams, he thought.

"In some ways," said Joseph.

"That means white," said Cassie.

"That would only be one way."

"She goes to uni," said Cassie.

"Not…" He stopped himself.

"Not now? Not any more? Oh, my God."

"What?"

"I know who it is," said Cassie.

"No, you don't."

"It's that pretty, twinkly dark-haired woman who comes in here. I could never work out what all those looks and smiles meant. I've seen women flirt with you in here. And sometimes you flirt back for a laugh. But you try not to with her, and she tries not to with you. Oh, that's fucking hilarious."

"It's not her," he said, but they both knew he was just going through the motions. "Why is it fucking hilarious?"

"I don't know. Just… Who'd have thought?"

"Why wouldn't you have thought?" he said aggressively.

It was easy to get Cassie off his back.

"Loads of reasons," she mumbled. "Not just one." And then, to make up, "What about tickets for something?"

"Tickets? For what?"

"She's an English teacher, right? A play."

"A play? What do I know about plays?"

"Give me your phone and your bank card," said Cassie.

"Fuck off."

"I'll have tickets for you by the time you've bought a sandwich."

"I can't buy a sandwich if I haven't got a bank card."

"Is that you saying thank you?"

She fished a fiver out of her pocket and gave it to him.

"Thank you," he said. "I'll pay you back."

"Yeah, I'd sort of presumed that."

"And thanks for doing this too."

"You're welcome."

He went off to buy a card and his sandwich, and when he came back, she had bought him a pair of tickets to see a Shakespeare play. He tried to remember whether he'd ever spent so much money on something he really didn't want to do. Maybe he wouldn't have to do it, but he didn't think that would be an option.

**Before they went out,** he asked whether he could use Lucy's printer, and then he folded up the two sheets of paper and put them in the envelope with the card he'd bought her. He'd spent ages choosing the card, which, in the end, said "Happy Birthday" and nothing else, and he'd spent ages thinking about the message, which, in the end, said "With love, Joseph" and nothing else.

He handed the card over in the restaurant.

"I hope," he said. And then, "I don't know." And then, "Anyway."

She made the face that people make when they're opening presents, like, oh, I have no idea what this could be. And then when she unfolded the tickets, he could see he and Cassie had made the right choice. She was thrilled, and excited, and maybe there were even a couple of tears.

"How did you know?"

"Know what?"

"Any of it."

That was what had moved her.

"Have you seen it?" he asked.

"Do you mean, ever?"

"Yeah."

"**As You Like It**? Yes. Of course."

Joseph's face fell, and she realized that this was the wrong answer, as far as he was concerned.

"But not this production. People who love Shakespeare see the plays over and over again."

"Really?"

"Yes. I've seen **King Lear** at least four times. There are hardly any I've only seen once. The big ones, anyway."

"Is this a big one?"

"Have you heard of it?"

"I think so."

"So there you go."

"I've never seen any."

"Not even on a school trip?"

"No."

There had been a school trip to see Shakespeare, but he'd hidden the permission slip from his mother, and told the school she disapproved of non-Christian entertainment. Looking back, he realized they believed any old crap if they were afraid of what they were getting into. He should have told his teachers that she didn't approve of French or geography, either.

"You don't have to take me, by the way. Maybe you should take someone who deserves it more."

"I'm going with you."

The play was in a month's time. He was almost sure he'd be going with her. He had never been in a relationship like this, where you presumed that things would stay just as they were for four weeks, and maybe even for the four weeks after that.

In the restaurant, the boys suddenly got excited about going with Joseph on the train to their grandparents' house, for reasons that Joseph couldn't quite understand.

"Sounds great," said Joseph, when he'd heard about the W.H. Smiths they visited at the station, where they were allowed to buy any sweets they wanted.

"Plus they've got a dog," said Dylan.

"Cool."

Lucy felt that she ought to explain, and to dampen the mounting excitement.

"We're going tomorrow," said Lucy. "We always go for lunch on my birthday weekend. They used to come up here, but . . ."

"But then Dad called Grandma the 'c' word," said Al.

"Ah," said Joseph. "That would have put them off."

"And they don't like coming to London anymore anyway."

"Where do they live?"

"Brexit Central," said Dylan.

"That's what Mum calls it," said Al.

"She didn't used to," said Dylan. "But then they went and voted out."

"Yay," said Al. "Out, out, out."

"I thought you'd changed your mind," said Lucy.

"Yeah," said Al. "I have. But I was supporting out on the day, so I'm still claiming the win."

"Anyway. They live in Kent," said Lucy. "They retired there."

"Where did you grow up?"

"Essex," said Lucy. "Same sort of thing, really. I don't know why they bothered."

"So you're not coming?" said Dylan.

"No," said Lucy. "He's got better things to do."

"I haven't," said Joseph.

That was true. He could make some music, but he and Jaz were still trying to find a date when he, she, and the recording studio were all free at the same time, and they hadn't even bothered trying during the summer. What else was there? Church, football on T.V., maybe a wander around Wood Green with anyone who wasn't up to anything.

"Good," said Dylan.

Lucy smiled. It wasn't a beaming smile, though. It was thin and awkward. There would be more to talk about later.

**"You don't really** want to come with us, do you?" said Lucy when they were plugging in and unplugging electrical devices, the last ritual of the evening.

Joseph laughed.

"It sounds like there may be a right answer to that question."

"I mean, what would your status be?"

"Does it matter? Would anyone even ask?"

"They'd probably presume you were some kind of hired help."

"What about if we started making out in front of them?"

"I can feel a panic attack coming on already."

"So let's not bother," said Joseph. He could do with some new jeans.

"Do we have to make out?"

"That was a joke."

"I know, but…"

"'But'? Where do you get a 'but' from?"

"Well. We are making out."

"Yeah, but not constantly. We don't have to rack up ten hours a day. We can give it a rest when we're visiting your parents."

"I think I would have to tell them. Before we went."

"Not by text, I'm guessing."

"They don't really do text. Oh, shit. This is **Guess Who's Coming to Dinner.**"

"You've lost me."

"It's an old movie. Spencer Tracy and Katharine Hepburn. Their daughter is going to marry Sidney Poitier."

"I'm guessing there's someone black in this movie. Or white."

"Sidney Poitier?"

"Nope."

"He was the most famous black actor ever for a while."

"So this nice white girl is going to marry Sidney Whatsit."

"Yes."

"What's that got to do with us?"

"Well..."

"That was a joke as well."

"Oh. So he's marrying this white girl, and her parents are liberals, but the dad doesn't want her to marry him because of all the prejudice in the world. But this film was made in 1967. And here I am, thinking about it in 2016."

"Well, don't."

"Why not? I'm not sure my parents are even liberals."

"First of all. I don't know about your parents, or Kent, but nobody gives a shit in London."

"Yeah. It's my parents in Kent I'm worried about."

"Plus we're not getting married."

"What difference does that make?"

"It isn't something they have to get worked up about."

"Won't stop them worrying."

"Worrying? What is there to worry about?"

"They're old. They worry."

"Right. I'm going to buy some new jeans and then I'm going to watch Arsenal on T.V."

Lucy didn't say anything. She wanted to say, "Are you sure?" but she had to time it right. If she said it too quickly he would know that she was the problem, not her parents.

"Are you sure?" she said eventually.

And Joseph knew that she was the problem, not her parents. He didn't stay the night.

There was nothing very beautiful to see on the bus home: neon-sick empty fast-food joints with names like L.A. Chicken, random gangs of Deliveroo drivers sitting on their scooters and motorbikes, talking and smoking, a group of teenagers running up and down and shrieking, a man taking a piss through the railings, three or four of the little shopfront churches that his mother lorded it over. This part of the city wasn't easy to love, he supposed. You wouldn't bring a tourist up here, anyway. But he did love it. He belonged here. And he didn't just belong to anywhere on the 134 bus route, either. He felt just as at home in Whitechapel, or Brixton, or Notting Hill. He loved it even more knowing that if he went to Kent, or to Italy, or to Poland, he would find people who didn't really want him to have a home anywhere, apart from countries and cities he knew nothing about and would probably never visit. Lucy couldn't do anything about that. Being with her somewhere that didn't have a London Underground station would probably make it worse for both of them. He felt stupid for even thinking about a family excursion.

———

**After the third** or fourth time that the boys mentioned Joseph— "Joseph said…," "Joseph can do…," "Joseph makes us…," "Joseph would like…" —Lucy's mother finally asked the question.

"Who's Joseph?" Al repeated incredulously.

"Well, how am I supposed to know?" said Lucy's mother.

Margaret Lawrence was not an easy woman. You could perhaps have predicted that just by looking around her sitting room (and it was very much hers, not her husband's); whenever Lucy visited, she was struck by the pinched primness of everything—the muted colors, the noncommittal art on the walls, the neat coasters on the little mahogany side tables. When the time came, Lucy would have to sell the entire contents of the house. There wasn't a single thing, a book or a piece of crockery, that she'd want to keep. When she despaired of the mess at home, she sometimes found herself thinking, yes! Good! It's not like Cordwallis Road, where nothing is out of place! Even the dog that the boys inexplicably loved seemed characterless. It simply lay there, in its basket, toning in with the room.

"I just thought you'd know," said Al.

"So who is he?"

"You tell them, Mum," said Dylan.

"They don't want to know about Joseph," Lucy said.

"Why don't you want to know about Joseph?" said Al, looking at his grandmother.

"We do," said Margaret.

Her husband smiled benignly. Lucy wondered whether Ken was all there, but she'd been wondering that since he was in his mid-fifties. He had checked out around then, not due to any illness or accident. He just seemed to decide that he'd had enough of engaging with the world around him, or the people who lived in it. Or maybe he had simply come to the conclusion that the people he knew best had said everything they had to say, but they said it again anyway, and he was unwilling to go around for a third or fourth time. He listened to choral music and, now he was retired, went on long cycling trips to do brass-rubbing. He'd talk about that, if you asked him, but asking him was always a mistake. Sometimes, when something engaged him enough, or he recognized the germ of a new experience in his inner circle, he'd check back in again, and say something shrewd, or at least pertinent. This was even more unnerving and depressing, in a way. It just made Lucy feel like she'd bored him stupid the rest of the time.

"They do," said Al. "Tell them."

"Joseph looks after the boys sometimes."

"And the rest," said Dylan, with a snigger.

"Anyway, he doesn't look after us much, because he and Mum stay in most of the time."

"We've been out," said Lucy. She didn't know what point she was trying to make. She certainly didn't seem to be denying that there was a connection that went beyond babysitting.

"Basically, they're going out," said Al. "But they haven't said anything to us."

"So a strange man sits watching T.V. every night and nobody says anything?"

"No," said Dylan. "It's Joseph. He's not strange to us."

Lucy could see that if she just sat gaping over the remains of the lamb, she wouldn't have to say anything. The boys would do it all for her—yes, in an unfortunate and cack-handed way, but one that had the virtue of requiring nothing from her. She wasn't sure that the boys understood how much older she was than Joseph, and why it mattered, but if they could somehow drop his age into the conversation, her work here was done.

Her mother looked at her, bewildered.

"What are they saying?"

"They are saying, I think," said Ken, "that Lucy has a boyfriend."

"Oh," said her mother. "Is it serious?"

"He's twenty-two," Lucy said. That sounded disloyal to her, as if she were answering the question in the negative because of Joseph's youth, but she was trying to chuck as much information as she could through the window while it was open. "And he's black." She didn't say that out loud. Joseph's age had already exploded right in front of her mother's face, causing shell shock and temporary muteness. Lucy didn't want to witness her mother's views on that other piece of information.

"Yeah," said Al. "So he plays FIFA with us and he still remembers maths."

"I remember maths," said Lucy indignantly.

"You remember numbers. That's different," said Dylan.

"Well," said Ken. "Fun for all the family."

"It really is," said Al with great enthusiasm.

"How did you meet him?" said Margaret.

"In the butcher's," she said. "He works there on Saturdays."

"And how did you go from that to this?" said Margaret.

"He babysat for us a couple of times," said Dylan. "And then BOOM!"

This made Al giggle uncontrollably. Even Lucy's parents smiled.

"Any further questions?" said Lucy.

"Are you happy?" her father asked.

"She's miles better than she was," said Al. "Can I ask you something, Grandad?"

There was a look on his face that Lucy didn't like. Permission to ask did not bode well. She was guessing the question would involve, or end up involving, Brexit and/or something worse.

"Now is not the time," said Lucy.

"You don't even know what I'm going to ask!"

"It doesn't matter."

"How can it not matter?"

All questions led to trouble, just as all roads led to Rome.

"Grandma wants to know about school," said Lucy.

"No, she doesn't," said Dylan. "Look at her face."

"Don't be rude," said Lucy.

"I wasn't saying that's her actual face. I'm saying she doesn't want to know about school."

"Tell me about school," said her mother, suddenly bright.

# 13

The play started before anything even happened on the stage. There were actors in the audience, shouting at each other across the aisles, blowing each other kisses, laughing, running around. Lucy never really enjoyed that sort of immersion; you needed time to yourself, she thought, between getting off a bus and settling into the evening. There was the queue for the loo, and the queue for ice creams and chocolate, and you usually had to say "excuse me" to an elderly couple who sighed heavily and looked at you as if you should have arrived before them, as they started to pick up coats and get slowly to their feet so that you could push past them. Also, she was afraid that an actor in the stalls would tell her she was a saucy wench, or wink at her, or ask her to buy a sweet juicy orange. She never knew what you were supposed to do. And the lights were on! There was no magic yet, but magic was being forced upon you.

**Joseph, meanwhile,** just felt that all his worst fears were being realized. If God had meant people still to be going to the theater, he wouldn't have invented T.V. And when you watched T.V., people didn't wander out of the screen and into your living room, embarrassing you. That, he now realized, was actually the best thing about T.V. There was a physical barrier between the viewer and the characters. That might even have been why T.V. was invented. "The theater is great, but is there a way of stopping people talking to us directly? It's awful when they do that." He thought he'd got away with it, but just as he was about to follow Lucy down the row, a man came up to him wearing a ruffle and carrying a tray, asking if he'd like to sample some venison-and-kidney pie. There were literal pies on the tray, cut into little chunks, and they stank. Joseph gave him a look that would have worked in Tottenham, let alone here, and the guy decided to try someone who didn't want to punch him. When he sat down, he looked around to see if there were any other black people in the audience. There were two, both girls.

He had tried to prepare. You could download Shakespeare plays for free onto your iPad, so he'd done that, and started to read it, but he couldn't focus. The play opened with a speech that seemed to go on forever and made no sense. "As I remember, Adam, it was upon this fashion bequeathed me by will but poor a thousand crowns," it began, and Joseph started to panic straight away. How much was a thousand crowns? Was that good? No good? "Poor" made it sound no good. He googled "How much thousand crowns in Shakespeare's time?" and found a website that both explained it all, and made him more confused. Three thousand crowns was a lot of money, it said, but one thousand crowns was only two hundred and fifty pounds, the equivalent of twenty-five thousand pounds now. Twenty-five thousand wasn't a lot? Why wasn't it? You couldn't live off it forever, but it would tide you over until you got a job. And then there was stuff about oxen and dunghills and gentility. If he spent a few hours on it, he could probably work it out, but that was the first page. How long would it take him to understand the whole play? He decided that reading the thing was too ambitious, so he went for a Wikipedia summary instead: **Rosalind, now disguised as Ganymede (Jove's own page), and**

Celia, now disguised as Aliena (Latin for stranger) arrive in the Arcadian Forest of Arden, where the exiled Duke now lives with some supporters, including the melancholy Jaques, a malcontent figure, who is introduced weeping over the slaughter of a deer. What the actual fuck? There was paragraph after paragraph of this stuff, so mind-numbing that he briefly reconsidered trying again with the iPad. Someone said **As You Like It** was just a crowd-pleaser, not a serious Shakespeare play, which, if he hadn't read the summary, would have raised his hopes a little. But Joseph found it hard to imagine a crowd that was pleased by slaughtered deer and Forests of Arden and Jove's own page.

He wouldn't mind sitting there, watching the people and the audience and thinking about something else. He could cope with boredom. It was the journey home he was afraid of. What was he supposed to say? Was he required to have some kind of opinion? About what? The actors? The production? He had nothing to compare it to. He googled again, and found discussion questions designed for students. **Lucy, in** As You Like It **is the pastoral life meant to seem ideal? Please provide quotes from the text to illustrate.** Maybe he'd forget about that last bit. It was supposed to be an evening out.

Once it started, it wasn't so bad. You didn't need

to know the value of a crown, really, and also he recognized one of the actresses from **Sherlock**. He didn't know why that mattered, but he hadn't been expecting to see anyone almost famous. But he had forgotten about intervals, which meant that the conversation he'd been afraid of was brought forward.

"What do you think?" said Lucy.

It was, he knew, an innocent enough question, but it was like a dagger through his heart.

"I wasn't expecting to see the woman from **Sherlock**."

"Which one is she?"

"The…" He wasn't sure which one she was. She was one of the women who'd started with one name and was now called something else, but he couldn't remember either. That was all he had, so far.

"But are you bored?"

"No."

"Really?"

He examined his experience of the previous hour again. It had gone quickly enough. He had laughed a couple of times, just to show willing, and to offer encouragement to the cast.

"Really. You?"

"It's good. I'd like to say more, but I'm bursting."

Joseph offered silent thanks to Lucy's bladder.

She stood up and pushed her way past the grumpy couple, who were even grumpier the second time, and probably wouldn't be thrilled the third. He looked around at the people who'd stayed put. They were reading their programs, talking quietly. He had never sat in a crowd like this.

The guy sitting in front of him, forties, wearing a suit, turned around and said something to him.

"Sorry?" said Joseph.

"My glasses. I think I've managed to drop them by your feet."

Joseph looked down, and there they were. He picked them up and handed them back.

"Thank you," said the man. And then, "It's a long old haul, isn't it? I only ever understand about one word in three."

"So you keep doing this?"

"She keeps doing this." He nodded his head toward the bar, or the toilet, or wherever she was.

Joseph smiled. He was tempted to ask the guy for his phone number so that they could keep in touch.

In the queue for the toilet, Lucy looked at the women ahead of her. She felt that somehow she had told Joseph that this was her crowd, even though he'd bought the tickets, and now she was beginning to doubt whether she had anything in common with any of them. There was Shakespeare, she supposed—but how many of them loved Shakespeare? Or even the theater? How many of them came because they thought they should, or because they had been brought up to do so? There were no young people in the queue, but that might have been because they didn't need to pee, and there were no black people anywhere. She looked at their faces, trying to discern whether any of them might have voted for Brexit, and concluded that it was hard to tell. Over half the country had voted for Brexit, and some of them must have been there. How would Shakespeare have voted? She supposed it depended on how old he was at the time of the referendum. If he was his actual age, four hundred and fifty-odd, he would probably have voted out. The older you got, the less tolerant you became, so he would have been very intolerant indeed. The man who wrote **Romeo and Juliet** and **Two Gentlemen of Verona**, however, might have had more time for foreigners. But what would he have thought of all the people who took his name in vain? To some English people, Shakespeare was a justification for never having anything to do with the rest of the world. He confirmed the nation's superiority. He might not have liked many of these people much. On the other hand, that kind of deification was hard to resist, she would imagine. She would never have thought about any of this if she'd come with Paul. (Fat chance of that. She couldn't remember ever going to the theater with Paul.) She'd have thought, I'm me, and I have nothing to do with any of these people. Or rather, she'd have thought nothing, apart from, what is that woman up to in there? Who does a poo in the interval of a play?

**"Perhaps this will** be the last time," said the grumpy man as he picked his coat up and rose wearily to his feet.

"I hope so," said Lucy, and gave him a grateful smile. When she got back to her seat, Joseph was talking to the man in front about whether Arsène Wenger, the manager of Arsenal, should go. They were both in agreement: his time was up.

**Outside the theater,** they talked about whether they'd go on somewhere for a drink (they wanted to get home) and where the nearest bus stop was (just up the road). But now they were on the bus, and conversation was unavoidable.

"Was it good?" he asked her.

She laughed.

"You tell me."

"No," he said, too quickly.

"You're entitled to an opinion."

"I know. But just because I'm entitled to one, it doesn't mean it's worth your while listening to it."

"It was a good production," she said. "In my opinion. It was sharp, and light on its feet. And Julianne Lawrence was fantastic."

"Which one was she?"

"Rosalind."

He stopped himself from repeating the question. Rosalind had to be the main woman.

"Oh. Yeah. She was great."

"I wondered whether Orlando was a little too dour, but I warmed to him. He was a slow burn. In a good way."

"Right."

He liked her talking about what she thought. It was sort of sexy, for some reason. Maybe it was because he'd never met anyone who would describe an actor as "a little too dour." It reminded him that this was new, and different. She'd been sitting there, thinking thoughts and making judgments, and having this access to them reminded him that she was both separate and part of him at the same time. He wanted to get back to her house.

"Would you go to another one?" she asked him.

"Another Shakespeare? Or another play? I like going places with you, so, yeah."

She wanted to kiss him, right there, on the bus, properly, but she resisted.

"That guy you were talking to about football..."

"Ah, he was suffering, man. His wife had booked the tickets."

"Do you think he wondered about us? When I came back?"

"No."

"Just no?"

"Just no. I think you wondered whether he wondered. That was the only wondering going on."

Maybe that was it, Lucy thought. Maybe there was only wondering about wondering, which had to be as good a definition of self-consciousness as any.

# 14

"Yeah, I'm not singing that," said Jaz.

Joseph sighed internally, and possibly externally too. He had e-mailed her the lyric, the track, and his guide vocal so that she knew what she was doing when they got into the studio; at no stage had she said that she was unhappy with anything.

"What?" said Jaz sharply, although that might have been because of the face that accompanied the internal sigh, rather than an indication that the sigh had slipped out into the world. It wasn't as if everything or anything had been easy up until this point. When they'd arrived, she'd said the room was too cold, and they had to wait for the heating to come on before she'd start. But then her throat was dry, and it turned out that she never drank water, tea, or coffee, which were the three options that were available in the studio, so she had to go to the nearest shop to buy a Coke Zero—with a fiver from Joseph, because she was fucked if she was going to finish out of pocket. She came back with the Coke and a ton of sweets, some of which had to be eaten for energy, and some of which got stuck in her teeth, which had to be picked with a fingernail. The engineer, an old hippy called Colin, went to sit in the little kitchen to read the paper rather than watch the picking.

And now the lyric was no good. It wasn't even supposed to be any good. He wasn't trying to write "What's Going On," or to flow like Kendrick. He just wanted the sound of a human voice over his track, so there were a lot of "baby's" and "yeah's." Once he knew the words were for Jaz, he tried to tailor them for her. He had written about female empowerment, kind of, using the metaphor of a car: "Gonna drive/ gonna sit behind the wheel/ gonna drive/ wanna check that life is real." He was pleased he'd avoided "feel." There were another couple of verses, but they were very small variations on the same theme.

"What's wrong with it?"

He regretted asking the question, because he knew it could be answered in many different ways, most of them unkind, but Jaz's objections were literal.

"I can't drive."

"Right. And you can't pretend?"

"I could if I'd had some lessons."

"So I have to pay for driving lessons before you'll sing."

"I'm not saying that. I'm just saying you wouldn't get the best out of me if I have to sing about driving."

"It's not about driving."

"What is it about, then?"

"It's about you being a powerful woman."

"Who's driving."

"Metaphorically."

"Can't I do something else metaphorically?"

"What do you want to sing about?"

"Depends which way you want to go. I was thinking either Brexit or oral sex. Receiving, not giving."

"They're quite different."

"According to men they are. One's disgusting and one's a human right."

"I meant the subjects."

"Oh. Yeah. One's more, you know, political. Topical. One's more sexual. Depends what you like."

"I can see that."

He thought that getting inside a recording studio, even one as basic as this, might make him feel closer to a music career, but Jaz seemed to be pushing him backward, right to the outermost edge. He could almost touch his mother from where he was now, and she wasn't interested in a music career.

"I don't have lyrics about either of those subjects right now, though. And we're recording right now."

"Well, we're a bit stuck then."

"What about 'fly' instead of 'drive'?"

"There's no wheel, though, is there?"

"We can find something else."

"How about this? 'Want you there/ Where I can feel/ Want you to taste/ my love is real.'"

"I'm a Christian," said Joseph. It had worked with the school theater trip.

"So am I."

"Well, behave like one."

Colin the engineer popped his head back through the door.

"Are we getting anywhere?"

"What do you think I should sing about?" said Jaz. "Cars, Brexit, or oral sex?"

"Cars," said Colin.

"Really?"

"There are a lot of good car songs," said Colin. "No Brexit songs. There are probably oral sex songs, but they don't get on the radio. Unless you want to sing about lollipops and so on."

"I'd be doing it the other way around," said Jaz.

"Ah," said Colin. "Well, then."

He had nothing else to offer.

**I hadn't thought** about the radio," said Jaz. "Why don't we do the car one then?"

She said it as if it were her idea.

"One more thing," said Jaz. "Maybe you should think about making it a bit more Afro Housey?"

"Well," said Joseph. "I'll think about it." He would have to ask £Man what the hell she was talking about. He didn't go to enough clubs.

"You're ready to start?"

The engineer took some levels.

"Whoa," he said, when Jaz sang, too loud, and too close to the mic, and his levels went haywire.

"I have a very powerful voice," she said. "Nothing I can do about it."

But she was brilliant. She found the melody, and then found a variation for the next verse, and all kinds of cool stuff for the fade, and she hung just off the beat like a much more experienced singer. When they played it back afterward, Joseph got a little shiver of excitement, and he could see she felt the same.

"Very nice," said Colin, as if it were just another day in the studio for him.

**355**

They walked to the Tube together.

"Are you on gray tings now?" said Jaz. "That's what I heard."

She was talking about Lucy, and for a moment he wondered if she was referring to her age, even though he also knew that the word "gray" was a reference to her color. Well, he thought. Now I know what I'm most paranoid about.

It never occurred to him that Jaz would know anything about her.

"I'm not on anything."

"So I heard wrong."

"I can't imagine who's bothering to talk about me."

"When a black guy goes out with a forty-year-old white teacher, people talk."

"Even with everything going on in the world?"

That was pathetic, like his mum telling him to eat his dinner because of the starving children.

"Especially because of everything going on in the world," said Jaz. "Who wants to talk about that? Anyway. What's wrong with us? Because you know I tried and got nowhere."

"I was with a black girl over the summer."

"Yeah. I was there when you met her. And she wasn't good enough either?"

"It's nothing to do with who's not good enough."

"What is it to do with?"

"People."

"What does that mean?"

It meant, of course, that some people he wanted to sleep with and some people he didn't, and that was that. But as Jaz belonged in the category of people he didn't want to sleep with, it probably wasn't the time to get into it.

"Some people I meet at the right time, and others I meet at the wrong time."

"So timing, more than people."

"Yeah. That would be a better way of putting it. Timing."

"And is it like a train? Once you miss it, it's gone? Or can you get on the next one?"

Joseph couldn't pick his way through the simile. Either way it was like a train, it seemed to him.

"I dunno."

"Well, we'll see, shall we?"

He gave her a smile, and though he couldn't look at his own face, obviously he could feel in his muscles that the smile was forced and nervous. He didn't want to see anything. He told Jaz it made more sense for him to get the bus, turned around, and walked the other way. "On gray tings." Fucking hell.

———

Lucy asked if she could hear it.

"Oh, you don't want to listen to it all over again."

"It's not like you've written a thousand-page book. How long is it? Five minutes?"

"Not quite."

"Well then."

"You see, last time..."

Was he going to get into last time? With the jigging, and the earnest enthusiasm? Had it really been that bad?

"What happened last time? Which last time?"

"When I played you the track."

"Did I say something wrong?"

"No."

He didn't want to hurt her. But he had a job to do too: the job was to stop her morphing into someone he couldn't sleep with. He couldn't sleep with his mother, or stepmother, or whatever she had turned into before. Their relationship was healthy, at the moment. If she jigged or nodded, it became unhealthy. Neither of them wanted that.

"Can you keep still?"

"What?"

"While you're listening. Don't move."

"Are you serious?"

"Yes."

"What happens if I move?"

"Nothing happens. Not really."

"It's for dancing to, isn't it?"

"Yes, but…"

There was no kind or easy way of doing this, that he could see. Either he played it and let her do what she wanted, or he told her that when she tried to express her feelings for the music, he felt every single second of the twenty years between them.

"Tell you what," he said. "I'll go upstairs."

"There's no need to be embarrassed. It was good before, without the vocals. It will be even better now."

"I'm just not very good at this yet."

"I understand."

He went upstairs and lay on the bed. He could hear the music through the floorboards. When it faded out, he went back downstairs. Lucy was flushed and a little disheveled.

"It's great," she said. "Jaz is a wonderful singer, isn't she? I had a proper boogie. I couldn't help myself. I'm glad you weren't there to see it."

"Yeah," he said. The word "boogie" set his teeth on edge. "But thanks for listening."

"I will always want to hear everything you do."

Joseph had once broken up with a girl because she bought a horrible coat. He hadn't realized that was the reason he couldn't go on seeing her until a lot later, when he started to wonder why, when he remembered her, she always had the coat on. He had seen her with nothing on, and in her underwear, and in jeans and a tight jumper, but the coat haunted him. It was fake fur, although God knows what animal it was pretending to be, and it drew attention to itself and to her and to him, and he couldn't forgive it. In every other way, the girl was nice, and she was really hot. He didn't want Lucy's dancing to become like that coat; Lucy was wonderful. She had just said something sweet, and supportive, and loyal, and maybe he was looking at things the wrong way round. Yes, she was oldish and he was youngish, but it was his youth that was the problem, not her age. He was too young to let stupid things go. But how were you supposed to learn?

**It started on** a Monday morning with the words "fuck off" and a vigorous nod, and Lucy worked backward from there. Of course, she could have been wrong. Year Eleven students nodded and said "fuck off" approximately every twenty seconds, so there was no reason to presume that Shenika Johnson and Marlon Harris were talking about her love life. But she was able to subtitle the scene so easily.

Shenika: You know Ms. Fairfax is banging a twenty-two-year-old black guy?

Marlon: Fuck off.

Shenika nods vigorously...

And they stopped talking the moment she came into the room, which nobody ever did, normally. (They weren't bad kids. She wasn't a bad teacher. But the lesson usually took a couple of minutes to get started.)

And anyway, it didn't matter whether that was where it started. By Friday afternoon, Ben Davies, the Deputy Head, was asking her whether she knew she was the talk of the town. They were in a corridor, and kids were streaming past them, and she felt it was not an appropriate moment to talk about it, and said so.

"Do you want to have a chat about it at the end of the day, then?"

"Not really, no. Why should I?"

"It's not great, when a teacher's private life is being openly discussed by the whole school."

"I'm not doing anything wrong."

"I didn't say you were."

Some of the students were stopping to listen. "Speak up!" one of them at the back of the small crowd shouted. There was laughter.

"I'll see you after school," she said, just to stop the hell of the public conversation.

———

**She found him** in his office. He was dealing with a Year Eight who had forged a toilet pass that enabled him to escape class whenever he felt like it, for medical reasons. Lucy leaned against the wall, listening.

"You don't mind people knowing that you're constantly on the verge of pooing yourself?" Ben was saying. He was an old-school teacher, in the sense that his main tools were sarcasm and ridicule. The kids seemed to find it funny, much to Lucy's annoyance.

"Not really, sir," said the boy.

"Why not?"

"Well, because I'm not, am I? It's a fake pass."

"But your peers think there's something wrong with you."

"No, they don't. They all know."

"Your teachers, then."

"I don't really mind about them."

"Anyway. I've told them all that you're never to go to the toilet at all during lessons, so..."

"That's not fair, sir. What if I really need to go?"

"You've cried wolf. You'll have to suffer the consequences."

"Everyone will have to suffer them," said the boy.

"Well, we'll cross that bridge when we come to

it," said Ben. "You'll be clearing it up, that's for sure. Off you go."

The boy left, and Lucy sat down in his place.

"And the next bollocking, please," she said.

"No, no. Not at all. I just wondered how you were doing."

"I'm OK," she said, but her guard was up.

"Before we go any further—is it true?"

"What?"

"Do you have a seventeen-year-old boyfriend?"

"God. No. No. Is that what they're saying?"

"The age has dropped during the week. He started off in his twenties."

"He's twenty-two. Ben, I'd never…Christ. Seventeen? He could be in Year Twelve? No. Never."

"I didn't think so."

"I'll have to leave," she said. "I'm mortified."

"By the time you've worked out your notice, he'll be fourteen."

"So what do I do?"

"I don't think there's much you can do. Apart from start going out with a fifty-year-old and bring him to the next school fair."

"The next school fair isn't until next summer."

"I wasn't being completely serious," said Ben.

"Oh. Yes. I see."

"And I don't think I can announce it in assembly, either."

"Please don't do that."

"'Contrary to what you've heard, he's twenty-two, not seventeen.'"

Ben seemed to be making the point that it didn't sound a whole lot better, but maybe that was her paranoia.

"If anyone says anything to me, I'll put them straight," said Ben.

"What will you say?"

"I'll say, I don't know... 'You idiots would believe literally anything, wouldn't you? If I told you Mrs. Marks was going out with Justin Bieber, you'd probably pass that round too.'"

Mrs. Marks had worked part time in the art department for decades, and the joke was therefore not a kind one, although Justin Bieber was unlikely to get involved with anyone on the school staff. But Lucy liked the scorn and the incredulity.

"Thank you."

"And I'll tell your colleagues the same thing."

"They all know, do they?"

"Oh, yes. They're as starved of excitement as the kids. Even more so, really."

Lucy liked to think that she had provided excitement occasionally, but only to a very select group of people, exclusively made up of lovers and children (her own, rather than anyone she had ever taught). But this was something entirely new: a procession of steps, most of them taken in an orderly and thoughtful fashion, that had resulted in very minor celebrity. She didn't like it much. She felt like someone who'd gone viral after she had been filmed walking into a manhole while looking at her phone.

On the way out, she saw Ahmad, one of Shenika's classmates.

"Hello, Ms. Fairfax."

"Hello, Ahmad. Detention?"

"Just a little one. Anyway. Just so you know . . . I'm not interested."

By the time she was home, she'd come up with three or four different responses, all of which would have killed him.

**"Seventeen?"** said Joseph. "How?"

He found the remote and turned the T.V. off again. They were about to watch another episode.

"Because kids make crap up."

"Are you embarrassed?"

"Yes."

"I could have been seventeen."

"Well, you were, once," Lucy said.

"I mean, when we met."

"And I wouldn't have gone anywhere near you."

"You'd have come to the shop. And maybe asked me to babysit."

"Well, yes. That."

"But you wouldn't have jumped on me."

"'Jumped on you.' Come on. That wasn't what happened. And of course I wouldn't have."

"What's the difference between twenty-one years younger and twenty-six years younger? I'd have been legal."

"Can we stop talking about this? It makes me feel uncomfortable."

"Well. I'm sorry for my age."

"It's the age they think you are that worries me."

"I'm sorry."

"Have I given you any troubles?"

"No," said Joseph. "Not really."

"What does that mean?"

"Jaz asked me if I was on gray tings."

"What does that mean?"

"Gray is white. Not gray."

"We're not pink?"

"Nope."

"So I'm a white thing."

"Not to me you're not. You're a person."

He said it cheekily, like, I know how to talk to modern women. She laughed.

"Thanks. And you're sure it's nothing to do with age."

"Nothing. Just color."

"Because I'm not going gray anywhere."

"I know."

"And how did you feel when she said it?"

"You know, 'Wow. She's right. I'd better stop.' What do you think I felt?"

"I don't know. That's why I'm asking."

"I think all that stuff is stupid."

"I've ordered a book from America called **Why Black Men Shouldn't Date White Women**."

"Sounds like you only need to read the title."

"I want to know why I shouldn't."

"You can do that in your own time. After you've finished with me," said Joseph.

"Why am I finishing with you?"

"Because you shouldn't be dating me."

"You shouldn't be dating me, the book says."

"Look," said Joseph. "I don't have a thing about white women. That's what they're all talking about. And you don't have a thing about black guys, as far as I know."

"No."

"Racist."

"I just meant..."

"Joke. Bloody hell. But that's what these people

get unhappy about. When people have a thing. Because then you're not looking at the person, are you? I probably won't have another forty-year-old white girlfriend. Not for a while, anyway. Not until I'm sixty."

"Ha ha."

She would be eighty when he was sixty, and all agonies of embarrassment, doubt, and desire would presumably be over by then. She would try to enjoy them while they lasted.

# 15

She invited Pete and Fiona first of all, because she owed them. And then, after careful consideration, she decided to call Nina and ask her and her boyfriend, Rav. Lucy used to work with Nina, before she got out of teaching, and she loved her, but didn't see enough of her.

"That would be lovely," said Nina.

"Just Pete and Fiona, you and Rav, and ... Well, I'm seeing someone. Joseph."

"Before we get into Joseph ... Rav and I are no more."

"Oh, no!"

"Yes. Sad. But there we are."

"What happened?"

"Ach."

"OK."

"But can I bring Andy?"

"Of course."

"Great."

She wanted to ask whether Andy was white, but she stopped herself. She could hardly disinvite him if he was.

"So," said Nina. "Joseph."

"Yes."

"Where did you meet him?"

"He works locally."

"Local to where you live?"

"Yes."

"Right." And then, "How does that work?"

"What?"

"Meeting someone who works locally? You're at work, he's at work…"

"Oh, I see what you mean," said Lucy, and hoped that this might clear up Nina's confusion, but Nina was waiting for more.

"He works Saturdays."

"Oh. Right. Is he a florist or something?"

Was a florist a better match for her than a butcher? Was that the implication? Was floristry artier than butchery? She had answered her own question. Butchery didn't sound good.

"It's a long story."

"Great. Look forward to hearing it and meeting him next Saturday."

Joseph had never been to a dinner party. He had eaten with family, sometimes extended family, and everyone had made an effort and made conversation and so on. But he had never sat inside a house with a group of friends and eaten food that one of them had cooked without a parent present. Was that the definition of a dinner party? He didn't object to them on principle, like some would. Jaz, for example, would have had a lot of fun with the idea of him going to a dinner party with his white girl-friend. "You're going to drink white wine and talk about Brexit? Fuck off." And he wasn't even going to the dinner party. He was throwing it, if you threw dinner parties. He was hosting it.

He sort of lived with Lucy and the boys now. To begin with, he'd stayed four or five nights a week, but he hadn't spent the night at home for a while now, and his mother had accepted that he'd gone, and she was alone at home. She still hadn't met Lucy, though, and the more she moaned about it, the less he felt like going back to see her. He didn't own very much, he had discovered over the months. What he had thought of as possessions turned out to be clothes he didn't wear, games he didn't play, kids' books that he'd never read again.

Most of his wardrobe had ended up at Lucy's, piece by piece. And now that he lived with Lucy, he was going to spend time doing what she did, which included eating with people he didn't know.

He wasn't scared of eating, obviously, but he was scared of the occasion. He already knew he didn't like wine very much, and though he might have a couple of beers, he wouldn't drink much more than that, just so he could stay sharp. But even that wouldn't help with the conversation.

"What will you talk about?" he asked Lucy as he was laying the table. The boys were with Paul and Daisy, and he missed them. He wouldn't have minded keeping an eye on them while everyone else chatted. He could have got up from the table, played a quick game of FIFA, chased them upstairs, stayed half in and half out, half partner and half babysitter. But Lucy didn't want halves of anything tonight. This was it, all or nothing, although nothing would be embarrassing.

"We don't decide in advance," said Lucy.

"But last time you saw them. What did you talk about then? Books?"

"Is that what you're afraid of?"

"A bit. Films. I mean, the sorts of film you watch."

"We haven't seen a film together yet. I've got nothing to talk about."

"You read a lot."

"I may recommend a book."

"So what do I do, when you're doing that?"

"I'd say you can recommend a book of your own, talk to someone else, or shut up and listen. It won't take long."

"What about politics? I've got nothing."

"You made me think about the referendum more than anyone else I know. They'd be interested."

"I can't speak for anyone."

"Nobody will ask you to."

"Shit."

"Meaning?"

"Just... general panic."

"What do you talk about with your friends?"

"I don't know. I've forgotten. Things come up. On Instagram. And then you show someone."

"Well, things will come up tonight."

"Shit," he said again.

"You're a clever and interesting chap," said Lucy. "I've never been bored talking to you. And they won't be either."

It was easier when you were having sex with someone, thought Joseph. You had to find something to say, before and after, otherwise nothing would ever work. Sex forced a conversational flow. The whole point of the dinner party, however, was conversation, and when the conversation was finished, everyone would go home. No sex, no phones—nothing, apart from the contents of one's head.

"They all know you're called Joseph," said Lucy. "So when they come, will you answer the door and introduce yourself? Then they can get over it straight away."

**He forgot, though.** Or rather, he opened the door and said, "Hi, come in." He was going to say, "I'm Joseph, by the way," after they had stepped into the house, but he was too late. Fiona said, straight away, I'm guessing you're not Joseph, and laughed, and Joseph said that he was indeed Joseph, and Fiona panicked and said, of course you are, sand stared at him while shaking his hand. Pete pretended to shoot himself in the head with his fingers, and rolled his eyes and said, hello, mate. He remembered the next time, when Nina and Andy arrived. Nina worked in magazines, and was quite glamorous, and when he said, "I'm Joseph," she said, "Oh, WOW," and sort of squealed with excitement, and said, good for Lucy, and then, good for you too, of course. Her boyfriend looked embarrassed. Joseph was half hoping he was going to shoot himself in the head with his fingers too, so there'd be two down even before the evening had started.

**There was a bottle** of Prosecco open and waiting for them in the sitting room, and they sat in a circle, on the sofa and the armchairs and a couple of kitchen chairs that had been dragged in for the occasion. There was a beer on the table too, for Joseph, but Pete picked it up and started swigging from it. Joseph was relieved. He thought that they would all go for the wine, and he would be forced to mark himself out as different straight away. He went to the fridge to get himself another one.

"Are you getting yourself a beer?" said Andy.

"Want one?"

"Yes, please."

"You're just afraid of not being one of the lads," said Nina.

"It's as good a way of choosing a drink as any," said Andy.

When they were resettled they toasted each other, and there was an awkward silence. Joseph wondered whether they'd be chatting away if he hadn't been there. His phone was burning a hole in his pocket. He'd never thought of himself as addicted to it before, but he remembered how his father once described his addiction to cigarettes: "I look down and there's a fag in my hand and I don't even know how it got there." It was just something Joseph did, everybody did, when they weren't feeling comfortable. Maybe he should start smoking. If he smoked he could just stand up and go into the back garden. Or maybe find one of those jobs where you got a call from your boss on a Saturday evening because there was a problem in the Istanbul branch. That had happened in the shop once. A customer's phone started ringing, and he said, "Hi, Steve. You'll have to forgive me, I'm just being served at the butcher's." And then he said, "Istanbul? When did that happen?" He'd seen the guy since, and he'd always wanted to ask him what had happened in Istanbul.

"So how did you two meet?" Lucy said to Nina. It was not a reasonable or thoughtful question, because Lucy would definitely be getting that one back, and then she'd have to talk about the butcher's, and all these people probably did something well paid and interesting.

"Andy's a photographer. He came to take a picture of a kitchen I had to write about."

That didn't sound interesting, but Joseph presumed it was well paid.

"I know, I know," said Nina. "There's almost no freelance work at the moment. And the money

I'm getting is what I got at the end of the nineties, when I first gave up teaching. I may have to go back."

"Oh, God. That bad."

"I haven't even got a teaching qualification," said Andy.

"Is it as bad for photographers too?" said Joseph. He was surprised to hear his own voice, but he'd said it now, and it seemed to be a relevant question, and Andy answered it in full, and Joseph asked him another one which seemed every bit as good, to him and to everyone else in the room, and the first part of the evening was up and running. When they got to the subject of how Lucy and Joseph met, it all seemed manageable.

**And he started** to see how things worked: conversation was not something imposed from above, like an examination. It was more like a sofa that worked out the shape of your arse and adjusted accordingly, except the dinner worked out the shape of your head. There was a conversation about books, a short one, but it was between Fiona and Lucy, and in any case some of it involved Michael, the writer whose house they had stayed in during the summer, so that was more gossipy than cultural. While that was going on, Pete was chatting to Nina about his kids, and it turned out that Andy, sitting next to him, was a season-ticket holder at Orient, so Joseph asked him about a kid who had just broken into the first team, the younger brother of someone Joseph knew from school.

There was a conversation about Brexit. Joseph imagined that there would always be a conversation about Brexit until it was all sorted out. There was a general agreement that it was a mess and a disaster and the country would be paying for its mistake for years; Joseph had heard all this. But then Fiona asked Joseph how he'd voted.

"Whoa," said Pete. "You can't ask that."

"He knows how we all voted," Fiona said. "Anyway, if he tells us he'd rather not say, that would be the end of it."

"And we'd all know anyway," said Nina.

This was the first time during the evening that he'd felt different from them. There were the five of them, and then there was him, and just the presumption that he might not belong to their gang, that he might have voted the other way, was enough to separate him.

Joseph looked at Lucy's face and her expression made him smile. She was trying to work out whether there was anything to be offended by.

"It's fine," Joseph said to her.

"You sure?"

"Yes. So, I had a problem. My dad voted to leave. He campaigned to leave."

"Why?"

"Because he thinks he'll be better off."

"What does he do?"

"He's a scaffolder."

"OK."

"And my mum—she voted to leave, because she works in the N.H.S., and she believed the bus and all that."

There were weary sighs around the table.

"But Lucy is a passionate remainer."

"Am I passionate?" she asked Joseph.

There was laughter.

"Yes, tell us, Joseph. Is she passionate?"

"A passionate remainer, I meant," said Lucy.

There was more laughter, at the obviousness and feebleness of the answer.

"So . . . Well, I came to a logical decision."

"Which was?"

Joseph shrugged. "I voted both ways."

"How?" said Lucy.

"Oh, I didn't cheat. I just put a cross in both boxes."

Nina and Andy laughed and applauded. Fiona, Pete, and Lucy were trying not to look scandalized.

"I didn't know you'd done that," said Lucy.

"I didn't tell you."

"Quite a silly thing to do," said Fiona.

Joseph felt a little sting. He could see that Lucy felt it too, or had at least recognized the danger.

"What if he hadn't bothered?" Lucy said. "What's the difference?"

Pete shrugged.

"There's no difference," he said.

"No," said Fiona. "If those are the choices. Apathy or I don't know what you'd call it. Pointless bloody juvenile rebellion."

"You're right," said Joseph. "I should have just voted out. I was like fifty-one percent Brexit, forty-nine percent remain."

"Oh, well, that's even worse," said Fiona.

"So his only choice was voting remain," said Lucy.

"In my opinion," said Fiona. She didn't seem to be joking.

"Trouble is, it was my vote," said Joseph.

"And you literally wasted it," said Fiona.

"And how do you feel about it now?" said Pete.

"Well, it's over, isn't it? We've just got to get on with it."

That seemed to bring the conversation to a close, and Joseph thought he detected a collective relief.

"I'd watch your step, though," said Nina. She was talking to Fiona.

"Why's that?"

"You started off by saying you wanted to listen. And then you told him you weren't interested in anything he had to say."

"When did I do that?"

"You just told him he'd made the wrong choice. And then you told him his second choice would have been wrong too."

"What am I supposed to do? I think he's wrong about everything."

"'MIDDLE-CLASS NORTH LONDONER LISTENS TO THE PEOPLE, DECIDES THEY'RE WRONG ABOUT EVERYTHING.' There's the way forward."

"Like you're not a middle-class North Londoner."

"Which is why I wouldn't dream of telling Joseph he did the wrong thing."

"What if he'd just voted in favor of hanging?"

"I didn't," said Joseph. "And I wouldn't. Two different things."

He got a laugh, then, and this time they did take the change in mood as a cue to move on—to food, schools, more football.

"How much did you hate that?" said Lucy when everyone had gone and they were stacking the dishwasher.

"Most of it was fun. And the tense bit was sort of interesting," said Joseph.

"Really? Interesting? Not insulting and really fucking annoying?"

"Oh, I didn't mind. You cared about it more than I did. I'm much younger than any of you. What do I know about any of this crap? Of course people are going to talk down to me."

"What do any of us know?"

"But see, I've never ever had an argument with friends about politics. I can't imagine I ever will."

"Really?"

"Yeah. Labor, Conservative, Brexit... Nobody I know gives much of a shit about any of it. Nothing much seems to change."

"Your dad does."

"Oh. Him. He's not a friend. He's your generation. Anyway, I wouldn't argue with him. I'd just be like, whatever. I don't see the point."

"You don't see the point of the future of the country?"

"Not really. Aren't we all fucked anyway?"

"Why?"

"Aren't sea levels going to rise a foot and we'll all be underwater? I care about that."

"Maybe you should vote for someone who'll do something about it."

"What, the Green Party? Isn't it all too late for that?"

"You're clever. You just ask questions instead of giving your opinion."

"It's not clever. It's because I never know for definite. I want someone to tell me the answers. I mean, yeah, that Fiona woman is hard to like. But she seems like she knows. She's so sure."

"Yeah. That's what a college education does for you."

"What, it teaches you everything?"

"No. It just makes you sure."

"So why aren't you sure?"

"I don't know. The older I get, the more I realize I don't know much about much."

When they went to bed, Joseph fell asleep within moments. Lucy lay there in the dark, still angry with Fiona, wondering how many of her friends she liked, and how many she would still like, by the time Brexit and Joseph were over.

**Joseph's birthday was** on a Sunday, which meant that his mother would be expecting him to eat at hers, with his sister. Neither of them had met Lucy and the boys yet. Both sides had asked, but he hadn't done anything about it, and his excuses and blocks, which had always sounded feeble even to him, were now being met with good-humored teasing (Lucy) and outright hostility (his mother).

"Are you ashamed of us?" said Lucy, secure in his pride and love.

"Are you ashamed of us?" said his mother, who since Joseph's disappearance lived in constant fear that he was ashamed of her, or the house, or the neighborhood, or something else that she could do nothing about. "Yes," he said to Lucy. "Of course not," he said to his mother.

"We'll go out on Saturday night with the boys," said Lucy. "And you can go to eat with your mum on the day."

"She'll want to know why you're not there."

"I've got kids."

"She'll want to know why they're not there."

"School night."

"She'll want to eat at six."

"So we'll come."

"Christ, no," said Joseph.

"Why not?"

Why not? They could both think of plenty of reasons why not. Lucy wanted to avoid the disapproval of a woman her own age, and for some reason she was worried that her children would be judged too. They probably owned too much, talked too often, used language that might horrify

Joseph's mother, a woman who went to church every Sunday. (Lucy wondered what difference church made, and whether disapproval was easier to come by as a result of attendance. It could go either way, in theory, but the churchgoers she had known, mostly friends of her parents, didn't seem to have had their minds stretched by their faith.) Joseph was afraid that his mother would feel intimidated by Lucy—by her confidence, her clothes, her figure, her curiosity. (Joseph wondered whether Lucy was curious because she was confident. She didn't mind where she looked, and she asked anything she wanted to know. He hoped his mother was different at work. He hoped she felt she knew what she was doing, and that her competence gave her the eyes and ears and voice that Lucy had.)

"So when am I ever going to meet your mother?"

"Dunno."

"Will I meet her?"

"I suppose."

"But not at any family occasion."

"If my sister gets married. You'll meet everyone then."

"Any sign of that?"

"No."

"What if I met her somewhere for a cup of tea?"

"What?"

He was genuinely uncomprehending, and Lucy laughed.

"A cup of tea," she said. "Me and your mother."

"Well...What for? What are you going to say?"

"I'm not going to say anything. It would be a chat."

"What kind of chat?"

"One where you know somebody a bit better at the end of it than you did at the beginning."

"Oh, God. Without me there?"

"Yes. Although if you wanted to come, you'd be welcome."

"Why don't I just pass on a message?"

"I haven't got a message," said Lucy. "I just want to understand more about you."

"No," said Joseph. "I'm sorry."

"Are you serious?"

"Yes. I'd prefer to split up."

"The thing is," said Lucy, "she wants to meet me, right?"

"Yes."

"And I want to meet her."

"So you say."

"And you gave me your home number ages ago, when you were babysitting."

"This isn't working. It's not you, it's me. I'd like to stay friends. I've met someone else."

"What is it? Seriously? What are you afraid of?"

"It's just normal. People don't want people to meet their mothers."

"Rubbish."

"Excuse me? You basically told me I couldn't go to your parents' house."

"I was protecting you."

"Well, I'm protecting you."

"From what?"

He was protecting everyone—Lucy, his mother, himself. He couldn't have articulated what made him so uncomfortable. All he knew was that God had put all those bus stops between his old home and his new one for a reason. It didn't matter what he felt, though, because Lucy called her anyway.

# 16

Is that Mrs. Campbell?"

"Speaking."

"This is Lucy Fairfax. I'm Joseph's..."

Why hadn't she thought of the right word before she'd called? She'd spent a lot of time thinking of venues, and reasons, and times, and dates, but for some reason she'd skipped through the hardest part of the conversation.

"I know who you are," said Mrs. Campbell.

She said these words neutrally, with neither warmth nor froideur, but all Lucy heard was the absence of warmth, which quickly became the presence of a chill.

"I was just wondering... Well, what with Joseph's birthday coming up, and then Christmas and so on..."

"Yes."

But it wasn't a yes that was encouraging any shortcuts. She was merely inviting Lucy to continue flapping and stuttering.

"Well, I wondered if you wanted to meet."

"Oh, I see."

"Without Joseph."

"I wouldn't want him there, telling me what I can and can't say."

"But if you don't want to..."

"No, no. I think that's sensible. He's moved out without ever saying anything. I suppose he's living with you."

"He wouldn't miss his night a week at home."

"He missed last week's."

"Last week, yes. But..."

"Where would you like to meet? Do you want to come round here?"

"Or shall I meet you halfway? In a, a café or somewhere?"

"Oh."

"I'd love to come to your house, though, if that's OK."

"Of course."

They arranged a date and a time, and when Lucy hung up she was slightly sweaty. She had met countless parents over the years, but none of them had ever discombobulated her like this. She didn't mind being judged as a teacher, not anymore, not since she got good at it. But now she was going to be judged as a woman and a partner, by a peer, and there was nothing to protect her.

**Mrs. Campbell lived** in a terraced house, ex-council, probably built in the 1960s, Lucy reckoned. When Paul had finally realized that he wasn't moving back into their old  marital home, and thought he should buy somewhere with three bedrooms and a back garden, he'd sent her a link to a house like this one, not far from here. It was on sale for £400,000. You couldn't buy anything like it near his former family home for less than £1.5 million. Yes, Lucy's new house had an extra floor, but that couldn't account for the million-pound gap. The difference was everything else—transport, schools, proximity to the large estates that had become notorious in the 1980s.

She walked up and down the road so that she arrived forty-five seconds after the appointed time, and then rang the front doorbell. She tried to recall the last time she'd been as nervous before a social occasion. It would have had to involve a teenage boyfriend, but the boyfriend would surely have been on the other side of the door, not in a leisure center a couple of miles away. Maybe this tea would go so well that she could make a complicated joke about teenage boyfriends and Joseph and how she'd never really moved on, and Joseph's mother would produce a scandalized chuckle.

Mrs. Campbell looked steadily at her before saying anything. There would be no scandalized chuckling. She was taking Lucy in. Lucy decided that she couldn't do much about being taken in, so she held the other woman's gaze and smiled. She was smiling at a large, unsmiling woman who, Lucy guessed, wouldn't warm to her for several years to come. Lucy had done some terrifyingly adult things over the last few years, some involving Paul, some involving school. She'd been to an inquest, changed her husband's soiled trousers, had several dealings with the police. None of it, however, had been her fault. Mrs. Campbell's obvious dislike was her fault.

"Come in," said Mrs. Campbell, and she ushered her through to the sitting room. The tea had already been made, and there was an empty cup waiting for her on a coffee table by the armchair that Lucy was guided toward. The steaming tea-pot on the tray seemed to suggest that Joseph's mother was tense too, that she'd been looking for a way to count off the last three or four minutes.

"This is a nice house," said Lucy, and she meant it.

"It belonged to my parents," said Mrs. Campbell.

"They were over in Ladbroke Grove with everyone else when they first arrived. But when they applied for a council house, this is where they ended up. And then Mrs. Thatcher let them buy it, cheap. I didn't agree with everything she did, but that was marvelous."

Lucy had strong views on the privatization of social housing, and she had expressed them many times. She had never expressed them to a beneficiary of Mrs. Thatcher's largesse, however, and she could now see that she never would. She'd save her bitter opposition for the ears of people with six- or seven-figure mortgages.

The room was spotlessly tidy. There was a matching gray three-piece suite, and photos of the children everywhere, on every shelf and mantelpiece and wall. If it had been up to her she'd have walked around the room, inspecting the place for every trace of Joseph; from where she'd been sitting, she could see an unbelievably cute picture of him in his school uniform on the mantelpiece. He looked fourteen or fifteen.

Lucy nodded toward it and smiled.

"Bless him," she said. "When was that taken?"

"Year Ten," said Mrs. Campbell. "So, what... 2008? What were you doing in 2008?"

"Pretty much the same as I'm doing now. Oh, and having a baby."

This was, Lucy thought, an attempt to shock her into grasping just how young Joseph was, and how old she was. But actually, 2008 and babies seemed like decades ago.

"So a bit more married than you are now."

"A lot more," said Lucy. Was that the right or wrong answer? Probably wrong.

"How married are you?"

"If you are looking for a percentage..."

"No." Not a smile.

"Well. I'm not at all married, but I'm not divorced. My ex-husband has a new partner. We are in the middle of divorcing."

"And then what?"

It wasn't teenage boyfriends who had produced nerves with this kind of twang. It was job interviews. This was a job interview, where you had to ignore what you might actually think, and suppress what you might want to say, in order to work out what the right answer might be. The trouble was, she didn't really understand the question.

"Well. Nothing. Just...No marriage anymore."

"Meaning you'd be free to marry Joseph."

Fucking hell. Now what was the answer? Was she expected to marry Joseph? Or was Mrs. Campbell suspecting her of some carefully set marital trap? She couldn't second-guess now. She had to give some kind of approximation of the truth.

"I have no intention of marrying Joseph," Lucy said. "He's too young, and he will want children one day. That won't be with me."

"So why slow him up?"

"Is that how you see it?"

"I don't think there's another way of seeing it."

"Mrs. Campbell..."

Lucy paused, so that Mrs. Campbell could say, call me whatever her first name was. That's what always happened, at least on television. But after a few seconds, with nothing forthcoming, she realized there would be silence forever unless she said something.

"He needs to find his way first," said Lucy. "He shouldn't be thinking about a family until he's thirty. And if we are still together, I'll get out of the way a couple of years before that. To give him a...a run-in."

"Well," said Mrs. Campbell. "That will be a very difficult thing to do. You'll be what? Nearly fifty?"

Lucy nodded and made the kind of face— HELP—that people always made when they thought about their age. It was a joke, of course.

"So by then you'll be looking at spending the rest of your life alone," said Mrs. Campbell. "Hard to give up a warm body in bed when you get to that time of life."

Lucy set her mouth firmly and nodded, in recognition of the tragic fate that awaited her, but she didn't believe it for a second. Where did her confidence and optimism come from? She knew her life would not be over at fifty. She would still be ambitious, in her private and professional lives. She might be single, but she would still be working on the assumption that she was attractive to somebody, physically and otherwise. This assumption might prove to be utterly baseless, but it was going to be there.

"I'll probably be ready by then," said Lucy.

"Oh, nothing prepares you for the loneliness."

"Anyway," said Lucy brightly. "Any ideas for Joseph's birthday? Would you and your daughter like to come to dinner?"

"Well," said Mrs. Campbell. She seemed to be examining the offer from every side, looking for holes, spikes, trip wires, light dustings of anthrax. And then, finding none, she accepted. They could move on to the photos.

A couple of Joseph's friends from the leisure center wanted to take him out on the Saturday night, to a club in Dalston. Lucy knew there were good clubs in Dalston. She'd read something about them in the **Guardian.**

"Do you want to come?" Joseph said.

Lucy laughed.

"What's so funny?"

"I don't think I belong in Dalston clubs. And you don't think that either, otherwise you'd have been able to make eye contact while you were asking me."

"You don't mind?"

"I minded about the eye contact."

"Sorry. I meant to look at you, but…"

"But then your enthusiasm failed you."

He didn't correct her. He was relieved that she didn't want to come. He didn't know what she'd wear, and he was worried about whether she'd want to dance. He shouldn't judge her on the kitchen-jigging, he knew, but he had nothing else to go on, and if it was representative of the way she might move on a night out, he couldn't take the risk.

"Will you get slaughtered?"

"Why?"

"I was just interested. I've never seen you worse for wear."

"I don't like it much. I'll have two beers and a lot of Coke Zero."

"What about drugs?"

"Nope. Weed when I was in my teens. But all that roadman stuff gets on my nerves."

Joseph had been a roadman for about ten days,

when he was fifteen, although he could no longer remember whether that's what they were called back then. It was the same thing, anyway: weed, hoodies, bikes. He was messing around with people he didn't like very much, people who did stupid things. He had ended up spending three hours in a police station. He hadn't done anything wrong, but the person on the bike next to him had robbed a kid's phone, so he didn't feel that he could complain too much about harassment and profiling and the rest. His mother had to come and get him out, and her distress and anger had ended his criminal associations on the spot. She also went to visit the family of the kid who pinched the phone, so Joseph couldn't have gone out even if he'd wanted to, for fear of what might happen when he did. Ahmaz was in prison now, as far as Joseph knew. Or if he wasn't, he'd be going back soon.

"So will you dance at the club?"

"Depends if I like the music. And whether I have more than two beers."

"So you won't drink much and you might not dance."

Joseph shrugged.

"So why don't you want me there? Is it anything to do with women?"

"No!"

His shock was genuine, she could tell.

"It's OK if it is."

Did she mean it? She had said it, certainly, but she wasn't entirely sure why, and it was hardly consistent with her recent behavior. One day she was visiting Joseph's mother, trying to demonstrate to her that she was genuine and solid, that Joseph was embedded in her life; the next she seemed to be suggesting some kind of 1970s Scandinavian arrangement.

"Why would you say that?"

"Because you're a young man, and..."

"And what?"

"I don't know."

But she did know, now. She just didn't know how to explain it. She had been worried about the dinner party with Fiona and the others. However much she tried to reassure him, she was afraid that he'd be uncomfortable, silent, alienated; and she was afraid that her friends would think he was dim, surly, inappropriate. None of that had happened, but the unease had been there. A night out in Dalston was his equivalent of the dinner party, and it seemed that his fear of embarrassment was greater than his desire to integrate her into his social life.

"Come," he said.

"You don't mean it."

He meant something, although he wasn't quite sure what. He meant that he loved her, and didn't mean to hurt her, and that she was worth more than any amount of funny looks in a dark East London nightclub.

**She looked great,** he thought. She was wearing a little bit more makeup than usual, but not enough for it to seem as though she was making too much of an effort. Skinny jeans, which she always looked good in. A top with a tiny bit of glitter. They met in the Six Bells opposite the club: Kevin B., also known as White Kevin, Kevan G., his girlfriend, Rose, Jan the assistant manager, her boyfriend, Azad, Suzie and Becca the swimming teachers who were or were not a couple, depending on who you listened to; Mikey West. Staff shortages meant they had to put a sign on the front door of the leisure center, CLOSED FOR A PRIVATE EVENT, which was sort of true. They didn't know what kind of trouble they'd get into, or even whether anyone at the council would notice.

Everyone was in there already when they arrived. They were at a big table in the back of the pub, and they all cheered when they saw him.

He had thought carefully about what he was

going to say and when he would say it, and he got
it out of the way.

"Everyone, this is my girlfriend, Lucy."

"Your girlfriend?" said White Kevin. It would
be him. Joseph and Lucy braced themselves, in
their different ways. "You never told us you had a
girlfriend."

"Yes, I did," said Joseph, but of course he hadn't,
he now realized.

Suzie and Becca made room on the bench for
Lucy, and Joseph sat diagonally opposite them in a
space between Azad and Rose. Lucy started chatting to Becca straight away, Rose joined in, and that
was that. Nobody cared. Azad had gone to the bar
to get them drinks, and Joseph watched how Lucy
operated: it was a beautiful thing. She smiled
encouragement when people talked, she laughed at
their jokes, the girls listened intently when she had
something to say. Nobody was going to ask what he
was doing with her. He could see, however, that
they might wonder what she was doing with him.

There was a queue outside the club, and when
Joseph looked down the line, he could see that
Lucy was not the oldest person in it by any means.
On top of that, the people who might have been

the same age as her looked years older, some of them—the men, anyway, black men and white men, all of them with younger women. He could see heads that had been shaved to deal with baldness, hats to cover the baldness up, gray beards. He began to see that his panic said much more about him than about Lucy, or London. When he tuned in to Lucy's voice, he realized that she was talking to Becca about sex.

"What about lube?" said Lucy.

"Maybe," said Becca.

"The thing with lube," said Lucy, "is that you should avoid flavors."

"There are flavors?" said Becca.

"Someone bought me a candyfloss one as a joke, but my partner at the time couldn't deal with it at all."

Who was her partner at the time? And how had this started? He had mostly been talking to Azad about what was wrong with rugby, and when he did hear anything of Lucy's conversation, it seemed to be about work and her boys. But somehow, during the second drink or maybe even as they were crossing the road, they had got on to the subject of feminine something—not hygiene, exactly, but a related field. Feminine mechanics, maybe.

"So what do you do now?" said Becca. "If you're, you know..."

"Well."

Joseph got out his phone and tried to become absorbed in his Instagram feed. Lucy lowered her voice.

"It turned out to be a partner problem, rather than a physiological problem."

Joseph wondered whether the people in front of him, who were not part of his group, would mind if he pushed in.

"Oh," said Becca, and then there was silence.

"Hey," Lucy said softly. "Hey."

Joseph still wouldn't look round, but if he'd had to guess, he would say that Becca was crying. Suzie was ahead of him, laughing with Kevan G. and Rose, but as nobody knew whether Becca was gay or straight, nor whether she and Suzie were in a relationship, he didn't think it was his place to alert Suzie to Becca's distress.

"I think that might be my problem too," Becca said.

"I'm sorry," Lucy said. "I didn't mean...I didn't know...Would you like to go back to the pub for a bit?"

"Would you mind?"

Lucy tapped Joseph on the shoulder.

"We're just going to the pub for a bit," said Lucy.

"Sure," said Joseph. He didn't ask why, which he realized proved he'd been listening to every word they'd been saying.

"Won't be long."

That seemed hopeful to Joseph, given the emotional and physical difficulties that she was trying to deal with, but he didn't argue.

The club seemed to be built of solid and impenetrable surfaces: sweating concrete, a wall of thick heat, metallic sheets of noise, flailing bone and muscle. Joseph and his friends pushed their way through to a corner, away from the bar, away from the D.J. and the dance floor, a little rural backwater that was of no use to anybody, but which at least provided sanctuary and air. They made a pile of coats and jackets on the floor, because the queue for the cloakroom was impossible, and suddenly Joseph was the center of attention.

"Fuck me, Joseph," said Kevan G.

"What?" said Joseph.

"Yeah," said Jan. "Bloody hell."

"What?" said Joseph.

"That's actually your girlfriend?"

"Oh."

He wouldn't say any more until he understood

the reason for the disbelief and the profanities, but he really didn't think it could be her age. She was older than them, yes, but not so old that she would provoke shock and outrage, he didn't think.

"She's so lovely," said Jan. "And so pretty."

"And hot," said White Kevin.

"That's what I just said," said Jan. "But in a less sexist way."

"I don't see why hot is sexist and pretty isn't," said White Kevin. "Men and women can be hot. Only women can be pretty."

"That's sexist as well."

"Oh, I fucking give up," said White Kevin.

"Good," said Jan.

"Where is she, anyway?" said Suzie.

"She went back to the pub with Becca," said Joseph.

"Why?"

"I don't know. I think Becca got upset about something."

"What?"

"I don't know."

He wouldn't know how to begin. If Suzie went off to the pub because she was worried, or angry, or to beat Lucy up, then at least they'd know whether Suzie and Becca were a couple. Suzie gave nothing away, though, and she didn't move.

"Anyway," said Jan. "I know your track record.

If you mess her about, or lose interest, you'll have all of us to answer to."

"Not me," said Azad. "I don't give a toss. She seems nice, though."

He'd had two more beers and was dancing when he saw Lucy come down the stairs. She was on her own. He pushed through to meet her, and led her to the coats backwater.

"Where's Becca?"

"She went home. I'm sorry."

"What are you sorry for?"

"If I hadn't started blathering on about lube, she wouldn't have got upset."

"You weren't to know. All your other lube conversations, it's probably been fine."

"She asked me. I never talk about lube."

"I heard the whole conversation. You started it."

"But she asked me about...Anyway. She's gone off to finish with her girlfriend."

"Her girlfriend?"

"Yes," said Lucy firmly, as if she were closing down an argument—which she was, sort of, but it was an argument between the staff that she knew nothing about.

"Not Suzie?"

"No. They split up months ago. But she regrets it."

Lucy had found out more in ten minutes than any of the people who worked with Becca every day.

"She was dying to talk to someone," said Lucy.

"She could have talked to any of us."

"Yes. But she didn't. Will you dance with me?" said Lucy.

"You don't want a drink?"

"No. I had two more in the pub. I'm already halfway to being pissed."

"Why not go the rest of the way?"

She just smiled and led Joseph by the hand into the middle of the dance floor. The D.J. was playing a remix of "Body Drop," which was basically a drum track, a synth note, and a rap, but which sounded great at that volume, spooky and futuristic. People were bouncing, arms up in the air, mostly because there wasn't much room for anything else. Lucy was making shapes in the sky with her fingers and pulling goofy faces at Joseph. He focused all of his energy on his toes, forbidding them to curl.

Some of their crowd were already dancing; the rest joined them when they saw Lucy. They all started doing her hand movements. They weren't taking the piss. Lucy just seemed to add to their enjoyment of the evening.

**Lucy roasted a chicken** for Joseph's birthday dinner, and while she was cooking, Joseph prepared the boys for his mother's visit.

"She doesn't like bad language."

"What are we talking about here?" said Dylan. "Fs and Cs?"

"Anything to do with sex or the toilet," said Joseph.

"Toilet paper?" said Al.

"You know that's not what I mean."

"Toilet brush?" said Dylan.

"Toilet seat?"

"Ladies?"

"Gents?"

"Shut up a minute," said Joseph.

When he told the boys to shut up, they did. Lucy found this simultaneously useful and depressing. She was consoled only by the knowledge that it was nothing to do with him being male, because Paul was even more ineffectual than her.

"Crap, shit, piss, tits, knob, dick, cock, any of it."

The boys knew better than to laugh, and this time their sobriety was straightforwardly depressing.

"So what words are we supposed to use instead?"

"Just don't talk about any of it. It's a meal. Nobody wants to hear about your penis during a meal."

Lucy wanted to repeat the word "penis," to see if she could introduce some levity into the proceedings, but that would be childish in several ways.

"Anything else?"

"Oh, no Christs or Jesuses, either."

"God?"

"If you must. You're clever boys. I want her to see it."

"Hey," said Al. "Maybe Dylan could ask me about the capitals of the world. I know most of them."

"Not that sort of clever," said Joseph.

"I haven't got a clue what to say now," said Al.

**In the end,** neither of the boys said very much for the first hour or so, because both of them fell violently in love with Grace. They wouldn't have admitted or even necessarily known that this is what had happened to them, but the signs were obvious: the occasional blush, the goggle-eyed attention whenever Grace spoke. Eventually the awed silence was replaced by a comical willingness to help, an exaggerated politeness, and the occasional spelling of polysyllabic words that came up in the conversation. Lucy didn't have to worry for a moment about inappropriate language, unless you counted the words they attempted to use to show their mastery of English. "Can I give you some assistance, Mum?" said Dylan. "A-S-S-I-S-T-A-N-C-E," said Al. And so on. Joseph rolled his eyes a lot. Grace was amused.

**Meanwhile** Lucy and Mrs. Campbell watched on fondly. They were, after all, in strangely similar situations: their boys were courting, with varying degrees of success. There would come a time when Al and Dylan would be sitting in somebody else's kitchen, trying to decide which version of themselves to present to someone who might or might not like them. Maybe she would be with them. She felt a little pang of anticipatory panic. She would be landed with important relationships not of her choosing. She felt grateful to Grace and her mother, at least for their apparent willingness to suspend disbelief. Perhaps her age made it easier for them; they were probably telling themselves that they wouldn't have to sit here in five years' time.

———

"We keep jumping over hurdles," said Joseph that night. He was reading something on his phone. Lucy was halfway through a book that she wasn't enjoying.

"What do you mean?"

"This weekend it was my friends and my family. That's a lot. And I've met some of yours, and... Anyway."

"There's nothing left," Lucy said.

"Well, my dad. But you won't get on with him because he's hard to get on with, and it doesn't matter anyway."

"And you still haven't met my parents, but ditto."

"So there we are. Sorted."

"I'm lying in bed with a twenty-three-year-old who is scrolling through his phone while I'm reading a tedious novel that was nominated for the Booker Prize. What could go wrong?"

"So stop reading it."

"I never give up on books," said Lucy.

"Why not?"

"Because... I don't know. I'm scared that once I start, I'll never stop."

"Do you always read boring books, then?"

She laughed.

"I try not to."

"Not sure you're trying hard enough."

Now that they were living together, and bed did

not always mean sex (although it meant sex much more often than Lucy was used to), Joseph knew that Lucy achieved oblivion quite quickly, and usually had to have a book removed from her chest and her bedside light turned off for her. Lucy now knew that Joseph's phone addiction didn't stop when he was under a duvet wearing shorts and a T-shirt.

He went back to his article, completely absorbed. She re-read the most recent paragraph of her novel, and then read it again. The book was about the relationship between a gardener working on one of Capability Brown's commissions and the daughter of the house. It wasn't even that sort of relationship. The daughter of the house was helping the gardener to understand that he might love men, "as the Greeks loved men." He seemed none the wiser so far. There was page after page about Brown's philosophy. She sighed when she turned the page and saw another long unbroken paragraph about landscaping as punctuation.

"If he wins, we're fucked."

"Who?"

"Fucking Trump."

"What are you looking at?"

"An article on **Ebony**."

"Who's fucked?"

"We all are. But I guess especially black people in America."

"And women."

"And Muslims."

"And Mexicans. Are you interested in American politics?"

"I guess. More than British politics, anyway. Ever since I was a kid, everything I listened to led me back to the Civil Rights movement somehow or another. You go from hip-hop to James Brown to Aretha to Martin Luther King. Or from Public Enemy to Malcolm X. It's not the same here. Boring. Nothing very inspiring, anyway. Brexit and, I don't know. Jeremy Corbyn. I don't care."

Since Brexit she had avoided the news. She was now mostly focusing on Capability Brown. Perhaps he was right: there were no hurdles. And then what?

# 17

He didn't know whether to wake her up, but he was angry, and he didn't want to be angry on his own.

"Lucy."

She looked at him, and then sat up in bed.

"No."

"Yes."

"Christ. I'm sorry," said Lucy.

"Why are you sorry for me and not for you? It's awful for everyone," said Joseph. "Awful for the whole fucking world. Awful for women. He goes on about grabbing pussies."

"I know. But I suppose it's like Brexit. The people who voted for him will be happy."

"It's nothing like Brexit. Brexit might turn out to be a good thing. This bastard retweets stuff from white supremacists."

"Racists voted for Brexit."

"Racists like my dad? This is different."

"I know," she said.

"You just said it was the same. Trump retweeted something with the Twitter handle 'White Genocide Now.' The Ku Klux Klan support him. You don't know. Really."

He was angry, and he wanted to pick a fight with the first white person he saw. This morning, like every other morning, it was Lucy. This felt personal, in a way that no other political event in his lifetime had. And if Trump was President, then he'd come to England, shake hands with the Prime Minister, and she was supposed to represent him. Wasn't she? Later, he wished they hadn't argued. He wished he hadn't had an excuse.

Success, when it came, was nothing like he'd imagined it would be. It was fast, and meant almost nothing, as far as he could tell. £Man remixed the track he'd made with Jaz, and put it up on Spotify, and because £Man had blown up, J. and J., as they called themselves quickly and without any thought, got ninety thousand streams within a few days. £Man was asked to remix another couple of tracks by people who were hot, and Joseph got swept up in the slipstream. A jeans company asked him to do something for an ad. "Gonna Drive," as they called the track quickly and without any thought, got played on Rinse F.M. a few times. And then the day that he had woken Lucy up to tell her the news about Trump, Joseph and Jaz went to a massive club in Leeds to do a P.A.

There was no money involved anywhere, although maybe the jeans company would pay him something if they used the track, and maybe the club in Leeds would give him a paid D.J. set eventually, and maybe the record company who'd set £Man up with a deal would be interested in a similar arrangement with Joseph, if the track continued to build. Someone was making a few quid somewhere, but it wasn't J. and J. That was the way the world worked now. Jaz was happy, though.

"I never thought I'd have a job where I got to stay in a hotel and other people paid the bill," said Jaz when they had found seats on the train.

"Yeah, I'm not sure it's a job yet," said Joseph. And they were staying in a cheap and crappy chain hotel way out of town, so they were unlikely to feel the glamour.

"Still," said Jaz. "It's all amazing. What you wearing?"

"How do you mean?" said Joseph.

"What are you wearing?" She repeated the question, but with more incredulity.

"You can see what I'm wearing."

"Tonight."

"Oh. Well. You can see what I'm wearing."

"You didn't bring anything else?"

"T-shirt and underwear for tomorrow. They haven't come to look at me." He was wearing Nike joggers, his red Adidas Gazelles, and a yellow retro Adidas T-shirt.

"You should try wearing a few more brands," said Jaz. "Can't you get some Puma specs or something? With PUMA in big letters on the lenses?"

She was being sarcastic, and he ignored her.

"You don't want to know what I'm wearing?"

"Why would I? I'll see it later."

"I think I'd better prepare you otherwise you might have a heart attack. It's a skintight black jumpsuit. No room for anything on underneath."

Joseph thought his own thoughts, and got out his phone.

When they went to the hotel to leave their bags, they found that the promoter had booked one room instead of two.

"We'll sort it out later," said Jaz.

When they got to the club, neither of them

remembered to mention the problem to the promoter. Joseph suspected that neither of them had forgotten the problem, though.

**The P.A. was both exciting** and stupid. People cheered when they came on, but Joseph had to sit behind a keyboard pretending he was doing something, and Jaz had to mime to the song. She was good at it, though, and completely nerveless, like she'd always expected to be gyrating in front of a crowd in a nightclub, and she couldn't understand why she'd had to wait this long. The skintight black jumpsuit was as advertised, and she moved well, and the crowd loved her. When they left the stage she was buzzing, and she kissed Joseph on the lips as they were walking toward their disgusting little dressing room.

"That was amazing," she said.

"Yeah."

He felt flat. You could look at it two ways: all sorts of people who were doing well had started out like this, with phony appearances in nightclubs. Also, all sorts of people nobody had ever heard of had started out like this, and ended like this, and that group was a lot bigger than the first group.

"I'm hungry," said Jaz. "And I want to get drunk. And I want to get you drunk."

"No need for that," said Joseph helplessly.

**Afterward he felt** so sick that he thought he might actually have to throw up.

"You OK?" said Jaz.

"Yeah. Good."

"We'll have time to do that again in the morning."

He didn't say anything. What was the point? He would either have sex with Jaz again or he wouldn't. Right now he didn't think he would, because he had had his fill, and he was feeling guilty and miserable as fuck. But he'd been pretty sure he wouldn't earlier in the day, and look what had just happened.

"Where have you gone?" said Jaz.

"I'm here," he said, but he wanted to be anywhere else.

"I knew we'd end up like this in the end," said Jaz. "And I knew you'd give up on gray tings."

When Jaz fell asleep, he got dressed and went out looking for something to eat. He was starving. That seemed like a metaphor: in his head he was sick to his stomach, but he was starving and he had to have food. He had no control over his appetites.

———

**Back in London,** he went straight home to his mother's house. She was at work. He had no clothes there anymore, so he washed everything he was wearing and everything he'd worn the day before, and sat around in an old dressing gown waiting for it all to dry. He didn't know when he'd have access to the rest of his wardrobe.

He turned the T.V. on, and watched **Sky Sports News**, and then an old compilation of Premier League goals, and then the teatime quizzes. Lucy texted him during **Eggheads**.

**You OK? What time are you back?**

**Staying at my mum's tonight.** Even remembering the apostrophe made him sad.

**Why?**

**Will explain soon.**

**Is everything OK?**

**Nobody ill.** He didn't want to use another apostrophe.

**But is everything OK?**

He turned the sound off on his phone and put it down the side of the sofa, just for a few minutes, and then fell asleep.

His mother woke him up two hours later.

"What are you doing here?"

"I'm staying the night."

"Why?"

"No reason."

"Has she thrown you out?"

"No." And then, because his self-loathing was uncontainable, "But she should."

"Why? What have you done?"

He sighed.

"The usual."

"You cheated on her?"

"Yes."

He didn't feel good about telling someone, exactly, but it was a relief to let some of his shame escape. He was beginning to think it might make him burst.

"Joseph."

"I know."

"No, you don't. You don't know at all."

Joseph had used those words when he got angry with Lucy about Trump. So he was thinking about her, and he knew his mother was thinking of her most recent, and maybe her last, relationship, with a man who had cheated on her, many times, just as he had cheated on his first wife while he was seeing Joseph's mother. This man had ended her marriage, and had replaced it with nothing that was worth having.

"You've told her?" his mother said.

"Not yet."

"When are you planning on doing that, then?"

"I don't know. The weekend, I suppose."

"You're going over there now."

"I can't."

"Because?"

"Because I can't."

"Because you're scared. You're not staying here."

"Great. Thanks."

"You can come back afterward. But you tell her first."

"I haven't got any clothes."

"Where are they?"

"In the washing machine."

But he'd put them in the dryer hours ago. They would offer him no relief, unless they'd shrunk so much that he literally couldn't put them on, and even then his mother would probably make him go on the bus in his dressing gown.

———

He **nearly got** off the bus at most of the stops. He
sat downstairs, near the doors, and he stood up
just about every time they opened. Alternative
plans were forming in his head: he'd go to his sister's, although she probably wouldn't let him
through the door if she found out why he was
knocking on it. Or to his dad's—his dad wouldn't
care what he'd done, which was one of the reasons
he couldn't bear to stay with him. Or he'd just
walk all night. He got three texts from Jaz during
the journey, and he didn't reply to any of them.
She seemed to be working under the assumption
that their night in Leeds marked the beginning of
a long relationship. The first text said, **What we
doing tomorrow?**

He wished he smoked. He wished he was a
proper drinker. He wished he took drugs. If nothing else, he'd have to go to a corner shop, or find
a dealer, and that would kill some time. Maybe
Lucy would go to bed early, if he spent ages looking for drugs. There wouldn't be many dealers
near her house. He'd have to go to Camden or
somewhere. What would he choose to become
addicted to? He googled "Best drugs" and found a
lot of helpful suggestions. He liked the look of
ketamine. He knew people who did it, but he
didn't really know what it was. According to
Wikipedia, it induced a trancelike state while

providing pain relief, sedation, and memory loss. He could take it just before he arrived at Lucy's house, say what he had to say, and collapse. And when he woke up he wouldn't remember any of it. Lucy would, though. He couldn't take a drug for that.

**He didn't do** any of those things. He didn't get off the bus, he didn't take any drugs. He did, however, arrive at her house in a trancelike state. He couldn't believe what he'd done, or what he was about to do. And she hadn't gone to bed.

He had a key but he knocked anyway. She opened the door cautiously, and then gave a big, loving smile when she saw him.

"I didn't think you were coming! Why didn't you text! Have you lost your key? It's so nice to see you!"

She stepped forward to kiss him and he stopped her, and she looked puzzled, and then anxious.

"I have to talk to you."

"Oh," she said, and her expression changed immediately. She knew. What else could the subject have been?

She ushered him into the house, and he told her before they'd even sat down. She was walking in front of him and he told her back, right between the shoulder blades. That was the last opportunity for cowardice, the not looking at her, and he took it. It was better than some of the others he'd been thinking of.

"Jaz?" she said.

"Yes."

She sat down on the arm of a chair and looked at him. He tried to hold her look.

"And now?"

He wasn't expecting that question. He thought now took care of itself, but apparently it didn't.

"Now what?"

"Are you with Jaz now? Is that what you're saying?"

"No."

"So what are you saying?"

He'd clearly forgotten that Lucy liked to ask direct questions.

"Does it matter what I say?"

"Of course."

"So you'd just, you know, forget about it?"

"No," she said. "Of course not. But there's not much point in me deciding to forget it if you're off anyway."

"I'm not off."

"OK."

For one blissful moment he thought that might be it—that in Lucy's world, people said "OK" and everything went back to how it had been, but he had veered too far in the other direction. Things weren't bad simple, and they weren't good simple.

"I think you should go home now."

He didn't try to argue, and he hadn't got an argument anyway.

**Lucy didn't know** when she would go back to Joseph's shop, but she wasn't buying her meat there at the moment. She went to the supermarket, in the car. So this was why local shops were neglected by local people, despite all protestations to the contrary: local people slept with the people who worked in them, and were then too embarrassed to go back when it all went wrong. She hadn't slept with anybody in Sainsbury's, and from what she'd seen so far, she didn't think she would. She used the girl down the road for babysitting, once when she went to the cinema, once when she went to a staff member's birthday drinks in the Three Crowns round the corner from school.

She was hurt but not bitter, sad but not angry. She felt foolish, above all. She'd entered into a steady relationship with a young man in his early twenties. What did young men do? They slept with other people. That's why nobody got married when they were twenty-three: they weren't done yet. Of course, it sometimes turned out that people weren't done at thirty-three, forty-three, or eighty-three, even though they thought they were, but the point is that they thought they were, and life—addictions, new people, whatever—got in the way. She'd known she wouldn't end up with Joseph because he wasn't done yet. So if she'd known that, why had she put any weight on him? He was a wonky table, a glass skylight, thin ice. But people enjoyed thin ice! They liked looking at it, or skimming stones across it, or cracking it! They just tried to avoid walking on it, when they knew it was thin (which Lucy had). So was there a way of skimming stones across Joseph, meta-phorically? Or chucking stones on him, just for fun, with no chance of causing damage? Even though she wanted to a bit? She had no idea.

He texted her most days, and she replied, but the conversations were brief, terse, polite. And then he called and asked her out to dinner.

"Just to talk," he said.

"As opposed to . . . ?"

"Yes. Sorry. That was a stupid thing to say."

"Anyway. I'd like to."

"I'll book somewhere."

"OK."

"Will I need to do that?"

"If you're taking me to the Ivy, yes. If you're taking me to Pizza Express, no."

"Is the Ivy very expensive? And where is it?"

"I don't want to go to the Ivy."

She'd never been to the Ivy, but she knew about it. Was that the difference between them? Neither of them could afford it, and neither of them would have been able to get a table, but she was aware of the reputation and the impossibility. It didn't seem worth a lot.

"Anyway, I don't want you to pay."

"I asked you."

"Yes, but that's enough."

They went to an Italian restaurant not far from where she lived, somewhere she'd been with Paul and the boys. Joseph was sitting there waiting for her when she arrived, and he was wearing a suit and a white T-shirt. The obvious effort brought a lump to her throat.

"I didn't even know you had a suit," she said.

"Yeah. Weddings and funerals, you know. Lot of them in our family."

"Well, you look very nice."

"Thank you. So do you."

She was wearing jeans, a jumper, no makeup. She had thought about what she wanted to say, and what she wanted to say, it turned out, was that she didn't want him thinking the evening was any kind of a big deal. Now she felt a little foolish, and a little cruel, in a way that she hadn't intended to be.

"This isn't how I feel," she said.

He looked puzzled.

"Nothing," she said. "Forget it."

They ordered drinks, and then looked at their menus.

"Have anything you want," said Joseph.

"I told you, we're going halves."

But she remembered what it had been like, when she was a young teacher on an evening out with friends who were being paid more—the anxiety while they wondered whether they wanted starters, the panic when the wine started disappearing faster and faster. She ached for Joseph a little, and wondered whether that anxiety would ever disappear for him.

"How's the music?"

"I haven't been with Jaz again, if that's what you're asking."

She laughed.

"No. I really did want to know about the music."

And he told her that he had nearly finished another track, but £Man had asked to hear what he was up to and hadn't liked it much, and he'd lost confidence, and he didn't know how to replace Jaz anyway. And then they talked about her work and the boys. They knew a lot about each other. There were a lot of questions to be asked.

"I'd like to see the kids soon," said Joseph. "I miss them."

"They miss you too."

But Joseph, she had decided, would be their last ex. If there was anyone else, he would have to be either permanent or secret. She couldn't keep introducing the boys to someone they liked and then withdrawing them suddenly. She didn't envisage a whole string of young men who enjoyed playing FIFA on the Xbox, but there might, at some stage, be someone who could offer wise advice, or help with maths homework. On the other hand, they were unlikely to become deeply emotionally attached to someone who was a whiz with fractions. (She wasn't sure that she'd be ripping his boxers off with her teeth, either, if that were his main hobby or interest.) Anyway, the subject was confusing, and needed more careful consideration than she had given it to date.

"What did you tell them?"

"I just said we weren't seeing each other at the moment, and you'd gone to live with your mum."

"Did they understand?"

"They understand that people split up."

"But you didn't tell them about why?"

"No. I just said we weren't getting on. And they said that wasn't true. And I said there was a lot they didn't see. And they said that wasn't true either. I'll give them the first one."

"We were getting on," said Joseph.

Lucy didn't say anything.

"Weren't we?"

"What do you want me to say? Yes. We were getting on. Apart from our little spat about Trump."

"That would have blown over."

"If what?"

"How do you mean?"

"Your use of the second conditional presupposes an 'if.'"

He sighed.

"You said 'would.' It would have blown over. If what?"

"Well. If I hadn't slept with someone else, I suppose."

"I think you were always going to sleep with someone else."

"I wasn't."

"You did."

"Yes, but..."

There were no buts, so he stopped searching for one.

"Did you think what it would be like for you if I slept with someone else?" she said.

"Yes. 'Course. Except…well, more afterward than before. I'd have hated it. I'm sorry."

"It's OK. It would happen again."

"No."

"Of course it would."

He shook his head, but he couldn't know for sure.

It was a time when everyone was vowing never to forgive people. Politicians were never going to be forgiven for what they had done, friends and family were never going to be forgiven for the way they had voted, for what they had said, maybe even for what they thought. Most of the time, people were not being forgiven for being themselves. Politicians who had lied every day of their professional lives were not forgiven for lying. People who lived in cities were not forgiven for being metropolitan, people who were poor were not forgiven for expressing dissatisfaction, old people were not forgiven for being old and scared. But was that all there was to them? And could you only love someone who thought the same way as you, or were there other bridges to be built farther up the river? Could you just tunnel under the whole mess, even? She hadn't ever been able to forgive Paul for what he had done to her and the children. Now she had to decide whether she could forgive a young man for being a young man, and if she decided she could, would she be able to follow through with it? Deciding to forgive, after all, was not the same thing as forgiveness.

"How is your mum?" said Lucy. She wanted to talk about something else.

# Spring 2019

# 18

Joseph had been asked to take his father suit shopping, and, if he had decoded his sister correctly, suit shopping meant he had been asked to buy Chris a suit. Brexit hadn't worked out for him financially, not because there was no work for scaffolders—there swas plenty—and not because wages had fallen—they had risen, just as Chris had predicted they would. There was a shortage of every kind of skilled worker in the construction industry, and the referendum had made it worse. But Chris was so angry about Brexit not happening that he had set work aside while he tried to put things right. Joseph wasn't sure what that meant, and didn't ask.

"Thanks for this, son," he said when they had chosen a dark gray suit from Fashion Man in Wood Green for eighty quid.

"Fine," said Joseph.

He had indeed decoded his sister correctly. They took the suit to the cash desk. The trousers would need taking up, but surely Chris could manage that.

"It's quite a cheap one, though," Chris said. "If I were buying, I'd have probably spent a bit more. Haven't you just had a promotion?"

Joseph had been assistant manager at the leisure center for a couple of months. He had given up working at the butcher's, and even though he still messed around with music, he no longer thought of it as a professional career.

"Yeah, and I worked hard for it."

"Cheaper in the long run, a good suit."

True, this was the sort of advice a father was supposed to offer a son, but it wasn't usually offered in this set of circumstances.

"Well, everything's cheaper for you, isn't it?"

"You know I'd pay if I could."

"You could have paid," said Joseph. He should have been bigger than that, but he wasn't.

"How?"

"You could have taken some work."

"How can I, when all this is going on?"

"Here's what I don't understand," said Joseph. "You voted for Brexit because the Poles and all that were undercutting you. But now they're not. Why aren't you out there coining it?"

"But Brexit hasn't happened, has it?"

"Why does that matter? The bit that you wanted has happened."

"It matters because out means…"

"Ah, don't say, 'Out means out.' Or, 'Brexit means Brexit.' Please. I'd just like to go one day without hearing that something means something that's exactly the same word. Of course it bloody does. How can it not? Cheese means cheese. Christmas means Christmas. But where does that get you?"

He still didn't know much about anything. He wasn't interested in customs unions or backstops, even though he seemed to hear those words every day. But Brexit seemed to have floated clear of its details. It was now like a religion. There were those who believed and those who didn't, and there were nutters on both sides, marching and shouting, and you could never prove that you were right and somebody else was wrong because nothing happened one way or the other anyway. He was beginning to wonder whether it was driving everyone demented, and the country was losing its collective marbles one by one.

"We've been betrayed. You and me."

"I haven't."

"Do you live in Britain? Were you one of the seventeen point four million?"

"Yes, but..."

Joseph had never told him that he was one of the seventeen point four million and the sixteen point one million. Chris would feel betrayed by that, as well as everything else.

"So you've been shafted."

"Meanwhile you haven't got eighty quid to pay for a suit."

"Some things are more important than money."

"You're right, Chris. I'm going to give up work and fight alongside you."

His father looked at him warily.

"But I won't be able to buy you this. I'll need some savings."

"I know what you're saying," said Chris.

In Joseph's experience, the expression "I know what you're saying" was always followed with a counterargument, but Chris just stopped there. Joseph got his bank card out. His father didn't seem embarrassed.

**The reason for the suit** was Grace's wedding, and the wedding was at his mother's church. Joseph hadn't thought of it as his church for a long time.

He hadn't been for months, maybe years now. He preferred being at home on Sunday mornings, and anyway he'd begun to think that going to church was weird. His mother was surprisingly reasonable about it when he said he had better things to do, and in any case he didn't believe in God.

"I wasn't enjoying you coming with me anyway," she said. "You always acted like you didn't want to be there."

"I didn't."

"He knew."

"Who?"

"Who do you think?"

"Not God."

"Yes, God."

"God knew I was acting as though I didn't want to be there?"

"No. He wasn't interested in the acting," she said scornfully. "He knew you didn't want to be there. He sees into your heart."

He wouldn't mind being there for the wedding, though. It wouldn't just be the usual lot, the walking dead that depressed the hell out of him. Some of his friends from back in the day would be there, the sons and daughters of his mother's church friends, the kids he and Grace had grown up with. And Joseph liked Scott's friends and family. He'd gone on Scott's stag weekend to

Bratislava, where he'd got drunk with Scott's brothers and mates and, in the absence of anything else to do, fired AK-47s on a shooting range.

And he was sort of excited about going with Lucy and the boys, probably because Lucy was excited about everything—the event, of course (she loved Grace and Scott), but the church too. She'd always wanted to go, and Joseph thought there was something suspicious about it, something romantic and maybe even patronizing.

"It's not one of those churches, you know," he told her when she was asking for wardrobe advice. "Nobody speaks in tongues, or starts rolling around on the floor."

"Please," she said. "Give me some credit."

"Nobody dances. They can't even sing, most of them. They're too old. They warble and croak. There might be a bit of swaying, if you're lucky. And it's usually half empty. Anyway, Scott's sister is going to sing 'Perfect' by Ed Sheeran, and her mum is playing the piano for that bit."

"Great," said Lucy, but Joseph could see she was a bit disappointed.

**But on the bus** up to the church with the boys, she couldn't help thinking that attending the wedding was an achievement, of sorts. For a start, it had been over two years since Joseph slept with Jaz, and as far as she knew there had been no other indiscretion since. They lived together, they celebrated family occasions together, and they never talked about next year, but they talked about next week, and the summer holidays, if the summer was not too far away. She didn't put any weight on him, but perhaps people were not meant to bear weight, and as a consequence, each day provided the pleasures of companionship and co-parenting, and each week provided the pleasures of sex, sometimes more than once.

Grace's wedding was a milestone, of sorts. There wouldn't be many introductions, or the nerves and self-consciousness that came with them. She would be Lucy, Joseph's girlfriend (his preferred terminology, not hers), and nobody would think anything of it.

When they got to the church, Joseph was in animated conversation with Chris.

"Hi," said Lucy brightly.

Joseph kissed her. Chris offered the boys his knuckles for a spud.

"You'd better give us a couple of minutes," said Chris. "We're having a domestic."

"We're not," said Joseph.

"We disagree strongly," said Chris. "We're related. That's a domestic."

"Chris wants to give Grace away," said Joseph. "And he's standing out here waiting for her."

"Oh," said Lucy.

Grace had asked Joseph to give her away, on the grounds that she disliked her father intensely.

"I've said we can both do it," said Chris. "But he won't even go for that."

"The point is that she doesn't want you anywhere near her," said Joseph. "She had to be persuaded to let you come at all."

"They're ashamed of me," said Chris to Lucy.

Lucy made a sympathetic face.

"Don't look at him like that," said Joseph.

"Why don't you come inside and sit with us?" said Lucy.

"That's a good idea," said Joseph.

"No, thanks," said Chris. "I'll be sitting with family."

"She is family."

Lucy appreciated the sentiment, but she still wished Joseph hadn't said it.

"She isn't what I'd call family."

He didn't elaborate.

"Maybe you should go in," said Joseph to Lucy.

She didn't like leaving him, but they were the last ones outside, and she didn't want to draw attention to herself and the boys by arriving late. They found a half-empty pew at the back and sat down, and after a minute or two Chris joined them, after looking for a space somewhere, anywhere else.

"He threatened me," he said to Lucy, at a volume that he knew would cause people to look round. "My own son," he said, when he was satisfied that he had a big enough audience.

"He's quite strong," said Al. "He could beat both of us up at once."

"Yeah," said Dylan. "I wouldn't get into it with him."

"He goes to the gym," said Al. "He works there, so he goes most days."

"It shouldn't come to that," said Chris. "It should never come to that."

"What about Hitler?" said Dylan, who was now at secondary school.

"Oh, we had to stop him," said Chris. "But he started it."

"Joseph was going to start it too," Al pointed out.

"You're right, son," said Chris. "I should have stood my ground. Like we did in 1940."

"He'd have beaten you up, though," said Dylan. "He's quite strong."

The circularity of it reminded Lucy of most conversations she had listened to in the last couple of years. Luckily the pianist started playing the "Wedding March," and Joseph and Grace walked into the church. Lucy watched, listened, and thought. She thought about her own wedding, and her marriage, which had made her happy and then very unhappy, and it suddenly seemed absurd to her that she had spent so many years with someone who had brought her so low, all because of the vows that she had made at a different time, to a different person. And for some reason that took her on to Chris, and Joseph's mother, and then Chris's peculiar obsession with Brexit, and then on to her unhappy country. Everything seemed to be about marriages and divorces until Scott's sister started to sing the Ed Sheeran song, when she was overcome by embarrassment and a little bit of rage, and all thinking stopped.

**Afterward,** Lucy and the boys watched the various permutations of photos: the bride, the bride and groom, the groom, the bride's friends, the groom's friends.

The photographer shouted for the bride's family. Nobody stopped Chris from joining the other three.

Joseph turned to her and the boys.

"He wants partners."

Lucy froze.

"It's all right," he said.

"Come on, Mum," said Al.

"Are you sure?" said Lucy. "What if we..."

Joseph stepped away from the others.

"Oh, what if what if," he scoffed.

"I don't want everyone to think, one day in the future, oh, that was weird, letting her in there."

"You're my life, now," said Joseph. "That's enough."

So Lucy stood on the steps with Joseph, and his mother, and Chris, and the boys, and Grace and tried to live in the moment, with these people, in this place. Joseph was right. There were no more hurdles. Now all they had to do was walk, and see how far they could get.

# ACKNOWLEDGMENTS

Thanks to Mary Mount, Georgia Garrett, Amanda Posey, Lowell Hornby, Venetia Butterfield, Joanna Prior, Mary Chamberlain, Farhana Bhula, Sandra Verbickiene, Zion Roache, Barney Sergeant, Sarah McGrath, Geoff Kloske, and Francesa Segal.

# ABOUT THE AUTHOR

**Nick Hornby** is the author of seven other best-selling novels, including **High Fidelity, About a Boy,** and **A Long Way Down,** as well as several works of nonfiction, including **Fever Pitch.** He has written numerous award-winning screenplays for film and television, including **An Education, Brooklyn, Wild,** and, most recently, **State of the Union.** He lives in London.